Salt of the Earth:

A medieval adventure of will

by

William N. Tindall

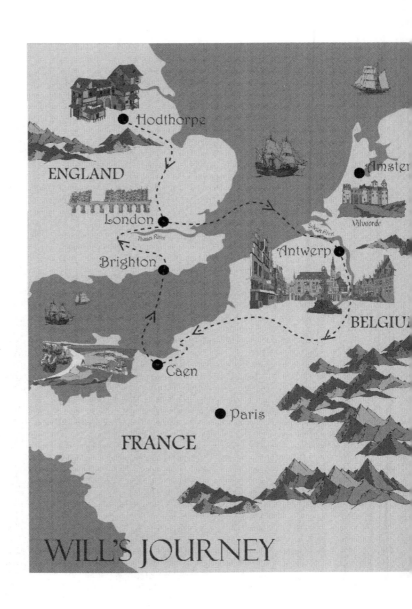

Hodthorpe

ENGLAND

London

Brighton

Thames River

Antwerp

Schelt River

Vilvoorde

Amster

BELGIU

Caen

Paris

FRANCE

WILL'S JOURNEY

Ye are the salt of the earth

- spoken by Jesus to describe his disciples when giving his Sermon on the Mount

- Matthew 5:13

"Two most important days in your life are the day you were born and the day you know why"

-Mark Twain

Written with love for the three brightest lights in my life; Aidan, Cameron, and Kendall Taylor

-prologue-

Tuesday 6 September 1536:
Vilvoorde Castle, Province of Brabant. The State Prison of
Belgium (Six miles north of Brussels, Belgium).

Looking much older than 42 years of age, a quiet and humble man awakened in a cold, stone-walled and stone-floored dungeon. His beard and threadbare clothing are unkempt. He is gaunt and emaciated. He has spent more than a year in this small single cell in the basement of Vilvoorde Castle. His only light is a small glassless window. Despite his unforgiving environs his deep blue eyes retain a quiet yet piercing spark of life.

His cell and its castle are modeled after the infamous Bastille in France, where escape was never an option and comfort never an intention. Without blanket, warm clothes nor overcoat, he has been shivering for many nights. Stirring, he tries to clear his head, but his shivering is exacerbated by excessive mucous in his throat. He feels miserable and has no medicine to provide him relief. He has had nothing to eat or drink since midday yesterday.

He shifts his focus and starts to pray, *"Dear Jesus, why have you let me languish here for 14 months? Is no help forthcoming?*

Three days ago you stood by as I was condemned a heretic even though I knew more about your Father's words

6

than my accusers…those papist-supporting theologians from Louvain University! Were you testing me during their many interrogations?

After a pause to cough he continues praying," So *now dear Jesus, I wonder how soon the day will come when I must die. Perhaps, not on a cross, but a day when you will be beside me. I believe in God's promise that I can be with you based on my faith. I have done my best to follow your commandment to be kind to each person I meet.. friends and enemies alike. Must I endure another test of my love for you?"*

His prayer is interrupted by another round of coughing which doubles him over in pain. He starts to pray again, "*Most Glorious Lord God, you must know my body is nearly spent. I am sitting in darkness and unable to continue bringing your Holy Words to English people so that they may discover how to acquire your grace. If translating your Holy Words is not enough for my own salvation, then I pray you forgive King Henry VIII for his temperament, and many lusts. I forgive the Bishop of London, Cuthbert Tunstall, the King's Lord Chancellor, Sir Thomas More, and the Archbishop of Canterbury, Thomas Crammer… whichever of them paid Henry Phillips to betray me.*"

A loud clank, the jangling of a bunch of keys followed by the click of his cell door lock interrupts the prisoner's praying. As the cell door swings open the prisoner is made more alert by the sound of its creaky hinges and by seeing the jail's warden step into view.

With a furtive, backward glance the Vilvoorde Castle Warden steps inside the cell, faces his prisoner and says, "Master Tyndale, hurry and eat some of this porridge. It is still warm, and it will it give your belly some comfort. My wife made it this morning."

Once Master Tyndale starts to eat, the warden continues," This is so little I and my family can do as thanks for all you have done for us. We have inner peace because you have led us to accept God's words by teaching us what is written in scripture. You have brought us closer to our living God by your gentle manner. Your kindness has truly been a blessing."

Before the prisoner can finish his porridge, they are interrupted by another loud creek at the door. This time both the prisoner and the warden are startled when two local and stern-looking constables' step inside the cell. The older of the two approaches the prisoner and says rather gruffly, "Get up. You are going outside with us."

Once outside, on the square in front of the castle, the bedraggled prisoner could not behold the beauty of the early morning sunrise as his eyes took a long time to adjust to its brightness. But soon his face bathes in its warmth. He is steadied by the constables who hold his arms as he squints against the brightness and struggles to walk in his emaciated state.

Once in the square's center he notices a throng of people, mostly theologians in their clerical finery. Before he can speak he is stripped of his tattered robe. Wearing naught but a loincloth he is tied to a stake already fastened upright in the dirt. Around the stake is a large pile of brush wood and logs. The logs and brushwood are sprinkled with gunpowder. Once he is chained to the stake, he lifts his head slightly to notice about 100 people coming closer to him.

On a platform beside the log pyre, another town constable, a rather portly man wearing a navy blue, twin-tailed coat and a matching fringed cap with a metal town seal over its small visor is standing with a stern look as he surveys the gathering crowd. His knee-high black leather boots make a clicking sound on the wooden platform as he walks around Tyndale several times before he stands behind the helpless Tyndale. He carries a baton, shield, and sword.

Putting the shield on the ground the constable shouts words penned on an official parchment he has withdrawn from his coat. He reads, "Hear Ye, hear ye, hear Ye, Here stands William Tyndale, an Englishman who has defiled and defied the Holy Roman Church. He has been examined by his peers, the Louvain University prelates. They have ruled him a heretic by his writings and his preaching against the teachings and traditions of the Holy Church of Rome. He has refused to recant his behavior and his errors in judgement. Thus, he has been stripped of his priestly position and is here for final punishment."

A hush falls over the crowd as the constable asks, "Do you have any last words Master Tyndale before your sentence is carried out?"

The prisoner coughed, groaned, then lifted his head feebly, and spoke. "It is my final wish," he said hesitatingly, "That the Lord would open the King of England's eyes."

Once Tyndale uttered his last words his executioner reached through a hole in the back of the stake, placed a thin piece of cordage around his neck, pulled the cord through a hole in the stake and tightened it with a stick. With all his force, the executioner garroted Master Tyndale. The pressure broke his windpipe, causing him to slump, cough, gasp, and gurgle.

When he believed Tyndale was dead the executioner ignited the gunpowder placed throughout the wood pile. He then cut the cordage that held Tyndale's neck and released the iron chain that bound Tyndale to the stake. However, Tyndale was not dead. He opened his eyes and one last time looked at the crowd as his burning body fell into the fire. Tyndale and all the wood were consumed within a minute rendering both into a small pile of ashes. Later, several spectators reported that Master Tyndale did not cry out as he endured the flames and most described him as being "resigned and patient" during his execution.

-Chapter 1-

Hodthorpe, Parish of Derbyshire, England The Blackham Apothecary Shoppe Friday 20 November 1536.

It is late in the afternoon as darkness descends on a small English village about 120 miles north of London. The town is in an area known as The Midlands and it boasts of being fortunate to have the only Apothecary within 10 miles.

Social life in Hodthorpe is sparse, strict, and proscribed but it does host two market festivals per year. Both festivals bolster civic pride and generate much welcomed coinage from all the trade and tourists they bring. Tomorrow is the day when one of the Festivals begins. It is known as the Annual Well Dressing Festival. This three-day event was created one hundred years prior to thank the Lord for sparing the town during the Black Plague because the town well supplied water for everybody who was sequestered during the plague. To continue this yearly tradition, biblical themed mosaics are created from natural substances such as flowers, seeds, berries, moss, cones, etc. and typically placed inside a three or four-foot square wooden tray. To hold a mosaic together each tray was filled with local clay which has been cleaned and mixed with salt and water. Next each mosaic is placed on an easel or mounted on a wooden form and placed in a large circle around the site of the town's original water well. Once all mosaics are in place a local priest blesses each one with a lot of pomp and circumstance. Once the mosaics are blessed visitors and towns folk gather to enjoy them as well as to enjoy much feasting, ale, and shopping.

The two men who run Hodthorpe's Blackham Apothecary are well-trusted and well-liked. However, many townsfolk still believe a life with no sin, coupled with great devotion to their Lord, is all they need to protect themselves from illness. The Apothecary is owned by Cyril Blackham whom a few locals suspect does the odd bit of witchcraft or sorcery. Of course, this is not true, but what is true is that Cyril does possess is a talent for observing various illnesses and for noticing what remedies and dosages work best to offset them.

The second person working in the apothecary is 24-year-old Will Tyndall, Cyril's journeyman apothecary. He has dark brown hair parted in the middle and of a length a little below his ears. His deep blue eyes and captivating smile make him instantly likeable. Will likes to keep his beard shaven in order to avoid odorous or colorful bits of medicinal agents that might stain it or put an unpleasant smell onto his face.

Will stands a little less than six feet. "But, I'm six feet tall when I wear my riding boots," he will boast. Will usually sports a course linen, open at the neck, half-sleeve shirt; knee length breeches, brown wool stockings, leather slip-on shoes with a brass buckle on top, and a white bib apron made of heavy cotton. Will is quite cognizant of his dress and deportment as he knows appearances often lead to a negative reputation in a small town, so he tries his best to keep his clothes clean as well as his language.

Will's mentor and boss, Cyril, is a white-haired man of indiscernible age, but many believe him to be over 60. Cyril never reveals his age but does joke his hair is thinning because, "the young children in this town give me so much trouble." Cyril is taller than Will but of slimmer build. Cyril has warm, inviting soft brown eyes framed by bushy eyebrows. With his kindly face Cyril is often mistaken for being older than his real age because his droopy white mustache and pince-nez eyeglasses do much to hide his real age and his cheerful smile. Lately, Cyril rarely smiles which has made many, including Will, to ponder, *"Why is Cyril so serious these days, He was never like that before."*

This past week Cyril Blackham joined a local Well-Dressing Festival team. Today, as he notices the daylight fast disappearing, he calls to his apprentice and states, "Will, please look after the shop for an hour or two. I am taking some supplies to folks creating a mosaic and I will likely stay to help them. If I am not back in an hour please lock the place up and go home. Remember I need you well-rested tomorrow and ready to work an hour earlier than usual. The Well-Dressing Festival is bound to bring us a lot of new trade."

"I agree, we will get lots of trade in the next few days." says Will, "We have already had many visitors as we have the best herb garden for miles around. Many come to us for the stems, roots, flowers, and leaves that will be used to make or refresh Well Dressing mosaics. I think it great that much of God's colorful and textured world is being be used to create characters and stories from his holy writ."

Once Cyril leaves, Will thinks, "I *started here seven years ago. I remember I was 17 at that time. I hope this is the year I become a Master Apothecary. I need that status if ever I want my own Apothecary. If that day were to come I would have to go to a town at least 10 miles away as it would not be fair to Cyril for me to be his local competition. Besides this town does not have the population to support two Apothecaries.*"

Will stays busy erecting displays of several items he hopes will attract buyers tomorrow. As he does he thinks to himself, "*I am glad to see this day ending. In fact, the entire week has been busier than usual. But one thing I do like about the shorter days of fall and winter is I do not have to deal with the annoying squint in my right eye when I am outside on the bright and longer days of summer.*"

Just then Cyril reenters the Apothecary and interrupts Will's thoughts. "Hey Will," he shouts, "Ready to close up for the day?"

"Yes, I am, why? What's happening?"

"While I was walking around the mosaics I made a decision. Now I want to talk with you about that decision. Go lock the door and let us sit awhile here in the back room."

"Straight away, Sir." Will locks the front door, walks to the back of the Apothecary, and positions two empty wooden crates for them to sit on.

"Will", says Cyril," I am not getting any younger. In fact, most men my age have already met their maker. It has occurred to me how quickly life is passing, and it is time for me to retire. I you are the son I never had I want you to have this business."

Will gasps. Cyril pauses until Will composes himself. Then Cyril continues. "When you go home tonight talk with your parents about settling down here in Hodthorpe. You have proven yourself a skilled healer and honest purveyor of the goods we sell. I believe you are qualified and ready to take over this shop."

"Well, thanks but…

Cyril spoke over him. "When I was in the town square just now, I asked several townspeople about you. What they said was very flattering. To a person they expressed their trust in your advice and especially in the trust they have about you never gossiping about their ills. They also said that any potion, lotion, pill, or unguent you made for them was of high quality and worked wonders. Will, the best kind of any praise comes from those you willingly and honestly serve. So, now what do you say about my offer?"

"Oh, my goodness," exclaimed Will nervously, "I do not know what to say, except I am honored to be so well thought of, but… more especially by you. Please accept my heartfelt thanks for the past seven years before I say anything else."

Will pauses, clears his throat, then says, "Yes, I have thought of someday operating my own apothecary, but not in Hodthorpe and never a thought it might be this one. I thoroughly enjoy helping our townsfolk and when they tell me they appreciate my help; I am at a loss to describe warm feeling their words bring."

Will again looks at Cyril, and says in a more level voice, "I have been saving much of my earnings. Yet I still do not have much coinage to bind any deal. I am sure you deserve a hefty price for this thriving enterprise. However, before I am allowed to own my shop I need to earn my

Master Apothecary certification and become a member of a Guild."

"Well, we can work out arrangements for financing later, I would be honored to support your advancement to Master Apothecary right away. But know this…Blackham Apothecary is thriving, and it is doing so in no small measure due to your hard work. Secondly, when I retire I will not live elsewhere. Thus, you will have me available for work as long as you want. My hope is that you would find a local lad to be your apprentice and pass on to him all of the art and mystery of our profession."

Cyril pauses then says in a fatherly tone, "Will, just as important as your becoming a respected shop owner, you also need to think about becoming a respected family man. I know of no man your age who is not already married. That is unless that twenty-four-year-old is as dumb as a fencepost, or is lazy, a bully, a drunkard, a simpleton, or someone with no prospects of supporting himself or a family. I swear that is not descriptive of you."

Cyril senses Will's discomfort and continues, "I know every single lady in this town and a few widows as well, I can safely say that every one of them will settle down with you in a heartbeat if you give an encouraging nod. Then, if you both moved in upstairs here, you would have a comfortable home to call your own. All this would enable you to move from your parent's home and be on your own. So, why have you been procrastinating about settling down, finding a wife, and starting a family?"

"Well, I never thought of it as procrastinating, I just thought I needed to be in a better position than being a farmhand working on my father's land. Becoming an apothecary was the only challenging work I ever saw for myself and it also offered wages to make settling down a more secure possibility than relying on the vagaries of weather to produce a healthy crop."

As Cyril smiles, Will continues, "But for me to settle down I need the right lady. I refuse to marry anyone just for convenience or because it looks good for business. And while I still live in my parent's home you know my father and I have had issues ever since I decided to become an Apothecary. I would hate to burden any girl with my unsettled family situation hanging over us."

Cyril, nods and says, "I can understand that."

Will thinks a second or two then continues, "Since I have been working here I have found true joy in helping people. Every day when I come here I know I am in a special place. This is very satisfying and more so than milking a cow or stacking wheat sheaves. I believe the poor relationship between me and my father is because he realizes he has no other male son to work or inherit his land.

My two sisters are quite young, and neither will inherit the farm."

"I understand your situation, Will, and I know my talking with you tonight is sudden. But it is just as sudden to me to have made my decision to retire. Please talk all this over with your family tonight. We can talk some more in the morning, Is that all right with you?"

"Yes," responds Will, "tomorrow morning we will talk some more. Again, I thank you twice over, first for the opportunity you have presented and secondly for the trust you have placed in me during the many years I have worked here."

The two men swing the window shutters in place and bar the front door. They also check the potbellied stove to be sure its fire has died down. Cyril then locks the back door behind Will and then climbs the narrow spiral stairs to his living quarters above to prepare his evening meal

Hunger pangs hit Will as he is heading home, but he is not sure what else he is feeling. But on his walk he tries to find answers to many questions, such as, *"Am I scared or am I happy?. Did I hear correctly what Cyril is offering me? Was my head swelled by the accolades from townsfolk? Why can't my father think as much of me as Cyril does? Is its time that I moved out on my own? Why have I never had feelings for a woman in his town that would make me want to settle down? Why do I have an ominous feeling that all this is a dream? Is there some dark cloud about to open up and wash away all this goodness in my life?"*

-Chapter 2-

The Tyndall Family Home: a thatch-roofed farmhouse on the outskirts of Hodthorpe. Supper time, Friday 20 November 1536.

Will's self-doubts, elation, fears, and ruminations disappear once he enters the Tyndale family home and smells his evening meal cooking in the hearth. He recognizes the smell of roast beef smothered with potatoes and carrots, cooking inside a lidded cast iron pot hung on an iron tripod in the hearth. He can also smell bread warming on the lid of the pot. Knowing his mother will soon make dark brown gravy his mood and muddled emotions are quickly altered as he realized his conversation with Cyril, and his ruminating over it on his walk home, has made him ravenous.

Will shouts to his mother as he walks into their kitchen, "Sorry to be a little late,"

"I am just glad you are home safe.' say's his Mother, "Besides, it will be another quarter hour before dinner is ready."

Will gives his mother a hug and kiss on the cheek then tells her about all the preparations he and Cyril did for the Well Dressing Festival. Seeing his father in an overstuffed chair Will continues talking. This time making sure both his folks could hear him as he says, "This event is only once a year, but don't think Cyril and I are not grateful because we are. The extra income artists and visitors bring to our community, and to the Apothecary, is great. Besides Cyril has always shared some of that revenue to bolster my wages. So dear mother, let me know if there is something special I can buy for you with my extra wages."

At the sound of Will offering to buy a gift for his mother, Will hears a small "harrumph" from the chair where his father is sitting.

After a quiet dinner with hardly any conversation Will looks at both his parents and says, "There is something I want to share with you. Earlier tonight Cyril took me aside and said he wants to retire as soon as possible. He also said he would like me to become the next proprietor. I have some money set aside but not enough to make a binding contract. I was wondering…is there is any way I could get some financial help from you?

Suddenly, Will's father turns red in the face, rises from the table, and growls, "Cyril Blackham is a fool if he thinks you have what it takes to run a successful business. Does he expect you to fund his retirement? I bet that within a year you will have given half the store away because of your generous nature. Then, you will have to sell it to someone else to pay your debts. There is no way I will put this farm and our meager savings at risk on your foolish dreams. You are too young and too inexperienced to own your own business. That's my final word".

Will's father pauses then he turns to face Will and says rather sternly, "Actually… this is my last word on it… if Cyril believes you should take over his damn business, then he should finance it."

"Damn it, Father" Will recoils, "You have never shown any faith in me nor in any of my decisions, especially those affecting my pathway in life. Cyril took me in as his apprentice when he recognized I had what it takes to become a great healer as well as a merchant of medicines."

Will catches his breath then continues, "I remember all too well your telling me that God put two hands on the end of my arms, so I could use those hands to make a living. Well God also put a damn good brain inside my head so that I could use it wisely to help people. That is not a slight on you, father, it is just that I know I am different from you and many of my relatives. And just maybe, just maybe I want more out of life than settling down like they all did to farm and raise a bunch of children and chickens".

Before his father can interrupt Will leans forward across the table and looks him in the eye and says, "Please know this, I thoroughly enjoy being able to help people as a healer. I have been praised for doing it well and my work is appreciated by those I serve. That is not me offering you a conceit, father, it is a fact. I wish you appreciated me as much as others do."

Will continues to look his father in the eye, and sees his father look down as if digesting what he has just said to him.

Will continues in a calm but firm voice. "Since I now know what you truly feel about Cyril's kind offer, our conversation on that topic is over. I am going to bed. I must get up early and open the apothecary tomorrow for it will be a busy day. Before you go to your bed, father, please answer one question. Why do you hate me so much? If I have all the virtues that my mother and customers see in me, why can't you see them? Have I wronged you in some way? Do you not want me as your son?"

Will's father balls up his fists, clenches his teeth, then slowly raises his hand as if to strike Will. But he stops short then says, "Son you go too far."

"No father, its time you know how I feel. All I ever wanted was to be a man like you and to show the same love of family, integrity, and what hard work can accomplish. You have been a great inspiration to many. But you never gave me any encouragement to follow in your footsteps. You only shouted commands at me without any kindness, explanation, or encouragement. All that ever did was cause me to resent you. You made me feel that I was not worthy of your trust and affection.

Will sees his father's face redden so he pauses a moment then says, "Whatever you see in me as a failure is the result of your being a failure as a father. All I ever wanted to do was hear you say just once that you loved me and that we were all right. Why could you not do that little thing?"

"Because…." He says with a bit of stutter, "All I ever wanted was to toughen you up so that you could face what it takes to become successful in a tough and cruel world."

Hearing his father blurt out his confession, Will gathers himself together, finding himself a bit ashamed of his recent accusation of his father. Now at a loss for words Will has no retort to his father's admission. So, he simply lowers his voice and says, "As I said a moment ago, there will be many visitors coming to trade in the Apothecary tomorrow. Good night to you both and thank you mother for another delicious meal."

Will climbs the stairs to his room, crawls into his bed but before he falls asleep, he ruminates over the encounter with his father thinking, *Damn, I don't know where I found the strength to stand up to my father after his years of berating me. But now I have told him how I feel I do not know if it was being disrespectful of him or respectful to myself. But now that I have said my piece, it feels like a heavy burden has been lifted."*

As the sleepless night progresses Will continues ruminating, *"I know the church is the center of this community and I and all of my family are good church goers. It seems to me I and my family have had to display higher standards than the rest of the community. Is it because of my uncle William Tyndale who when he became an Oxford priest left for Europe on his quest to translate the Latin, Greek, and Hebrew Bibles?*

Tossing and turning some more, Will continues to ruminate over his life in Hodthorpe and concludes *"Yes, our family has social standing but if so why do I not have more friends? My only true and honest friends are my mother, Cyril, my sisters, and old school friends, Richard, and Robert. My cousins, aunts and uncles live far away. I just wish God had given me the fortitude to up and leave this place. My father may be right I do need toughening up and maybe Blackham's offer is just too much for me to handle."*

Will continues to ruminate but before he falls asleep he ponders several other questions, such as," Why *did today have to end like it did? Why have I never experienced so many ups and downs in a single day? What will tomorrow bring?. Will all the goodness I was given today be replaced with something dreadful tomorrow?"*

-Chapter 3-

After a fitful night with little sleep Will stumbles out of bed before the sun is up. Once he is fully awakened he remembers his need to leave early to open the Apothecary. He knows he is in for a chilly walk because at this time of year the sun has brought no warmth to the day. Will skips his usual breakfast of oatmeal and milk with raisins sprinkled on top, as he did not want to disturb his parents nor have another confrontation with his father.

On his half hour walk to the apothecary his mood is distracted by several town folk. They are heading into town to complete their religious themed mosaics for the Well-Dressing Festival. But this small distraction does little to calm Will's ominous feelings over the lack of support and confidence shown by his father.

Will's despondency over something "dreadful" about to happen is interrupted when he hears the sound of a horse and wagon coming up behind him. The driver of the wagon is a man the town's people call "John's son". Will has never ascertained who John was and if he ever had a son. But still it is "John's Son" who once a week drives the back streets of Hodthorpe to pick up human waste from the privies of folks who have paid his fee. The odorous work "John's son" performs has earned him the moniker, "Master of the Honey-wagon."

As the honey wagon passes, its driver gives Will a nod But as it passes Will's nostrils are assaulted causing Will to conclude, "*I know this is a sign I am in for a day that will likely smell as bad as that wagon. I never should have stood up to my father and told him how I feel. I hope God is not going to punish me for that. I pray Cyril has not changed his mind. I just can't think straight wondering what else could happen today.*"

As Will continues walking he again makes an assessment about his life in a small town ending with the hope, "*If only I could leave here and live in a larger town where nobody knows me. Then I could be myself and do whatever I want.*"

By the time he has reached the front door of the Apothecary Will's thoughts have reversed, "*Life in a small town is the only thing I know. Perhaps it is ordained that I stay here. Perhaps I can work an arrangement with Cyril that allows me to do just that?*"

Once Will enters the Apothecary and closes the rear door behind him, he quickly starts a fire in the center stove to drive off the chill in the air. He then starts thinking about how many out-of-town visitors will arrive that day. *"I can remember how in past years the Apothecary was really busy during every Well Dressing Festival. Today should be no different."*

Will continues to muse as he puts more wood into the stove. *"I bet we sell more soap and unguents this year than last. There seems to be a real liking for our lavender and sandalwood soaps. I hope we have enough bag balm in stock. I better check our supply.*

After inspecting the supply of bag balm Will decides to make more." *I think I will make up a supply of three dozen jars as last year we sold out. It is great for calloused, split, and chaffed hands from milking cows. It is such a simple formula of yellow wool fat, a little water. grated beeswax, almond oil, and witch hazel. Then I add either a little lavender, mint, or lemon oil to make it smell nice. Hard to imagine this old formula goes back to the ancient Egyptians"*

Once Will measures out his solid ingredients, using a brass balance scale mounted to a marble base, he transfers them into a large porcelain dish. Next, he places the porcelain dish on top of a double boiler sitting on top of the pot-bellied stove. As the ingredients meld together he slowly stirs the mixture waiting to watch the yellow mass turn into a white creamy consistency. Next he places his cream into small four-ounce porcelain jars while smiling and *thinking, "It's funny how this stuff protects both cows and people. I have recommended it to new mothers who use it on their babies' bottoms when they do not change nappies often enough."*

As Will focuses on packaging his skin cream he is startled when his work is interrupted by two visitors coming through the front door. One is a well-tailored man whose clothes and demeanor exude a gentleman of means. He politely holds the door open for a pretty woman who has arrived at the same time. She rushes past the gentleman and greets Will with a cheery, "Good Morning Will."

She is clad in a thin cotton dress but with a rough woolen shawl about her shoulders. She is slim with blond hair cut much like that of a pageboy at court. But her hair reaches down to her shoulders and looks like it has not seen a comb or brush in a long time. Her eyes are a hazel color and her pug nose and thin lips make for an attractive face but for the smudges on her forehead and cheek. Will looks up and addresses her saying "Good Morning, Audrey"

As she approaches Will he remains curious, but silent, knowing that Audrey has never come to the Apothecary early in the day. Will has known Audrey since she was about five years old. He believes her age is now about or nineteen or twenty, but her demeanor and unkempt look make her appear much older.

Audrey looks at Will and flips some hair from her forehead. Her clothing and speech suggest she is from the lower class of townsfolk. While her eyes appear sunken and somewhat sad for Will they have always been captivating.

Will smiles warmly and then notices Audrey has a dirty cloth wrapped around her wrist. "What brings you here so early on this chilly morning, Mistress Audrey?"

"My Mother has sent me to get some of that special cough medicine that you and Cyril are so well known for," she replies. "It seems to be the only stuff that keeps her raspy cough quiet. I believe you make it from something called laudanum."

"Yes, I have what you need", Will responds, "But first, why is there a dirty piece of cloth wrapped around your wrist?"

"Oh that," Audrey demurs, "It's really nothing, I scraped my wrist on a rock."

"How did you scrape your wrist on a rock?"

"Uhm! Silly me, I fell off our horse when I forgot to duck when I rode too close to a tree."

"I can see you are in pain," says Will. "May I take a look?"

"Oh, Master Will I have no money for you to attend to my foolishness. Please, just sell me the cough medicine for my mother then I can be on my way," says Audrey. "Besides, there is another gentleman here in the Apothecary who must need your help more urgently than I. I am sure he has important business otherwise why would he be up and about so early?"

"No, there will be no charge to you, I just want to see how bad your scrape is," says Will, "Then I will tend to this gentleman's needs."

Audrey reluctantly holds up her hand. Will takes her hand, holds it gently, and removes the dirty piece of cloth. The wound is about the size of a tuppence coin, but it is deep. He can see enough skin has been scrapped off to expose a part of her wrist bone. Audrey blanches at the site but Will remains calm. He furrows his brow and raising one eyebrow responds in a clear but low voice, "Hmmm, thanks for letting me see this, I know now what I must do to help it heal."

Will then walks Audrey to a basin and fills it with water. He then grabs some soap and rubs it onto a clean wet cloth. He next washes the dirt, debris, and pus out of the wound and all around it. He then tosses that cloth into the waste hole in the floor along with the dirty water he used to clean the wound. Finally, he dresses the wound with a piece of clean linen strips but not before he pours a dollop of honey onto the dressing.

Will tells Audrey, "I have learned over the years that wounds will heal better with either being washed in fresh urine or packed with honey. In your case the honey will work best. I want you to apply honey when you change this dressing every couple of days. Keep it up for at least ten days or until the skin closes over the wound."

With his work complete he asks her, "Where did your mother get that cloth used to wrap around your scrape?

Audrey replies, "She ripped it from one of her petticoats."

"It must have been a piece from near the ground because it's filthy."

"How did you know that honey helps close a wound?" Audrey asks

"It's been a staple treatment that physicians and apothecaries have used for a long time. It was learned from soldiers who used it to heal wounds suffered from being in battle.

"Do you have a fresh jar of honey at home? If not I have a small jar hear that should last for as long as you need. Any leftover you can pour onto some bread and enjoy," He adds with a smile.

Will pauses to be sure Audrey is listening attentively, then continues, "If you have some honey at home you also need to keep changing the dressing every day or so and especially so when the honey seeps out through the dressing. You must keep this up until the wound closes over with some new skin. Do not continue to use any of your Mother's cloths or you will find the wound attracts a bad air we call a miasma. There are a lot of miasmas around and farm air is especially noted for harboring them. Should you let some miasma find its way into that open wound you could lose your hand, or arm . . . or worse."

As Audrey nods her understanding Will continues, "I am going to give you some clean linen strips to use as new wraps. I have enough here for several changes but come back and get more later."

Will then turns to the gentleman, "Sir, if you would be so kind and be a little more patient I would like to finish with this young lady. Then I can give my full attention to your needs." Will again looks at the man and thinks, *"This must be a man who is well-to-do by his fine clothes, posture, clean boots and neatly trimmed hair and beard. But he has a friendly face with piercing eyes.*

The gentleman looks at Will and in response says, "Take all the time you need Master Will, I have plenty to occupy myself by looking at all these wares on display."

Will stops suddenly and wonders, *"How did this fellow know my name? Perhaps he is a friend of Cyril. It is obvious, by his dress he knows a good haberdasher. Did he overhear Audrey call me by my name?"*

Will then turns to Audrey and produces from a drawer a roll of fine linen bandaging about an inch wide. He tells her, "This roll of linen is to be used exactly as I instructed you to replace the one on your wrist. Be sure not to let any dirt get under it or on it. I want you to come to me in three days and I will check the wound and change the dressing and apply a new one. Do you understand?" Audrey nods.

"There will be no charge to come to me but someday you will be able to do a favor for someone else and I hope when that time comes you will remember when a favor was done for you." Audrey nodded her assurance to Will that she would.

As he finishes tending to Audrey's wound Will's mind searches for an answer to just who his second visitor of the day is and how he knew his name. As Will finishes with Audrey he says, "Here is a special soap I want you to also use to keep your hands clean and to help keep dirt from getting inside your bandage. Now remember this and remember it well, I want you to come back and see me in three days."

"Uh, Yes, Will, I promise I will do that," she says.

"Each time you return I will also change your bandage if you haven't. Remember also to wash your hands with this soap every time you use the privy, cesspit, chamber pot, or whatever sheit-hole you have. Also wash your hands every time you prepare food for you and your mother. How well you keep both hands clean will determine how quickly your wound heals. I believe Mother Nature wants our wounds to heal but she wants us to help her by keeping things clean. Is all that I have said clear? Will you follow my instructions?"

"Yes, Master," Audrey says demurely as she looks at Will with a wistful longing in her eyes.

Audrey wraps her shawl closer around her shoulders and heads to the front door. As she nears it Will calls after her, "Don't forget this medicine for your mother."

"I won't" she says," And Will, thank you. You are a real blessing both to this town and to me" Then Audrey turns to leave, hesitates a second, then turns to Will, stands on her toes, and kisses him on the cheek.

Will blushes at the warmth of her lips on his cheek. But before he can think about his somewhat embarrassed reaction to Audrey's kiss, the unknown gentleman comes up to Will and says, "I do not believe we have ever met. My name is Humphrey Monmouth."

"Well, well, well. My goodness. May the saints preserve us," Will stammers in astonishment," I know your name… even though we have never met. My uncle William and my Uncle Arthur have talked about you."

"All with good and polite language I trust," says Mr. Monmouth

"Oh, yes, very much so. But not publicly for obvious reasons. Its a well-kept secret in our family that you have been funding and supporting my uncle's self-exile in Europe.

Will pauses then looks at Monmouth and gets a quizzical look on his face and says, "We have not heard from Uncle Will in several years. As you know his situation so very well, you also know it's quite risky to communicate with him."

"Well, it's nice that you know who I am."

"Mr. Monmouth, you especially have to be careful around here. There are zealous papists hereabouts and they have many spies and informants. All they want is to curry favor with Catholic Church officials by betraying a friend or neighbor. Usually they cry out "heretic" because they dislike a man or covet someone's land or even his wife. They are like rats in a feeding frenzy and they exist everywhere, even way up here in this little town far from London."

Humphrey Monmouth raises his finger and interrupts. "Will, you're a well-informed young man but the worst bastard of all is the Lord Chancellor, Sir Thomas More. That man professes piety, but we know he has placed more people under the executioner's torture, rope, garrote, and sword than anybody. He probably has ordered more bones be broken for heresy than anyone else in this country. And he has also ordered the burning of good people."

"I can't imagine why pious people are so cruel to others" says Will, "Even in this small town our entire family has had to be careful with what we say and to whom we say it. In fact, some family members have changed how they spell our family name. They do so that they might live elsewhere and not be bothered with questions about being related to Uncle Will. Even changing our names to Tindall, Tyndall, Tindell, or anything close to it, we find ourselves harangued by questions about whether or not we are church reformists or worse... a breed of heretics."

Monmouth interrupts Will and says, 'Believe me Will, I know your situation well and yet still I continue my support of the reformist movement. When I first started funding your uncle's endeavors, I was proud to fund his room, board, clothing, travel, and printing fees through a society known as The Christian Brethren. Using them as a conduit for funds we were able to smuggle Tyndale Bibles and treatises into England from Worms and Cologne,

Germany. Additionally, since I am a haberdasher, I was able to hide over three thousand Bibles in bolts of cloth imported from Europe. This led to a fortuitous outcome as I then sold and made my best quality fabric into clothing for London's high society folk. Doing so was ironic, as I was making a profit from the same folks who were working to stop the spread of Tyndale Bibles."

"Not to change the subject but my curiosity now begs me to ask, what brings you here to Hodthorpe?" Will asked.

"I am afraid my smuggling days are over. In fact, you should talk to your Uncle Arthur about how he once smuggled Tyndale Bibles into England by hiding them in barrels of flour.

I have heard some tales of that. Can you give me an instance?"

"Your Uncle Arthur used the ruse that he was importing flour to make large batches of buns. You know the ones filled with raisins and embellished with a cross on top? You know them as Hot Cross Buns and as a treat during Lent. Your uncle really did make his buns for celebrating the Catholic Feast of the Exaltation of the Cross held on Good Friday weekend. But while he was baking buns he was also distributing Bibles out the back door of his bakery. Some of those Bibles were given to me or to one of my trusted servants for distribution in London.

Monmouth smiles, then looks at Will and says, "Ask your uncle someday about the irony of having his flour barrels emblazoned with the emblem of the Poor Sisters of St. Clare in France. It was these sisters who first created Hot Cross Buns. Your uncle had their logo placed on the flour barrels to avoid raising suspicion by a custom house agent. But we never thought that more times than naught your Uncle did not pay import tariffs because that emblem was recognized by a Catholic customs agent who wanted to show his support of the catholic church.

"I can see that is pretty ironic, but you did not answer my question, so please don't change the subject. Why are you really here?"

"Well, I am looking for a good man," says Monmouth, "But before I say anything more tell me about the girl who just left here."

"Oh! Audrey! I have known her since we were kids. She and her mother have fallen on hard times since her father was killed in a coal-mining accident a couple of years ago. Since then she has become a little promiscuous in order to acquire a few coins from time to time to help feed them both. She is known by the local lads as "Easy Audrey," if you get my meaning."

Will pauses, and Monmouth gives a curt nod of the head indicating his understanding.

Will continues, "I think Audrey lifts her skirt more out of being angry with God rather than doing so to find pleasure or raise money. This really started once her Mother took to drink because of her husband's death. But to me, Audrey is still one of God's daughters and deserves a better life than the one created by her circumstances."

Will looks at Monmouth for a reaction then continues, "As they say, but for the grace of God go I. Thus, I treat Audrey as anyone else who comes through that door seeking help. We are all God's children despite our circumstances. She is quite pretty if you overlook the dirt on her and on her clothing. Despite her circumstances she is not a woman that interests me beyond her being a childhood acquaintance."

Monmouth turns his gaze to Will and says, "I am glad to hear what you have just said about that poor woman. It makes my decision to be here even more sound. But first I have some distressing news to relate about your uncle."

"Which is?" asks Will

"Let me be direct. Your uncle, my very dear friend ever since we first met when he was a temporary preacher at Saint Dunstan's Church in London, was executed three weeks ago outside Vilvoorde Castle in Belgium."

Will displays shock and gasps for air. Obviously distressed and at a loss for words, Monmouth gives him a moment to compose himself. Then Will stutters, "What in God's name and by all that's good and holy has happened to Uncle William?"

"Master Tyndale was held a prisoner in a cold, stone dungeon for well past a year while he underwent an arduous sham trial at the hands of theologians from Louvain University. Those corrupt and well- paid theologians, led by Ruard Tapper and Jacob Latamas argued with, cajoled, and tortured him. They also deprived him of clothing, food, and light. This was done to get Master Tyndale to recant his writings and return into the fold of Catholic faithful.

Catching his breath Monmouth continues, "Those rotten theologians were paid likely with funding from the Pope or with funds supplied by Sir Thomas More at the behest of Henry VIII. However, they were unsuccessful in breaking your uncle's will nor in arguing against his knowledge of the Bible. Then, having failed to break him they levied charges of heresy against what he wrote in a few of his treatises of several years ago. But Tyndale's real undoing was his stand against Henry VIII's desire to seek a divorce from his then Queen which in turn really angered the King and set in motion Tyndale's capture because of a price put on his head."

Monmouth gives Will another moment to let what he has just revealed sink in.

Then Monmouth continues with, "Since Master Tyndale had been embroiled in all the controversial mess surrounding Henry's divorce, no appeal by me or by several others was going to work because Tyndale opposed Henry's divorce in print. Thus, while his superior intellect and knowledge of the Bible could rebuff any inquisitor's tactics, especially those used by the Louvain theologians, he was still found guilty of heresy, stripped of his priestly status a month before his execution, and then dragged into a public square and burned at the stake."

"OH MY GOD," stutters Will. "Is this really true? Never in my wildest imagination would I have believed such a holy and pious man, and especially one with true and honorable intentions as Uncle Will, would be tried and executed for heresy."

"Yes, it is true," replies Monmouth, "These damnable inquisitors from Louvain convicted him of heresy, not because he translated the Bible in English but because he eloquently defended his other writings which in turn stirred dissent among Catholic church elders. But his treatise on "The Practices of Prelates" in which Master Tyndale took a stand that the King was being selfish by how he approached his divorces and that he should stay with his first wife was what really got him killed.'

Will nods his understands and thinks *"The truth behind all of this is.. Henry VIII had no other way to silence my uncle other than to destroy him."*

"Master Tyndale died with his integrity intact," Monmouth says. "He was truly a pious man who was not going to recant his beliefs just to play politics with the King and the church. Unfortunately, too many have crumbled under torture and recanted their position when faced with charges of heresy. But do know this, Will, if Henry VIII could not stop the several thousand Tyndale Bibles already in England, nor could he stop Tyndale printing his treaties, especially the one with your uncle's belief that Henry should not divorce the woman Henry called his "Spanish Cow, then your uncle has started a reformation movement in the country that will only grow because of his example"

"That's a lot to take in all at once", says Will.

"It's pretty simple really. Now that Henry VIII is infatuated with a young French lady known as Anne Boleyn, he has only one recourse…use his position of power to send out his hounds to destroy Tyndale. This is what he has done but it took nine years of Tyndale's living in exile before the Church and Henry were able to catch him."

Humphrey stops and takes Will by the hand, looks at him, then continues, "I and others are honored to have been part of that man's life. His loyalty to the meaning of friendship, doing God's work, and his actions were absolutely above reproach. Your uncle was a fine example of why a society's strength comes from its people when they are living in harmony and being kind to one another."

"Well, let's send Henry and all around him into Hell and damnation," says, Will, almost breathless, "Now I know why I have not seen my uncle in nigh on nine years and now I never will. I remember my uncle as a kindly man. He exuded a grace and a wisdom that made me hang onto every word he said. I still remember a lot of the profound things he said. The fact he spoke and wrote five languages and was Oxford trained would have put him head and shoulders above any prelate that I know and especially those who owe their comfortable paid positions to a prelate above them no matter that prelate's lack of piety and integrity."

Monmouth grits his teeth and interjects. "What a shame all this has become so dramatic and so political. It is really tearing the country apart. It's pretty sad when you see how some folks use superstition and Catholic ritual to argue against those who found religious enlightenment by understanding the truth about salvation being freely given by faith alone in God."

After another short pause, Will calmly and quietly asks Monmouth, "Have you told anyone else in the family about what has befallen Uncle William?"

"No, I wanted to come tell you first as I have an idea how you can help me finish your uncle's work."

"Oh my", thinks the startled Will, *"Now what am I getting myself into? Just when I thought my life was going in one direction Cyril comes along and pulls it one way with his offer, my Father pulls it another by making me stand alone, and now Humphrey Monmouth comes and upsets my life again by his news and his hint of something likely to pull me in a third direction."*

"What are you thinking?" Humphrey asks observing Will's silence.

"I have been thinking…that…. I need a little time to digest what you have told me. As the blessing of the Well Dressing mosaics will happen in a few moments.... would you like to attend it? It would give you a chance to see all the beautiful mosaics in their best light. Also, this Apothecary is about to get really busy which means visitors and locals will be dropping by in droves to purchase the many wares we have prepared for this event. My suggestion is it would be best if you come back here at midday as then it will be quiet, and we can talk undisturbed in the back."

Monmouth says, "I agree."

Will adds, "I want to mull over some ideas on how best we should share your news about Uncle William with my family. I have uncles, aunts, and cousins here in town, I want to be sure everything is planned out for you to tell them the news in the best and kindest way possible."

"I appreciate your careful approach to a delicate situation. I have travelled three days from London, so I might as well partake of the Well Dressing Ceremony and its Festival. Perhaps seeing some local culture will be good for me and it will give you a chance to do some preparation," says Monmouth, "But do not misunderstand me, I would travel through a month of hardship if I thought it would return your uncle back to us."

Monmouth walks to the door but before he leaves he says to Will, "I will be back here in time for your mid-day break. Do you have your own food? Can I take you to a pub for bangers and mash? Perhaps add a nice pint of ale or a shandy to wash it all down? Does anyone about here offer a poor traveler a good feed of Corned Beef and Clap-shot?

"Thanks, but no outside food for me. My Mother left me some bacon, cheese, and bread. Why don't you bring some food back here for yourself? Then we can just sit quietly on the back stoop and talk."

"I can tell you want some time to think about all of this," says Monmouth, "I will see you in a few hours."

As Monmouth leaves the Apothecary and the doorbell gives off its usual tinkle. Will turns to see Cyril coming down the stairs from his living quarters above the retail shop.

Cyril looks at Will and says, "Sorry to be late, but an old man must be able to oversleep occasionally. All the fresh air yesterday while working on the Well Dressing Mosaic really tired me out. I really am looking forward to this day. Oh, I heard some voices just before I came down, have we already had visitors? Did they buy a lot?"

"We had two visitors," answers Will, "The first was Audrey. She purchased some cough medication for her mother. The second was, Humphrey Monmouth, an important gentleman from London."

"Well, well, well, "Cyril retorts, a smirk on his face, "I have not heard that name in years. What brought him here and is he returning to our Apothecary?"

"He brought sad news about my Uncle William and yes, he is coming back here about mid-day to share lunch with me. But first he is taking in the Well Dressing Ceremony and viewing the mosaics."

After a short pause, Will approaches Cyril and asks, "You made a little crooked smile and a raised eyebrow when I mentioned Monmouth's name. Is his name familiar to you? Will knew from working with his boss that what he left unspoken often revealed more about his thoughts and feelings than what he did speak. "Am I right, did you recognize Monmouth's name?"

"I do not think I am telling tall tales, but several years ago Monmouth was caught smuggling Tyndale Bibles into England. After a trial he spent a few months in a dungeon before making a large donation to a Catholic relief fund in order to get himself extricated from that hell hole," Cyril explained.

"Oh my," murmurs Will quietly to himself. *"that explains a lot. It's likely he is still being watched just to be sure he does not get back into the business of smuggling Bibles into England."*

-Chapter 4-

Mid- day Saturday 21 November 1536
The Blackham Apothecary

Henry Monmouth returns to the Blackham
Apothecary carrying a Cornish Game Hen Pot Pie. He
purchased it from a street vendor's cart. It is wrapped in
brown paper. Monmouth asked the vendor, "Since these
savory pies have been around for a hundred years, did you
use an original recipe from either Devonshire or Cornwall
to make them?

"I used neither mate. These were made using a
family recipe of my mother's," he replied rather curtly.

"Well it better be jolly good. If it is I will be back
for another!"

Monmouth walks back into the Apothecary, and
says to Will, who is standing behind its counter weighing
out a powder, "Let's sit in the back so I can eat this pie
while it's fresh and warm, and we can chat privately and
uninterrupted."

Will is amused a man as wealthy as Humphrey
Monmouth would indulge himself with such simple fare.
Cyril notices Monmouth and tells them both, "Go ahead and
sit in the back room you two. It has where we do our heavy

compounding, but I am happy to stay out here and keep watch, so you are not disturbed. Take your time and enjoy."

As the two men sit on a barrel using a third barrel between them as a table, they eat in silence. Midway through their meal, Will breaks their silence. "I think you came here to say a lot more to me than just the news about my uncle's death. Am I correct?"

"Yes," answers Monmouth, "I really wanted to meet you as I believe you are the perfect person to help me, and those who support your Uncle's work. We are hopeful you will agree to help us retrieve the last of his Bibles and bring them to England. Remember, when your uncle once said he wanted his work to grow and continue until even a plowman has the opportunity to read the scriptures? Well, there are not enough Bibles to go to every ploughman but there are a thousand sitting in a printer's warehouse in Antwerp, Belgium. I believe you would be perfect to go and fetch them."

"You're kidding.. aren't you?" gasped Will, "I do not have a clue about how to accomplish such a thing. It's nice you would think of me but it's totally beyond my capabilities."

"I need someone smarter than most to pull off this scheme. I do not need some clod who walks the streets looking for work, or a member of city or town council, or a member of the clergy. I need someone whose integrity is intact. These turbulent times are times when family turn on family hoping to find favor in the Catholic hierarchy by exposing friends, strangers, and even family as heretics, witches, and sorcerers. But even more so, there is widespread ignorance of the scriptures that must be eradicated."

Monmouth continues, "Look Will, I watched you carefully and respectfully bandage the young woman's wrist. I also saw the trust she had in you. You treated her as a worthy human being. I would not send anyone on such a mission without all the pieces of a viable plan in place beforehand. I would also provide some training so you would know how to respond in sticky situations should one ever arrive. I believe we can minimize the risk of any real danger. So, Will, are you willing to help so many who believe in your uncle's work?"

Will wipes his mouth, rubs his eyes, then slowly speaks hoping to be out of earshot of Cyril, "Holy Mother of God, you're testing me, is this not so? Did Cyril put you up to this? Does my father or anyone else know you are here? Really Mr. Monmouth and please, if I may, can I call you Humphrey? This is getting really personal. What is going on?"

"First, Yes, you many call me Humphrey. Second, nothing untoward is going on Will." says Monmouth as he gestures to Will to calm down.

Once Will catches his breath, Monmouth continues, "You must maintain this information is strict confidence. A plan is being put together to smuggle the last of your Uncle's Bibles back into England. We want to hide them as part of a shipment of herbs and other drugs being imported from Europe. This is a legitimate importation and is being done under the auspices of a London Guild of Apothecaries, so the risk is absolutely nil."

"But why someone like me", asks Will, "Are there not many Apothecaries or others in London who could do this for you?"

"We need a smart and dedicated Apothecary to pull this off, preferably someone not known in London circles. Spies are everywhere and such scum would like to earn a fat reward or curry favor with the Lord Mayor, The Lord Bishop or any one of the King's hang-around clergy by exposing us and our plans."

Will thinks for a moment, then looks Monmouth in the eye and says, "Humphrey, your being here places me in the middle of a moral dilemma. When I got up this morning I thought God had finally put in place his plan giving direction for the rest of my life. I can assure you becoming a smuggler was not what I saw him offering as an option."

Will pauses for a moment, then again looks straight into Monmouth's eyes and states, "I need a little time to think. Can I give you an answer tomorrow? In the meantime, I have sent a messenger to my mother telling her there will be one more guest for dinner tonight. Because of the Well-Dressing Festival several aunts, uncles, and cousins are gathering at our home and I am sure they would rather hear of Uncle William's martyrdom from you than from me. Please say that you will join me?"

"Already I can see you are thinking ahead and that is reaffirming to my decision to ask you on this quest," says Monmouth. "Yes, I will meet you at your home tonight and I will tell your family about your uncle. If you accept my offer you will have to give them another reason for why you are coming to London. Is that all right?"

"Yes, that would be fine."

Will thinks to himself, "*Already the lies have started. This is not a good beginning. Am I better off accepting the quiet and safe life of my small town? If so, then why I am so intrigued by the offer of Monmouth? Is this the itch I need to scratch if I am ever to find some purpose or meaning to my life?*"

Will and Humphrey leave the back room and go out into the public space in the front of the Apothecary. As they approach Cyril he speaks to Will saying, "Will, you look worried about something. I have enjoyed my time this morning at the Well Dressing Festival so why not take a couple of hours and go enjoy the beautiful artwork. Perhaps being in a crowd of people will do wonders to improve your mood. I know some of your childhood friends would love to spend a little time with you."

With an approving nod from both men, Will takes this unexpected small respite. As he exits the front door he notices Cyril and Humphrey in conversation.

"Hmmm," thinks Will to himself, "It's as if those two know each other. No, that cannot be right. All this news and intrigue is causing my mind to play tricks on me. I have to decide, am I a qualified Apothecary? shop owner? or a smuggler?"

As Will walks around the town square with its public well his nose is assaulted by the smells of many familiar organic materials used to make the Well-Dressing mosaics. He also smells street vendors with their myriad foods for sale. His eyes are also distracted by people wearing colorful bits of garb and the crush of them all trying to crowd around a favored mosaic while chatting about its biblical-themed message.

The general cacophony of the crowds is a distracting drone to Will's ears and allow him to give each mosaic only a perfunctory glance. Will quickly moves past each piece mostly distracted however by thinking about Humphry's invitation and by asking himself several times over," Should *I accept this dangerous adventure, or should I stay here where my life is safe and predictable?"*

Later, as he heads back to the Apothecary, Will has convinced himself, "*Smuggling Bibles into England is a damn dangerous business and if I accept Monmouth's tempting offer, I will be totally risking everything, perhaps even my life, in this undertaking. I have never done anything like this before. I have no skills as a smuggler."*

But once he and Cyril serve a flood of customers later that day Will has concluded, *"It must be God's will calling me to help with my Uncle's important work. As Uncle Will willingly risked his all to see God's words revealed to England's people, then so must I."*

-Chapter 5-

The Tyndale Farm home
Early evening, Saturday 21
November 1536

That evening Will introduces Humphrey Monmouth to his family as they gather to enjoy each other's company and chat about the weather, each other, and a favorite Well Dressing mosaic or experience. Before the family sits around a large wooden table and wanting to escape the sounds of women preparing a meal, all the men move outside to share mugs of ale.

Once outside Will, Humphrey, Will's father and his two uncles, Victor and Arthur, enjoy Humphrey's reading from a thirty-six-year-old copy of The Miller's Tale from Geoffrey Chaucer's Canterbury Tales. Will's father asks, ""How, under heaven's green earth, did you ever get a copy of that ribald book?"

"It was not difficult. I found a copy on one of my travels to Europe," replies Humphrey.

"Well, it certainly paints a true picture of how the landed gentry, high society, and even English church leadership behave," retorts Will's Uncle Arthur bringing loud laughter and guffaws from the men.

The men are interrupted when Will's mother calls, 'Come inside gentlemen, your meal is ready."

Once their meal of roasted potatoes, boiled young carrots, and a lamb roast with mint sauce, has been washed down with wine and ale for the adults and milk kept cold in a root cellar for the young, Will's mother asks for their attention. She states, "Before we share any news from our guest from London, let's share some bread pudding with raisins and hot custard poured over it."

Then with cries of "Delicious!" they dig into the pudding.

With bellies sated from a full meal and special desert, Wills calls for his family's attention, "Please be quiet as we hear from our guest, Humphrey Monmouth. He has brought special news we all need to hear."

And so, Humphrey shares the news of the death of William Tyndale while some of the family sit stunned and others are visibly shaken.

After a few quiet moments, Arthur speaks, "Mr. Monmouth is a genuinely good man. Several years ago, we both were smuggling my brother's Bibles. I was using barrels of flour to conceal them in order to get them through the London customs house. Monmouth was also smuggling Bibles by wrapping them in bolts of cloth. We both were successful even as we faced persecution from the Lord

Mayor of London and Sir Thomas More. I was not caught but Mr. Monmouth was, and he spent several months in a dungeon. The persecution of folks wanting to read a Bible has gotten worse and it is harder on those who engage in helping bring God's words to the common man."

Arthur's last remark did not go unnoticed when both he and his nephew exchanged glances.

The family next chatted among themselves about the Reformation and how dangerous it had become for anyone with the last name of Tyndale to evade "heretic hunters". They ended their evening wishing they could do more to stop Sir Thomas More and his widespread campaign to stop folks from reading the Bible. Then they said a prayer for their martyred relative.

Will retired for the night after everyone had gone and after he and his female cousins and sisters cleaned up the kitchen. But Will did not sleep as his mind raced over the events of the last few days. He decided to head downstairs for another bite of left-over pudding hoping it would settle him. He was surprised to see his mother sitting at the kitchen table. She beamed at her son's presence.

"What are you doing up so late? Was Father snoring again?" Will spoke first as he knows snoring is an issue between them because of how the beds in their home are built into alcoves along an outside wall. Each alcove has a curtain drawn across the face of it to help keep body heat inside the alcove more than relying on blankets alone. Unfortunately, it also keeps sounds echoing inside the alcove and when someone is snoring the sound can be pretty loud and unnerving.

Will's mother, whose Christian name is Constance replies, "Will, your father usually snores, and when he does is so loud he can awaken the dead and perhaps devil himself. But not tonight, as it was I that had trouble sleeping.

"Oh! says Will, "Any reason for that?"

"Yes, I was thinking of my poor brother-in-law and the terrible ordeal he must have gone through. I just cannot imagine the deprivations he endured in order to uphold his integrity and convictions. Many folks see the Tyndale's as a stubborn lot, but they are even more so when ideals, integrity, and family are threatened."

Constance is a well-suited name for Will's mother. It was introduced into the English vocabulary by Normans and was derived from a Latin word meaning "steadfastness" or "one who is constant." It is also the name of William the Conquerors daughter and Will's mother bears her name proudly. Will adores his mother because of her steadfastness being the rock he can always rely upon for an honest answer.

Constance is a freckle skinned, short-statured woman. Her blue eyes, freckles and auburn hair speak to her Irish heritage. Will's father met her when he was on a trip to Ireland trying to earn a living as a travelling salesman of farm tools. Though smart and practical, Constance, like so many of the women of her time, is not well schooled but has great practical insight, especially about people. Her ability to manage the farm's finances has done more to keep the farm afloat than Will's father. Constance accepts her place as a dutiful housewife and loves her husband and three children equally. She supported and encouraged Will's decision to become an apothecary without hesitation.

"Will, I believe in you and have told you before you will be successful in life no matter what you do. God put a great intelligent head upon your shoulders and filled it also with a curiosity about the world around you. I have seen how much enjoyment you get applying the knowledge Mr. Blackham has taught you. However, sometimes being smart can be a burden and a hindrance when it when it causes you to ruminate over decisions, specially life-changing ones, like buying Cyril's apothecary." Constance says to Will as she reaches out to take his hand.

"Mother, you know me pretty well, you know I am not the type of man who can snap his fingers and make a quick decision. I truly wish I were more like Father or Uncle Arthur."

"Well, my dear, if you were more like them then you would not be you. You can see the consequences of your actions long before others. However, once you make a commitment you always follow through until you find success."

As Will lets her words sink in, she continues, "I often have wished you had more faith in yourself and I blame a lot of that on your father. He likely pushed you too hard when you were younger by expecting you to perform like a man before you had a chance to grow into one."

"Do you think father treats my sisters as he treats me? It's hard for me to see and differences as I spend so much time at the Apothecary"

"No, he treats them well. They are smart like you. But, both your father and I worry they might not be able to marry well. There is a shortage of decent, hard-working men in this area who would appreciate your sister's companionship and not be intimidated by their intelligence. But in my heart and soul, I just want all three of my children to marry for love, like I did."

"You seem to be somewhat pensive, Mother."

"Will, I have a feeling that Mr. Monmouth came to do more than visit the Well Dressing Festival and bring news of your uncle's martyrdom. What is it you know that we do not?"

Will smiles at her directness and replies, "Mother, you know me well and you are correct, there is more going on than just a simple visit.by Monmouth."

"My dear son, I can read on your face that something is amiss. What is bothering you? Someday when you are a parent you will be able to tell when your children are worried about something."

Will has always been able to talk to his mom about anything. Their special bond has always been based on direct talk and unshakable trust. And so, he replies," Well, Mother, three things are bothering me: First, if Mr. Monmouth knew Uncle Arthur in days past why did he not go to him as Uncle William's brother? Wouldn't Uncle Arthur, a brother, be the most appropriate person to approach rather than me as a nephew?

"Perhaps Mr. Monmouth lost touch with Uncle Arthur over the years and perhaps he did not know he lived near here," Constance replied.

"Perhaps. But, secondly, I got a small inkling that Mr. Blackham may have known Mr. Monmouth in day's past. Cyril seemed a little bit secretive and protective of Mr. Monmouth. You know that both have London backgrounds. Do you know anything about that relationship? Some idle gossip from days past?"

"No son, I know of nothing to connect those two."

"Thirdly, I have a huge decision to make." Will took a deep breath and confided, "Mr. Monmouth asked me to retrieve a thousand of Uncle William's bibles from a printer's warehouse in Europe. It terrifies me thinking of all that foreign travel and becoming a smuggler.

Will sees his mother's eyes widen.

"The risk," as Will shudders, "Is my being caught and being burned at the stake like Uncle William, this whole matter I find most daunting."

Will looks into his mother s eyes, "On top of everything else, no news of any of this can be shared with anyone especially my blabbermouth sisters and aunts. It is just too damn dangerous. I do not even want Father to know. I promised Mr. Monmouth I would not tell anybody of his mission, but with you I know I can share anything, and you will keep it to yourself."

"I will keep your secret," replies his mother, "It makes sense that Cyril and Humphrey Monmouth could have known each other in London. As I think on that a little more I remember both are merchants who could have belonged to similar guilds. However, Cyril is older than Humphrey and that old fellow has been here for thirty years, so whatever the connection between them is, it has to be one that is quite a way back into the past. I would say to trust your instincts if you feel there is more to their relationship than meets the eye."

Constance pauses then speaks again. "My dear son, have you considered how dangerous smuggling Bibles can be during these rough and anxious times. What seemed to Uncle Arthur as just a game a few years ago is now a deadly serious business."

"I agree Mother, but Monmouth says he has a very workable plan with all the pieces to make it work in place," Will replies.

"Maybe so, but no matter how well something is organized and no matter how much Monmouth has planned for every conceivable issue, something will happen to spoil the best of plans," answers Constance with a stern look and raised voice.

As she takes Will's arm she lowers her voice and says, "You're not serious about going on this wild adventure, are you?"

"Hush, Mother, let's not wake father."

After a pause Will says, "By God's truth, I don't know what to do. On one hand I want to finish Uncle William's legacy; yet on the other hand I do not want to uproot my life here. Cyril wants me to settle down and get married. Father wants me to quit everything and be a farmer. I am so weary of having my life dictated by the whims, fancies, best-intentions, and rules of small-town living.

Will takes his Mother's hand and says, "A few days ago I was convinced I would open my own Apothecary, once I became a Master Apothecary, and move to a different town. If that were to happen I would want it in a town close by and one that permitted me to come home on holidays and festival days. And it would be a town far enough away that I would not be competition for Cyril. But now, that plan has gone askew as Cyril has given me the opportunity to replace him and not move anywhere."

Again, Will pauses to look at his mother, "The prospect of going to London would be a chance to really test my mettle. But the risk and the dangers are most unnerving. So now, what sage advice do you have for your troubled son? What do you truthfully think I should do?"

Will's mother again takes her son's other hand and speaks slowly, "My son I could not be prouder of you and the honest and moral man you have become. The local townspeople, whether I meet them in the market, on the street, or in church, all say they admire your skills at healing, Your fairness in dealing with them, and especially your integrity in listening to them and keeping their confidences is what I hear over and over. Many say they prefer your advice and skills on medical matters more so than Cyril's."

Will blushes at the accolade and can only say "Uh!"

Will's mother continues, "Many have told me you are an old soul in a young person's body. There is not one mother I know who wants to see her son move away or take a position that might bring danger to him. But to my way of thinking there are two considerations you need to resolve. The first consideration is the quest that Monmouth brings to you. It is honorable and it opens up to a world of new experiences. To accomplish what he is asking would be a huge contribution to completing your Uncle's legacy and a huge test of who you are. However, I pray others will take up the cause of seeing to it the whole country someday has access to a bible written in English."

"Now, also think about this" she continues, "You are not a huge risk-taker. However, without some risk in life people never change, nor find happiness, nor find satisfaction in their work, nor see themselves as worthy human beings."

After another short pause she addresses what she believes is Will's biggest concern, "My son, this is your second consideration, Your Father's rough and gruff manner comes from his inability to show his emotions. In many ways he loves you very much he just is unable to express it. You are like him in many ways. When he made his decision to settle on this farm, it was a decision he made alone. You too must make you own decision as to which path you will take. But if you stay to work a deal with Cyril you will have to live with that decision the rest of your life."

Will embraces his mother. "Thank you for all your wisdom and insight. I can go to bed now and think about my life ahead. You will be the first to know in the morning. Then, I will be off to tell both Cyril and Monmouth my decision. However, I do wish father would have been more forthright over the years about his behavior. I understand him better now but my feelings towards him remain strong. I promise to work hard at overcoming them."

Will pauses before climbing the stairs to his room. Calmly he turns and says to his mother, "I have been a little naïve these past many years when it comes to my life and work. Maybe I am as smart as you say I am, and I have let my imagination run amuck and let it keep me from seeing my father as he really is. If I decide to follow after Monmouth it will be because I want to, because I want to see some of the world beyond Hodthorpe, and because I want to learn how to be happy on my own terms."

Will kisses his mother on the cheek, hugs her and says, "Mother, I genuinely love you and I am truly proud to be your son. Someday, I hope to meet a woman who will be as forthright and as smart as you."

"One last thought before you retire, Will. We are a family of faith and especially so after understanding the scriptures because of your uncle's extraordinary work. I know you have been thinking that perhaps God has a plan for your life, and you are patiently waiting for it to be revealed. It seems to me that you cannot see what God has in store for you until you step out and trust him to guide you. God does favor the risk-takers."

At that they both extinguish the household candles and lamps, bank the fireplace, and retire for the evening. Constance makes her way to her sleeping cubicle and lies next to her husband; a tear runs down her cheek. She is overtaken by her anxiety about what Will may have decided by the next morning.

-Chapter 6-

Morning Sunday November 22, 1536

The Blackham Apothecary

The next morning Will leaves the family farm before anyone arises so he can arrive at Blackham's Apothecary "a little early" just as Cyril requested. Once he enters the apothecary he sees Cyril Blackham already behind the compounding table. He approaches Cyril with a cheery "Good Morning!'" and then asks him, "Would it be possible for you to delay your retirement for a few months?"

Cyril responded, "Does your query have anything to do with why Humphrey Monmouth is here? Who, by the way, did he indicate to you he was leaving today on a three-day coach trip to London? I can only presume he has pressing business."

Will responds quickly by saying, "Cyril, before I answer you, please answer me this. I have an inkling you two might have known each other in the distant past. Did I read that correctly?"

Cyril asks, "Why do you ask?"

"I have been thinking I may want to go to London before I settle down and get tied up with all the details of running this shop six days a week. Also, perhaps a nice trip away from here would help me clear my head about the need to settle down… as you have been so quick to point out."

Cyril scratches his ear, rubs his nose, adjusts his pince-nez, then he looks at Will, "If you have something extra you would like to say then go ahead and say it. As for you going to London I could manage here for a couple of months if you want to go and see what a filthy, loud, and smelly town it is. You will find it filled with loose women and ruffians who will lift your purse and likely stick a knife in your ribs as easy as if they were peeling an onion.. You may wish you had never gone away from the safety and comfort of home."

Will shudders at Cyril's comment. "Well ... It sounds like you know that city well if I may be so bold to assert."

Dodging Will's suspicion, Cyril says "If Monmouth has put some foolish ideas into your head I think you should run over to the stagecoach station and talk to him. But do so now before his coach leaves for London."

Will sees Cyril's remarks as an opportunity to finally bring closure on his decision. He dons his jacket, turns to Cyril, and says, "Thank you" and heads to the station.

He quickly leaves the Apothecary and heads briskly across the six streets to the edge of town where the stagecoach is loading freight and a few passengers.

Will finds Humphrey perched on a crate. As he approaches Humphrey, Will blurts out in a manner that is as much of a surprise to him as it is to Monmouth, "Mr. Monmouth, I accept! I will come to London right after Christmas. We can talk more when I get there about those special plans you mentioned. Staying here until the holidays are over will allow me to put my affairs in order and conclude some family issues as well as resolve my position with Cyril."

"That would be simply fine Master Will,' says Monmouth, "I am pleased you are coming to see me. We will meet eight weeks hence on this same day. Come to The Drapers Guild at noon. Later that day you will be a guest in my home."

Monmouth adds, "Besides, Will" as he smiles and leans forward to shake Will's hand," London always smells better at that time of year anyway."

Will notices only one of the three folks standing around the coach is boarding. The other two are saying their farewells to the man. The coach driver and its six horses seem eager to get going. Other people standing about are placing luggage and freight on top of the coach for either delivery to stations along the route or to London itself.

As the coach's driver starts to step up and onto his seat Will helps Humphrey step up and into the coach. Will then stands alongside the coach's open side door and whispers, Really and truthfully Mr. Monmouth, I appreciate the trust you are placing me. I will work hard not to let you down. But before we say goodbye, is there any connection between you and Cyril that I should know about?"

"Oh my," says Monmouth, "I think the game is now afoot, your astute powers of observation will hold you in good stead on our quest. But let me answer your question Cyril and I are related…but on my Mother's side"

"Well! I'll be damned," mumbles Will, "I suspected something was amiss yesterday as he treated you with behavior I had never seen before, even after seven years of working with him."

Humphrey closes the stagecoach door, leans forward through its window and says to Will, "Your astuteness, intellect and integrity plus your ability to observe and read people have again convinced me my invitation to have you come to London is well warranted."

Humphrey shakes Will's hand then adds, "May you have a great upcoming Holiday with your family. Good-bye for now Will. Rest assured; all will be ready for your visit when we meet in London after the New Year. At your convenience just send a letter addressed to me at the Drapers Guild Hall should anything be amiss as well as the exact day on which you plan to arrive. That special cargo we spoke of earlier will be quite safe until you retrieve it."

The men shake hands again just as the coachman hollers at his six horses to move forward. Once the stagecoach leaves Will watches it until it travels around the first curve on the edge of town and then onto a deeply rutted dirt road heading south.

As Will walks back towards the shop, he thinks, "*I can't believe I just made that huge commitment; I must be out of my mind thinking I can do this."*

Back in the Apothecary Will busies himself in the back room by grinding some cochineal in a brass mortar using a brass pestle. He is using the brass mortar, rather than a wood or porcelain one, as he does not want the cochineal's carmine dye to stain any medicinal by being a residue in any porous apothecary equipment. He likes to do this when he is alone as customers are often upset seeing him grind up the ugly little dried-out insects who secrete the dye.

Later when Will returns to the shop front to be with Cyril Will asks, "Since you do know Humphrey and are aware of what he is up to, do you think I could trust him to do what he says?"

"There is not a finer man in all of England," Cyril replies. I would trust the man without question. We have kept each other's secrets for more than thirty years. I am not sure what he has in store for you, but whatever it is it will be well planned and thoroughly tested. Personally, I will not tell you what to do nor when and how to do it".

Cyril then leans into Will and says," If you do go to see Monmouth in London I may have to find another Master Apothecary to take over this shop as I want to retire and do so before summer of next year. Either way you will have my heartiest endorsement, my blessing, and prayers for your success. It's also been my privilege to have tutored you these many years."

With a tear in his eye, Will's voice cracks as he says to Cyril, "I am sure now of what I must do. Let us work together on a plausible reason that we can use to quell any suspicions from townsfolk who may query my absence after the Holiday Season."

"Oh, that will be easy," chimes in Cyril, "We shall say to anyone who asks that I am sending you to London to learn some new compounding skills and to become acquainted in the use of the latest medicines, especially those for the treatment of syphilis."

"Excellent," says Will, "Let that be our common story. I cannot say it enough, but I truly am grateful you are such a large part of my life. I assure you I will do all I can to make my mission with Monmouth something we can be proud of."

"No thanks are needed. It is I who is proud to have you around, even if it has been seven years since you walked in here and showed interest in medicines. I have watched you grow into a fine young man."

-Chapter 7-

On the road to London England,
Saturday 16 January 1537

There was no snow on the ground when Will left Hodthorpe for London. But it being England, January was cold, damp, and overcast. Will hoped his four-day trip would be uneventful and he would not have to converse with anyone. He was alone the first day but on the second a travelling preacher and schoolteacher joined him in the coach. When the preacher asked where he was going he sheepishly replied, "I am going to London to undertake some training with the London Guild of Apothecaries..

On the fourth day Will arrived in London tired from all the bumping along on dirty and well rutted roads but once there the reality of what could lie before him had him excited. He spent his last two nights trying to sleep in rooms above a travelers' inn and was dismayed by those experiences. Both rooms had either two or three men sharing a bed and four or more sleeping on the floor. While the sounds of snoring reverberated throughout the room this did nothing to make Will's two nights anywhere near restful. But Will convinced himself, *"Yes, I am tired from my travel but this is better than walking or riding alone on a mare. Besides there is some safety in numbers."*

As Will's coach quickly entered the center of London the driver headed straight for his home stables Will is lulled by the rhythm of the horse's hooves and their rhythmic and distinct clackety-clack on cobblestone streets, But soon Will is aware of many odd and pungent smells as they drove further and further into the city. At one-point Will leaned forward and pulled back one of the coach's curtained door windows curious to see out at what he thinks will be a beautiful city with wide boulevards and stately homes. *"After all,"* he muses, *"I have been led to believe all 100,000 souls who live here* are wealthy."

Instead Will is dismayed at all the smells, noises, and the crush of street people who must dodge his coach and horses. He is also taken aback by street people pushing carts full of wares while others are begging coins for a meal. He sees others offering meat pies, nuts, and other foods for sale… most of which Will can smell as he passes. By the time they reach the coach's home station Will's emotions are running high because of the squalor he has witnessed and especially the piles of human and animal excrement he has seen, but especially by the look of despair and hopelessness on the faces of countless pale and gaunt street urchins..

Will is also disturbed by the lack of smiling faces among London's crushing, noisy, and bustling street people, *"I was naive to think London was full of people like*

Monmouth: well-spoken, upper class folk wearing fine clothing. However, peasants back home have it much better than many of these poor sods, at lease those back home appear cleaner and happier

Once Will steps down from the stagecoach, retrieves his two travelling bags, he asks the driver for directions to the Draper's Hall. He is told, " It is but a short distance away, walk along that street in front of you for three streets, then go left for two streets, as you cross the street you will see an open square and it will be the three story, grey stone building second on your right."

As Will walks London's streets his eyes, ears, and nose are again assaulted by all he sees, especially the crush of people with no one smiling or stopping to say hello or "good day." Scrunching his nose, Will thinks, *"When this trip is over I will never think Hodthorpe as bad as I make it out to be. At least it is cleaner, quieter, smells better and not every person looks like they want to assault or rob you. God Almighty if I do not get to that Drapers Hall soon I may turn around and go home. I better hang on tight to my valises as you never know how attractive they could be to a thief."*

As Will walks along to the end of the route he was told, he finds a street a little wider and cleaner than those he travelled before. Now the street opens into a square and he can readily see the Greystone building he was directed to.

He feels relief he has found the correct building as he sees a brass sign to the right of its front door announcing it as home to "The Ancient Guild of Drapers."

Will muses, *"This has to be it, why don't they just update this sign and call themselves by the more appropriate "Haberdashers" instead of "Drapers." Oh well, I sure hope Monmouth is inside."*

Will finds the door locked. He hesitates and thinks, *"What the hell is this? No public building back home is ever locked. Have I come here on a feast Day or Holiday?*

Just then he notices another brass plate just above the center of the door: It reads, TO ENTER RING BELL BY PULLING KNOB.

Will pulls the brass knob under the sign and can hear a ringing sound on the other side of the door. A moment later a man in a bright green livery uniform opens the door and snarls at Will saying, "What do you want?"

"I have come a long way to meet Humphrey Monmouth at your fine establishment. We made an appointment to meet here today and at this time. Is he here?" Will asks.

At the mention of Monmouth, the doorman smiles and his eyes brighten. He then turns to face Will and he says, "Why most certainly. You must be the young man Master Monmouth has been expecting. I see you have two valises with you. You can leave them here in the cloak room and I will take you through to where Mr. Monmouth is waiting for you. And for lunch, today we are having steak and kidney pie. Would you like to join him for our mid-day meal?"

Will gazes past the open door and is startled by the opulence he sees. Dark wood paneling, huge candelabras, several oil paintings on the walls, and dark wood floors that seem spotless and freshly waxed. He is awed, but manages to utter to the doorman, "Thank you, it's nice you would offer a meal. I have been travelling three days and have had little to eat and most of that was cold. It will be nice to sit with Mr. Monmouth and partake of your hospitality. Will you please take me to Mr. Monmouth?"

The doorman takes Will into an enormous dining room containing a dozen and a half white-linen covered tables with place settings for six at each. Even with the room's capacity of near a hundred Will can see only about a dozen folk engrossed in either a meal or hiding behind a newspaper. Once Will recognizes Monmouth sitting by himself at a corner table, Monmouth has already seen him and rises to great him.

"Ah! Master Will, how good it is to see you. I trust your journey was uneventful. Please sit down as we have lots to talk about."

Monmouth extends his hand to shake Will's. After which the two men sit as the doorman retires from the room to fetch Will his meal and a flagon of ale to help wash it down.

Once the two are alone Monmouth turns to Will and they exchange some pleasantries about Will's trip to London. Monmouth inquires about Will's health and that of his family and Cyril Blackham. Then With pleasantries dispensed with Monmouth leans closer to Will and says in a quieter voice, "Will, I know you are anxious to get on with why you are here, but this place is not the best place to talk about such things. Once we leave here I will take you to my home on the outskirts of London where you will stay for a couple of weeks as my guest and until I am sure you are comfortable with our quest. A lot of detail must be put in place… and most are. So, let us enjoy our meal then I will get you comfortably settled."

Will looks at Monmouth with a certain degree of trepidation and says, "I know you have many details to put into place. I am overwhelmed by all I have seen since I got to this huge town. This Guild Hall is gorgeous. There is nothing like it in Hodthorpe. I believe it is good we have time to get used to our quest."

Their conversation is interrupted when Monmouth and Will look up at a wait staff bringing their food. Again, Will is impressed at seeing their food served on a silver tray with a silver dome. When the dome is lifted Will sees their food on blue and white porcelain plates he recognizes as being made by Delft craftsmen. Two pewter tankards of brown ale are also on the tray.

The two men eat their meals in silence, but Will tackles his with gusto. Once finished he wipes his mouth with a linen napkin then turns to Monmouth and says," I do not know when I have had a finer meal, I certainly did not eat like this on the trip down here. This meal is delicious. And it was served piping hot. The ale was cool and refreshing."

"Don't go too hog-wild gulping down your food. Once our wait staff see you push your plate away he will rush to replace your plate with a dish of egg custard," says Monmouth

"My favorite! I hope it's as good as my mother's," says Will, "I have to believe it will be like everything else around here, first class and delicious."

After their desert Monmouth says, "Come with me. Will I want to show you something, after which I have a carriage ordered that will take us to my home. Be sure to collect your travel bags before we leave. For now, it is my plan to have you eat all your meals at my home. I have great staff who will look after your needs as if you were family…in fact probably better than many in my family…

as I have some family for whom my staff and I bear a great dislike."

With a smile Monmouth leads Will to a storeroom in the back of the building. There he shows Will a few bolts of cloth and some cotton bales. "Here are how these bolts of cloth were used by me and others to smuggle Tyndale Bibles and his other tracts into England,"

While Monmouth demonstrates he continues "Now I cannot do this anymore. As you may know I was caught and imprisoned for a short time. I had to pay several high officials in the church heavy bribes to extricate myself out of prison. However, there are still spies and some clergy who remain suspicions of me. They would love to determine if I am still in the business of supporting the reformation. Please be careful to whom you talk with while you are here, while on your quest, and especially when it is over."

-Chapter 8-

London England, The Estate of Henry Monmouth
Tuesday 19 January 1537

The hired carriage takes Will and Humphrey from Drapers Guild Hall to a London suburb about half an hour away. As the driver takes them over a few miles of cobblestone streets Will is again lulled with the rhythmic clop, clop, clop of the horse's metal shod hooves.

Then as the carriage slows down Will notices the change in pace and assumes they are at the Monmouth Estate. Will peers out his side window to see iron gates and an iron fence around an estate likely about three acres. Once through the gate they drive the estate's long, curved, tree-lined dirt driveway to a graveled pad in the front of an elegant three-story, red bricked house. Will knows the pad is graveled with small pebbles of quartz known as "chert.", but he has never seen so much of it nor a house so opulent

The driver pulls the coach into a covered porch built out over the middle of the front of the house. The porch is providing shelter for those using its large carved oak front door. Once under this roofed porch the driver jumps down from his seat and opens the coach door for Will and Humphrey. Once both men alight onto the ground, the front door swings open and a maid, cook, gardener, liveryman, two young children and their governess, rush out to greet them.

Will is immediately introduced as," a protégé who will be staying here for several weeks," and to the children as "Master Will. He is an apothecary just like Cousin Cyril. He also works for Cousin Cyril who you remember lives far away in a small town in the midlands called Hodthorpe."

Will stares through the door wide-eyed at seeing this stately home's opulence. Then at Monmouth's invitation to "come inside" Will picks up his bags and walks across the thresh-hold. It is then he notices carved wood-paneling, well-framed and positioned oil paintings and watercolor scenes hanging on hallway walls. He can see also that candelabras and fireplaces are placed strategically around a dining room on the left and a "receiving room" on the right. The receiving room has chairs and settees furnished with green velvet cushions. He notices all windows have regal patterned, maroon themed, heavy damask coverings… among which a few have been opened to reveal lace linings and to let in some late afternoon sunshine and light..

Will's scrutiny is interrupted by a young girl. As she approaches she says, "Good Day kind sir. My name is Mary."

Mary gives a small curtsey then says to Will, "I will take you to a bedroom prepared for you. It is on the second floor. Just leave your two bags here and the butler will bring them up to you. When he does you can put your belongings in the wooden chest beside the bed."

Once they are upstairs Mary points to a ceramic blue Delft basin sitting on a wooden stand with towels draped over a brass rail on each end. The basin is one-third filled with clean water.

Mary says, "You can use this to wash off some of your road grime and city dust before dinner. There is a Thunder Mug under your bed, and it will be cleaned and emptied every day. Your towels will be changed every other day."

Will is impressed with the trappings of his room but finds himself enamored more so by Mary. As he stands near her, he senses a whiff of lavender from her hair. Will has surmised she is in her late teens. He also is fascinated with how pretty she is but also by the fact she has not once looked at him.

"What is your full name, Mary?" Will asks.

"I am just Mary," she says demurely.

"Mary, why do you not look at people when you talk to them?"

"Oh, Sir, that would not be proper."

Will thinks, "I hope when I talk with people I always look at them. I guess what she is saying is, it is her way of being prim and respectful. She certainly knows her station. Now while I am here I guess I better watch my manners and my use of earthy language. I sure do not want to offend anyone in this household, after all I am their guest and not some village idiot or dog in heat."

After Will's two valises, one small and one medium, are delivered and his things put away, he washes up and sits back on the bed to rest. He drifts in and out of sleep for about an hour. He is abruptly interrupted by the sound of a tinkling bell which he concludes is the call to dinner.

Will jaunts downstairs on a massive curved staircase to join Monmouth and his family in an elegant dining room. The dishes one which they ear are imported, and the utensils are heavy silver. Candles light the room. After another large meal, and with much idle chit chat with the family, the two men retire to an adjoining sitting room.

Once comfortable in two overstuffed wing-back chairs, situated to catch the warmth emanating from a fireplace and with both men armed with a small snifter of brandy, Monmouth explains the details for Will's journey to Antwerp.

"This time we will not be hiding Tyndale Bibles in sacks of flour or bolts of cloth," says Monmouth, "rather this time we are transporting those bibles by hiding them in a false floor and in false sides of a specially designed …wagon."

Will looks at him wide-eyed as Monmouth further explains, "This wagon is to be a distraction created to avoid fully being searched by English Customs House officials. You will pay an import duty on the foreign herbs, spices, and medicinal products listed on the wagon's manifest. This manifest also has papers that say you are an emissary of the London Guild of Apothecaries.

"I understand that, but why," asks Will

Monmouth continues, "I and we believe the wagon will get little scrutiny especially with you as a real apothecary entrusted with its care. Being a real apothecary, you add credibility and integrity to any challenges towards the importation of these drugs, herbs, and medicines. Cyril has told me you are professionally qualified to talk about anything stored inside. I am sure you can understand why we cannot trust a local apothecary, nor a fake one, for this risky task for many obvious reasons."

"Yes, I can understand your reasoning", says Will, "but I am not a real Apothecary. I am but a journeyman. How would that look?"

Monmouth continues "Do not to worry. It has been arranged for you to become fully vested into the Ancient Order of Worshipful London Apothecaries and becom a Master Apothecary. This we will do during an initiation ceremony in their Guild Hall.. Once that is over you will be issued papers that identify you as one of their members and as their emissary. These papers will give you a new name. You will become Will Hutchins. Your real last name might arouse unneeded suspicion."

As the enormity of his mission begins to sink in and before Will can question anything he has heard , Will hears Humphrey say, "Your trip to Antwerp will also include your attendance at a series of lectures given by the German physician known as Paracelsus. Do you know of this notable German who lectures at the University of Antwerp.?

"Yes, I have heard of him," replies Will

"Well, in anticipation of your being there the London Apothecary Guild has sent a letter with your credentials and your appointment to represent them. Should anyone ask your story is… you are returning to England with many supplies and medicines advocated by Paracelsus and which are unavailable here in England.

"What's missing from all what I have heard," asks Will

"Oh!, just this, we will give you enough coinage to pay and import taxes and tariffs asked for on either end of your journey. You will also be given funds for your living expenses."

Speaking a little more forcefully Will turns to Humphrey and says, "I admire the thoroughness of all this planning. When we met in Hodthorpe you promised you would have it planned before I got here. I congratulate you for the impressive work you said you would do. This quest is starting to fit together in my mind as being safe and accomplishable. But truthfully, is there anything that can go wrong?"

"Not really," says Humphrey," However I must warn you, the man who betrayed your Uncle, Henry Phillips, might still be in Antwerp.

"What are the odds of running into that poor excuse for a man?"

"Not much odds of that happening," Says Monmouth, "Here is why. Over 5,000 Englishmen live in Antwerp and Phillips cannot engage with or know all of them. So, I believe you will be safe as long as you stay away from public houses and brothels.

Will nods, and Monmouth continues, "Remember this and rely upon its truth. Antwerp is a massive trading port, the largest in Europe, so a wagon full of medicines is not an uncommon sight and especially one leaving the continent for England. There are countless many who make this trip without incident. It your trip goes as all who have contributed to its planning have anticipated you will be all right. Don't forget, however, your knowledge as a true apothecary will be your saving grace should anyone question your right to be there."

"Where are my Uncle's bibles now?" inquires Will.

"They are stored safely in a printer's warehouse. Since the Guttenberg Press was invented a half century ago, Antwerp has become a well-established hub for publishing. Already Europeans have access to Bibles printed in German, French, Swedish, Dutch, and now English. Your uncle's Bibles are quite safe as they are in the hands of reformist supporters, but the longer they stay in Europe the more likely they are to be discovered.

Will nods his understanding and Humphry continues, "Once we get close to your departure date I will give you more detail about where you will stay and with whom you will meet. Believe me, you will be well prepared before I finish your training."

"Training?" Will asks?

"Yes, young man, I want you fully prepared, and comfortable" smiles Humphrey, "And that starts tomorrow. So, let us get a good night's sleep."

After saying their goodnights, Will goes to bed wondering if he has made the right decision to be part of what could become a dangerous and convoluted mission. After a fitful night comparing what his life was like in Hodthorpe, to what he has seen in London, and to what is expected of him in Antwerp, he sits upright and finds himself fully awake ..but in the early morning.

Will feels the need to relieve himself, because of drinking wine during the evening before and having brandy after the evening meal. Putting on his clothes Will goes outside looking for privy. Will finds a gardener who informs Will, "Upper class folk have no need for a privy. You should find a "chamber pot" or "thunder mug" under your bed."

Will reddens, having forgotten that Mary told him of this amenity tucked under his bed. As he returns back to his room using the back door or servant's entrance he hears a clatter in the kitchen. He realizes servants have arrived early and must be readying for their day's work. He finds his "thunder mug" where he was told it would be and snickers at the sound he makes while using it.

-Chapter 9-

Morning at the Home of George deBergdorf, Antwerp
Belgium Thursday 21 January 1537.

While Will belabors over his mission in England, in
Antwerp Belgium a mother, daughter and son are enjoying
each other's company and a simple breakfast of porridge
and milk.

The mother, Margareit deBergdorf, finishes her
porridge and says to her son, Ahren, and her daughter, Elke,
"You both have worked hard helping keep your father's
shop a business able to support us. I know how difficult it
has been not having your father here. He would be proud
knowing he taught you well. His passing was too sudden. I
know you miss him as much as I."

As the siblings pause, Margareit breaks their silence
saying, "Now, let us move on to another matter. I have
received a notice that in a few days your father's good
friend, Humphrey Monmouth, the English merchant, will
send someone here. It will be his task to pick up the
remaining Tyndale bibles left behind when Tyndale was
martyred. You must be quiet about this. No one must know
about our involvement in getting those bibles out of this
country."

Margareit then gives her children a stern look to
which both nod their assurance they understand her words.

She then turns to Elke saying, "I believe it best if you, my daughter, meet this new fellow when he arrives. He is coming by boat from England. Your ability to speak his English language is better than mine or Ahren's. I will give you the details of who he is when it's close to his arrival."

Elke thinks," *Knowing Monmouth I bet he will send some stodgy, old, and ill-mannered servant from his drapery business. I hope he has not asked mother to lodge him in our home. Good Lord above, I pray his stay in Antwerp is no more than a day or two for all our safety and our sanity.* "

Margareit seeing the look on Elke's face says, "I can read your mind like an open book, Elke! I am sure this man's stay will likely be no more than a couple of weeks. Monmouth has indicated he is sending a real Apothecary."

"Oh great!, Elke muses, "Likely some tottering old fool who would rather reminisce about the way things used to be that the way things are today," she cringes.

Her mother notices the furrowed brow on Elke but continues," This fellow will be attending lectures at the University while we ready the Bibles for transport. We honor both your father and his friend, Master Tyndale, by seeing these Bible safely leave our country. It would cause a danger to us and to all printers in this area if those Bibles were found as I can assure you the long arm of the Catholic church would reach out and punish us."

Margareit is a petite woman who when standing erect is about five foot three. While she is of slim build with short cropped gray hair she has twinkling eyes that can turn stern in a flash. She wears the white linen cap and horned headdress so fashionable with women of that day so that its up and outward facing cones completely conceal the front of her hair as do its starched white veil… attached with pins to the back of her head.

Physically, Margareit is not at all like her 20-year-old daughter Elke. Elke is five foot eight, shapely and with long curly brown hair cascading down to her shoulders. Elke's bright blue eyes and warm smile make her instantly likeable. Her outgoing nature and beauty have made many a man's heart flutter, but most were intimidated by her head strong, well-read, intelligence and quick wit. Elke has not had any long-term suitor or short-term beau because she finds most men boorish, humorless, and unable to carry on a civil or intelligent conversation without using crude language or sexual innuendo.

Elke adores her brother Ahren. Ahren, who is four years older than Elke, is muscular and six feet tall. It is obvious to all who meet the two siblings that they care for each other. They are almost capable of finishing each other's sentences when they speak. Ahren's soft face, blue eyes, curly brown hair and smile also tell the casual observer the two are brother and sister, even with their age difference.

As the family continue to engage in light conversation, a sharp knock is heard at the door. Ahren goes to see who it is. As he approaches the door, it opens and a short, portly, dark-haired, and bushy bearded man enters their home. His eyes are mere slits and dark. He is wearing a uniform consisting of a brown jacket, brown leggings, brown knee-high boots and brown leather cap with a visor. The emblem of an Antwerp constable is embroidered on his jacket

"Don't get up," he blurts in a commanding voice, "Its only me, Raymond Gagnon."

He walks into the kitchen and looks at Elke saying, "I was going about my rounds and thought I would stop in and have a friendly chat."

Then ignoring Ahren and his mother, he continues to look at Elke, this time saying "So, what say you girl? Will you come outside and sit on the door stoop so we can visit?"

His voice has a bit of a menacing tone. It is obvious Elke finds the man boorish and almost disgusting. She looks at her mother and then her brother for their assistance.

Elke's mother nods her head and says, "Constable Gagnon, you know Elke is still a maiden. She needs to be chaperoned. If she sits on the stoop with you, we will have to leave the front door open and her brother will need to sit with you. Opening the door will let out all the heat from the fireplace. I think the air is still a bit chilly, and since we have a lot of work to do before the day is done I believe it best we keep Elke to her work schedule"

Gagnon looks almost stunned at what he perceives is a rebuke at his "command" but before he can say anything Margareit says, "Perhaps you have pressing civil duties to attend to today. After all you are such an important man here in Antwerp. Perhaps it would be best if you call again when we are all not so busy."

Elke feels herself caught in the middle of a now win situation and not wanting to escalate the conversation between her mother and Gagnon thinks to herself, "*My family knows Gagnon is a bully and ruthless. He is also too lazy to work an honest trade. Everyone knows he is corrupt and accepts bribes by preying on the weak and on itinerant folk who simply want to be left alone. I can't cause an ugly scene today or this mangy son of a dog may take it out on my brother or mother.*"

So, Elke does what she thinks best. She grabs a large shawl from the back of a stool, puts it around her shoulders and head using it to hide as much of her womanly features and face as she can. As she does this she now thinks, "*Perhaps if I look more like a nun it might cool this man's bluster. The last thing I want is for him to turn amorous when his stink assaults my nostrils. With the loss of my father we are somewhat unable to fight this man's intrusion into our lives. It falls on me to keep peace."*

So now wrapped in her shawl Elke speaks, "Mother! Just leave the front door open. I will sit there with the constable for just a few minutes. Then we can all get on with our work as he too must have responsibilities that will take him all day to complete."

Elke looks at constable Gagnon and says, "May I remind you this family is still in mourning. The loss of my father has been unbearable. Church rules are such that we will likely be in mourning for over a year before we are able to enjoy social engagements. I will spend a few minutes sitting on the stoop, because my Mother is right, the air is chilly, the heat is escaping, and we all have work that needs to be done. Do you understand?"

"Yea, I do," he replies rather condescendingly.

Once Elke and Raymond are sitting on the stoop, Elke silently prays, *Please God, bring your divine intervention to this place and make this visit calm and short."*

Raymond interrupts her prayer and tells her, "Now that you father has gone you need a real man about your house. I believe the best man to do that would be me. I can win your heart if only you will give me a chance. You will soon be old enough to be called a spinster. Once that happens then no man will want you. I have a good job and I can support you, your mother, and your brother. I will protect your family in a manner that only an officer of the city can. So, what say you? What hope can you give my petition?"

"I really do appreciate your interest in me, but it would be unseemly if I were to enter into any arrangement with anybody right now. My family and I are still mourning the loss of my father and it may take more than a year to mourn him and to straighten out all the affairs associated with his printing business," says Elke under low breath and with gritted teeth.

"Maybe so, but I will not wait forever. I will have you," says Raymond in a threatening manner. He grabs her wrist and gives it a twist. "I know no other man will dare come near you. I have made my intentions known to every man here in this town who might dare oppose or meddle in our future union."

Just then Elke's mother breaks into their conversation saying, "It is time, dear daughter, we have a big day ahead with much work to do. Please say goodbye to the constable."

Grateful for her mother's intervention, Elke walks inside, shuts the door, slides the lock then says to her mother, "Thanks for rescuing me from that awful boorish man. He is the personification of evil. I cannot imagine any women wanting to lie in a bed with him. It would make me vomit. I would rather stay a spinster than endure his touch. I cannot be alone in my thinking like this otherwise why would a man twice my age still be single. There is just so much about him that defines him as the perfect horse's ass. God, I pray I have a good day ahead after sitting next to that pond scum."

-Chapter 10-

Early evening, The Estate of Henry Monmouth –

Sunday 24 January 1537

As they start another evening meal, Monmouth introduces Will to a new guest. This man is a Carthusian Monk, named Brother Gregory. Will immediately takes a liking to the man who he assesses as being similar in build and height as him but perhaps about 10 years older. Will is silent during the meal as a few pleasantries are passed around making Will all the more curious about who the visitor is and why he is there. His only conclusion is Brother Gregory is somehow part of the plan Humphrey has set in motion

Once their dinner is finished Humphrey turns to Will, saying, "I invited Brother Gregory here to meet you, not only because he and his Monks support the Reformation, and your uncle's work, but because you will need some instruction on how to answer questions about being a good Catholic. It's possible you might be challenged at some time to prove your faith either here or in Antwerp."

Once they are seated comfortably in the adjoining drawing room, a fire is lit, and brandy is shared. It is then that Brother Gregory says, "Will, I am going to spend the next several hours with you. It may be a long night."

Will replies, "I am ready, so let us get started. We have full bellies and we are quite comfortable here in this warm room with its fireplace and brandy."

Brother Gregory nods, smiles, and says, "Our order is currently under suspicion by London authorities, and especially the Lord Cardinal, the Lord Mayor, and the Lord Chancellor to Henry VIII."

Will nods that he understands then listens as Brother Gregory continues, "The reason for all this intrigue is because my brothers have challenged many of the Catholic dogma and ritual. However, we want reform to come from within the church rather than see it come from without and especially so with all the incivility and violence that will bring. You are wise enough to know all I institutions rot from within, especially when its powerful turn corrupt, and we would like to stop reverse that within the church."

Again, Will nods his understanding

Brother Gregory proceeds, "Our goal is to stop all the bloodshed when good citizens are charged with heresy and often face a death penalty for having read a Bible in their native tongue. Additionally, this country is losing some of its best and well-educated citizenry who flee to other lands, like America, where they find peaceful lives and toleration in their relationship with God and Jesus Christ."

Will is mesmerized by Brother Gregory's eloquence and sincerity as he is instructed in some deeper understanding of Catholicism. A few hours later, as they conclude their visit, Will asks, "Brother Gregory, before I leave on my mission to Antwerp would it be proper to visit with you again. This time, I would like to come to your Monastery."

"Without a doubt, Master Will. You would be welcomed at any time."

Once Brother Gregory has left, Will notices the silence in the house and climbs the wide staircase to his bedroom. When Will is comfortably tucked into bed, with its feather comforter wrapped around him, his mind starts racing over his mission that appears to be fraught with intrigue and downright danger.

The following morning Will awakened later but still tired. Hurrying downstairs, he finds staff waiting for him with a hearty breakfast of scrambled eggs, sausage, fried tomatoes, toast and jam and a large pot of tea. As he gulps it down he hears Monmouth approach.

Monmouth says to him, "Today we will travel into London. We are going to the Harbor district along the Thames River. There you are to meet some men in charge of the docks and the Customs House. They will make you familiar with what you will face when you return from

Antwerp with our precious cargo. This should help allay any fears you may have."

An hour and a half later, they alight from their coach, Will's eyes sweep over a massive and bustling harbor with perhaps twenty tall-mast ships at anchor. Some are tied up alongside large wide docks where the water is a little deeper and where block-and tackle pullies on large tripod wooden overhangs are being used to unload cargo.

A number of close-in piers are rimmed with dory boats and sailors shouting orders to shore-men for help with unloading small cargo boxes or freshly caught cod, herring, and shellfish. Will's nose and eyes are assaulted by the smell of fish and at the assortment of seafood, most of which is cleaned right on the dock. As the blood, guts and other fish-waste are dropped into the Thames River, Will muses, *"When all has been said this has to be the most stinky and most filthy place I have ever seen."*

Will notices that Humphrey, who has walked a few paces ahead of him, seems right at home among the harbor's crushing crowd of workers, push carts (some with boxes and some with street food for sale), dollies, cranes, and horses. Walking behind Humphrey Will almost bumps into him because of constantly twisting his neck trying to take in all the sights and sounds. Just then the two men walk up to a large wooden door on a large red brick building. Will notices it is three stories high with its top floor jutting out over the Thames River by about 10 feet... giving anyone looking out its windows on three sides a commanding view of the entire harbor.

Monmouth leads Will up a wrought iron staircase attached to the side of the building. At the top of the stairs, and ignoring the etiquette of knocking on the door, the two enter an exceptionally large wood paneled room lined with many cabinets and about a dozen work tables. Will notices about ten men working at the tables and about another ten at windows. The men at the windows are looking down over the busy harbor using telescoping spyglasses. Will stops at the door but Monmouth walks across the room and sits down in front of a portly but official looking man. Will thinks the man must be well into his fifth decade of life. He is bald and wearing wire-rimmed spectacles, but he has a pleasant face, brown eyes with wrinkles at the corners, and he is clean shaven.

Monmouth, seeing that Will is not behind him, turns and motions to him, "Come over here Will, I want you to meet somebody."

Will stumbles across the floor and notices that one of the worktable men are writing furiously on what appears to be official forms, *"Likely Bills of Lading."* Will concludes.

"Will, this is my friend Oliver Pemberton,", says Humphrey. "Oliver is Harbor Master of the London's entire Shipping Docks and Port of Entry. Oliver oversees all management of this, the largest port in England. It is also Oliver's job to put the agents you see at these tables to work. It is their job to collect import taxes from those bringing foreign goods into England. They also are charged with seizing contraband."

Will extends his hand and with a smile, says "It's nice to meet you sir, my name is Will Hutchins and I am an Apothecary. Are there import taxes paid on items used to make medicines? Are any agents I may use in making medicines considered contraband?"

Harbor Master Pemberton says, "Yes Will. There are import taxes on all things made in foreign lands when brought to England. including medicines. In fact, if anything is foreign made, we will collect an import tax on it. However, you may bring in free of tax some of the seeds used to grow natural herbs and similar substances. There are a few poisons that we do not want to see in England, but I am afraid we cannot examine every ship's cargo that comes up the Thames."

Pemberton continues, "Getting much needed medicines from distant lands makes them expensive, however, items used in perfumes and soaps get taxed the most because they are used to make items only the wealthy can afford. So why not tax the rich folk on non-essentials? Sometimes you will also find no matter what an item is, if it is foreign made an export tax is also collected as it leaves its country of origin. That tax also applies to many natural substances used in medicines. Thus, many goods get taxed twice, both from their coming' and there going."

Will smiles, then winces and thinks," *I would bet a shilling against a pound note that a lot of those collected taxes never benefit the poor because of the graft bribes, and corruption that gobble them up before being used to do good."*

As Pemberton pauses, he notices another gentleman enter the room and calls him over, saying "This is Jack Sampson! Please meet Monmouth's new protégé. This is Will Hutchins."

"Hello, Jack says and shakes Will's hand. "I am second in command here, and I oversee all the work that occurs outside this building while Oliver oversees the work inside the building."

Pemberton motions to Sampson, "Please take Master Hutchins here on a tour of the harbor. He needs to become familiar with how larger ships are loaded and unloaded at our docks. Also show him some of the better methods by which we inspect cargo for unpaid tariffs and how we often find and seize any contraband that comes up the Thames."

"Are you coming also?" Will asks Monmouth

"No, I believe it best if I stay here. I would like to share a cuppa' tea and a biscuit with my friend, Harbor Master Pemberton. Besides, you two would walk my poor feet off if I came along. I am quite familiar with all you will learn on your tour. So, toddle off the two of you and I will await here for your return."

"I will be sure to have Will back here in an hour," Jack replies.

Will and his guide leave and return in an hour. Will is exhausted and foot-weary but being a quick learner, he is pleased with obtaining a working knowledge of how his "cargo from Antwerp" will be handled upon his return.

Humphrey ends their visit saying to Will, "Let us both leave these kind folks to their important work. We have used enough of their time today."

As they say their good-byes, Will notices the familiar way in which Pemberton and Sampson shake Monmouth's hand and his own, He muses, "*It's as if these men are more than quite simple business acquaintances but rather are old friends. I bet Monmouth has been here a lot more than he indicated to me when he set up this meeting.*"

Reflecting again on his observation of Monmouth and the two men, Will smiles and says to himself, "*Monmouth must be one of the most well-connected and influential men in this town. I have to believe he does have all the necessary elements in place to make our quest be successful."*

Will is silent on the coach ride back to Monmouth's estate and also during most of the evening meal. This time the meal is shared with Monmouth's two children and Mrs. Monmouth, Humphrey's wife, Barbara. Will finds Barbara well-spoken and delightful. She shares with him her knowledge of several medications she grows in her household garden besides its vegetables and spices.

Barbara tells Will, "If something we grow is not used for food preparation it will likely be used in remedies, unguents, potions and lotions for our estate staff."

Will and Barbara talk enthusiastically about medicines he and Cyril grow in a garden back in Hodthorpe. He asks her, "How did you acquire such a full knowledge of many herbs and spices?"

She simply says, "First I learned to read then I acquired this book," and shows him her copy of "The Good and Obedient Housewife's Herbalist." Which Will tells her he knows about.

After the evening meal, Monmouth and Will again engage in another quiet conversation in the adjoining drawing room and over more evening brandy. As he sips his brandy Monmouth tells Will, "I find this brandy aids my digestion."

"Will replies, "I do so agree. It is really a nice finish to a superb meal. Thank You."

Monmouth senses Will's hesitation to speak, "I think you are a bit worried about what may happen when you return up the Thames River with your wagon. Rest assured Will, the two men you met today, the Harbor Master and the Customs Official, will be on duty the day you arrive from Antwerp. You can expect them to conduct a cursory inspection to avoid any suspicion of either them or you. You will also be paying any taxes which they suggest are due. Paying those taxes openly will also avoid raising suspicions from spies and agents of the King and Church."

Will responds "Once again you have demonstrated your thoroughness in planning for every contingency.

Will then looks at Humphrey and asks, "What you have said makes me feel better. But how will I pay for any taxes, either coming or going if you are not there with a purse full of coin to do so?"

"Not to worry, Will. Before you leave for Antwerp, I will give you a purse with enough money to pay shipping fees, all taxes at both ends, and your lodging and food while in Antwerp."

"But isn't all this going to be very expensive?" asks Will.

"Not really" says Humphrey, "The London Guild of Apothecaries wants the medications herbs, spices and all other goods stored inside the wagon. And they also want the wagon. They plan to outfit it as a travelling apothecary. Their goal is to use this travelling apothecary to visit towns that have no access to medicines. They also want to use it in a campaign to counter quackery and unscrupulous men selling worthless medications at county fairs and markets. So, whatever the cost of smuggling these Bibles will be, that sum will be well recovered and more by using the wagon's legitimate cargo to divert attention away from its cargo important to us... and so many others."

Humphrey sips his brandy then adds, "To tell you the truth Master Will, I used a similar scheme with bolts of fine cloth and cotton. When the fine cloth was made into fine clothes and then sold to the gentry, the profits I made funded your Uncle's printing fees and lodging for these past nine years. You would be amazed as the fine clothes I created for upper class clergy who at the same time were fighting against the Protestant Reformation. These poor fools never realized the fees I was charging them brought in much funding for your Uncle's exile and printing fees. It's all kind of ironic, don't you think?"

"Yes, I really do understand," says Will smiling at the irony, "But sincerely, I do appreciate all you continue to do to preserve my uncle's legacy and my safety in this quest."

"Thank you, I also thank you for taking a chance on an old smuggler like me." At that point, both men smiled, clink their glasses, and finished sipping their digestive.

Once both men have said good-night pleasantries Will retires to his room. He is feeling a little warm from the brandy. His head is also buzzing with what he is feeling for the first time... a little smug but with a firm and newfound confidence in his mission. Once he readies himself and climbs into bed, he realizes, *And praise Jesus, Mary, and Joseph, I can't believe I also get my Master Apothecary credential out of all this. I wonder what Friday night will be like at the Apothecary's Guild Hall.*

That night, for the first night in many, Will slept soundly.

-Chapter 11-

*The Worshipful Society of Apothecaries, Potts Livery Hall,
Black Friars Lane, London*

Friday 29 January 1537.

Will rises early to once again meet with Monmouth, who has spent the he better part of the week grilling Will on the Bergdorf family, others who he is to meet in Antwerp, and how he will exit Antwerp with the wagon.

They discuss thoroughly how Will is to behave and act when he is in Antwerp, including his attendance at the Paracelsus lectures and details of how he will obtain the wagon with its herbs and medicines and get them through the Antwerp port.

Satisfied with his knowledge of the plan, Humphrey tells Will he will be leaving London the following Monday morning on an overnight voyage. It is to be on a merchant ship sailing directly to Antwerp and that he is to proceed directly to its large open market square, known as Grote Markt to rendezvous with his Antwerp hosts.

Monmouth has bought Will two new suits made from fine cloth, so he is appropriately dressed to travel as a middle-class member of a trade and thus be looked upon as any other skilled merchant or tradesman.

Finally, Monmouth also admonishes Will," Stay away from drink and loose women. Do nothing to embarrass the London Guild of Apothecaries by engaging in unseemly behavior. Remember your vows that are to be taken inside their Guild Hall when they elevate you to the status of Master Apothecary."

After a pause to let those words sink in, Will is further admonished, "Will, you must remember this is serious business. Keep your wits about you at all times. It not a disaster that would bring hardship onto many would occur if you fail."

Finally, Monmouth gives Will a hefty purse with coins that jingle if he walks a certain way.

"Now go and prepare yourself for this evenings event," asks Humphrey," Wear one of the suits I have brought you. You must impress a lot of strangers tonight and must look the part of a Master Apothecary. We leave in an hour."

An hour later Will and Humphrey leave the mansion and take the estate's coach to Black Friars Lane. Once in the heart of London they meet several top officers from London's Worshipful Society of Apothecaries. Humphrey explains, "We are invited to an afternoon meal, across the street. It will be in a private room in the back room that public house known as The Crown and Anchor Inn. The Guild officers will tell you of all they expect of you and likely as well their struggle to separate themselves from both the Guild of Grocers and Paperers. And the Guild of Physicians"

Once are all seated in a dark paneled room and its heavy wooden door a man is posted at the door. Will hears him called a Tyler. Will whispers to Monmouth, "What is a Tyler?"

Monmouth whispers back, "His job is to listen for any eavesdroppers.".

For the next while both men listen as the Guild officers talk about plans to end their relationship with the "Guild of Spicers and Pepperers" which has lasted almost 400 years. Will discovers the belief that the Reformation has helped Apothecaries become more modern and medical oriented such that it is time to separate from those seen as mere purveyors of a commodity.

After a short while the Grand Master of the Guild turns to Will and explains,: "Master Hutchins, you will be doing more than just bringing us back medicines. While in Antwerp you will learn from the illustrious and distinguished physician Paracelsus, his knowledge about certain diseases, especially syphilis, and the medicines he advocates to cure them. That knowledge will help us solidify our quest to become independent under Royal Charter. We especially want to free ourselves from encumbrances proposed by the Royal College of Physicians, especially their addled notion that every Apothecary and his shop is to undergo yearly inspections by a team of Physicians."

The Secretary of the Guild interrupts and says with a bit of hope in his manner, "Our real goal is to remove the monopoly held over us by the College of Physicians. This is because it is we Apothecaries who provide the only healing hands for poor and common folk. As you well know physicians only serve the wealthy who can pay, but we serve anyone who comes into our establishments and where it is also well known that apothecaries have far better healing rates than physicians who bleed them or priests who pray over them."

"Besides," a third officer of the Guild states, "One well-trained Apothecary may compound prescriptions for ten or more local physicians. Thus, any observant Apothecary knows what works and what doesn't work because the sick always return to praise and give thanks to the person who gave them medicine that works."

As the afternoon lingers on Will learns many members in the Worshipful Society of Apothecaries are reformists, however only a few trusted officers know of his mission to recover his Uncle's bibles.

"Be careful with what you say in and around the Guild Hall as spies and papists are everywhere," he is warned by the Grand Master of the Guild

Once Will receives the papers identifying him as a representative of the Worshipful Guild of Apothecaries and the papers that admit him into the Paracelsus conference, He turns to the assembled officers and says, "I truly want to thank you for all you have done. I have no problem traveling abroad under the identity of ...Will Hutchins. When I return will I be able to get new papers issued in my rightful name?"

The Grand Master of the Guild replies, "We will be proud to do that. We are sorry for any subterfuge we are putting you under, but I am sure you can also understand the stakes are high."

Will is then asked, "Please return with us to the Guild Hall. Perhaps a hundred or so apothecaries will have gathered for our monthly business meeting. During that meeting Will, you will be asked to undertake a public and solemn oath in a short ceremony. At the end of it we will confer upon you full status as a Master Apothecary with all the rights and privileges of that honor"

The Master of the Guild pauses, then states, "Will, this is not being done solely because of how it would aid in our plan for you to go to Belgium. You have also brought honor to our profession first as an Apprentice and then as a Journeyman. You truly have earned the privilege and have been found to be well learned in our profession and a man of virtue and good report."

A few moments after leaving the Crown and Anchor Will and Humphrey find themselves in a quiet room in the back of the Apothecaries Guild Hall.

"It's been a long afternoon and several hours since we met across the street and shared a meal. I can see that some of the Guild members have brought in some food from street vendors. If you would like one of those Beef Pasties, and a pint of Ale, better do so now as it may be a long evening", Humphrey says to Will.

"Thanks, but I am fine "Will answers.

Soon they hear a jumble of voices as the main guild meeting room begins to fill with men. The two men rise from their seats and enter the room from a side door. They find themselves in a large red, wool carpeted meeting room, whereupon Will notices two rows of benches lining three sides of the room. Will quickly figures the room has seating for about sixty to seventy people. The wall directly across from a beautiful set of carved wooden doors has a dais with seating for the officers whom Will and Humphrey met with earlier. As they are walking in they are warmly greeted and also escorted by an official looking officer who returns to a station near the entrance door. In the center of the room is a small table on which are placed two books and a brass mortar and pestle.

The Master of the Guild spots Will and Humphrey and motions for them to take a seat on a bench at his right. He then raps a gavel on the table in front of him and announces, "Gentlemen, please be seated, our guest has arrived and it's time for us to get down to business."

Once the room has quieted and all are seated, the Master looks at Will and asks that he stand at the table in the middle of the room. Will complies, marches quietly to the center of the room and stands erect behind a square table. He thinks, *"this looks like an altar of some kind, I better pay attention to what's going on here."*

The Master speaks so all can hear, "My fellow Apothecaries, tonight I am pleased to introduce to you our newest candidate for membership in our Worshipful Society of Apothecaries. He has been examined and your officers have found him worthy of the rank and privileges of a Master Apothecary. Is there anyone here who would like to speak on his behalf?"

Two gentlemen stand, Will can see one is Humphrey Monmouth but then he goes weak in the knees. He gulps as he hears Cyril Blackham saying," All of you know me and of my many years as a member of this esteemed body of Apothecaries. It is with great pride and humility that I recommend this young man be admitted into our Guild."

Cyril then gives a lengthy talk describing Will is and his relationship during the past seven years. He waxes eloquently about Will and his passion for learning, his empathy towards all who enter his Apothecary, his skill as a healer, and his integrity as a true Christian man, and how at such a young age he is considered a pillar in his community.

The Master then calls for a vote for which all hands rise on the resolution to accept Will , whom they still believe is named "Will Hutchins", on his being of "sound of mind, appropriate age, temperance, temperament, training, and of good report."

Will is asked to place his hands on each of the two ancient books sitting there on the small table before him. As he bends to do so, he sees one contains the writings of Avicenna, the other the writing of Galen. He then is asked by the Master to repeat a solemn oath which Guild members have been repeating for at least 200 years.

Will repeats his oath in a clear voice. "I promise to keep and only compound medicines I believe are necessary for the health of man and which are not corrupt or foul. I am willing to allow yearly inspections of any shop I may own by Guild officers. I will avoid any chicanery or spurious arrangements with other apothecaries, physicians, or patronage. I promise to always extend wisdom, truth, hope, and charity to my brother apothecaries, to practice temperance, and to subdue any irregular passions."

Will is welcomed into the Guild with a long round of applause, and then each Apothecary comes forward to shake his hand and offer a friendly welcome.

After a few business items are discussed within the Guild Hall, Will leaves with Humphrey. The two return to Humphrey's estate in his waiting carriage. As they bump along Will feels a swell of new confidence in his ability and the details placed before him to complete the smuggling operation.

Will thinks "I *just have to believe in myself as much as these good fellows do. If I follow Monmouth's plan, nothing should go wrong.*" At which point he sighs, draws a deep breath, and the two men ride the rest of the way home in silence.

Once into bed Will is both tired and happy. Before he falls asleep he reviews the day's and night's events. His last thoughts, before falling asleep, were of the words in his vow wherein he agreed "to subdue irregular passions."

-*Chapter 12*-

The London Charterhouse, Monastery of the Carthusian Monks, London

Sunday 12 January 1537

Because it is Sunday morning, the Monmouth family and Will are up early to enjoy a full and hearty English breakfast of eggs, toast and jam, bacon, and tea. Monmouth is dressed in fine clothes and so are his wife and children.

During the meal Monmouth turns to Will and asks, "After breakfast we are all going to church. The children have asked if you would like to join us?"

Will turns to the family sitting quietly around the table and says, "Please accept my gratitude and thanks for your kind invitation."

Then turning to Monmouth Will continues, "However, if it is alright with you, after this delicious breakfast I would like to go visit Brother Gregory at his Order's London Charterhouse. I am hoping he will provide some additional spiritual comfort before I leave England. I truly would like to spend some more time with him and if possible, meet a few of his Carthusian brothers."

Monmouth nods "That sounds like a good idea. Any time spent with Brother Gregory is always comforting. He has a gifted way of strengthening ones resolve and relationship with our Holy Father."

Later, as the family drives off to church in an open carriage Will walks towards the Carthusian monastery. An hour later Will has threaded his way along London's winding streets to the Charterhouse, in an area of London known as Islington. His first impression of the monk's100 year-old home is, *"it's really a rambling, run-down walled-estate."*

Will walks up to the monastery's wall and finds he is tall enough to peek over it whereupon he can see three rows of four or five cottages in each row. Will surmises they row of cottages must be a residence for either one or two of the 25 monks who he was told live there.

Will can also see each cottage has a garden behind it and thinks, "I *bet each monk or monks in each cottage must attend his or their own garden."*

Will then notices the door of each cottage faces toward the entrance to a larger building and thinks," *Perhaps that building is the one where they cook, dine, hold chapel, and conduct business. I will head over there and perhaps that's where I will find Brother Gregory."*

Will steps through a worn iron gate and onto a path that takes him to the larger building "I *wonder if there is any truth to the rumor that Sir Thomas More once came to this monastery seeking spiritual recuperation and sanctuary. It would be quite interesting to know how More became determined to fight the reformation, unless that's the outcome of his paid patronage and blind loyalty to Henry VIII."*

Will hesitates before stepping inside and thinks, *"Why is it I feel so drawn to meet with Brother Gregory? Should I really be here? Am I taking a risk asking Brother Gregory for spiritual advice? I really do not care a fig for the rumors that these good and pious Monks are being watched by the King's authorities and high-ranking Catholic Church officials. So, what could happen if one of their spies is watching me? It's more likely that the church only wants to see the dissolution of this monastic order so they can gain possession of its land and buildings."*

Not seeing Brother Gregory after a cursory peek inside the   hall, Will starts to walk around the grounds. As he walks around he finds Brother Gregory in his garden.

"Good Morning, Brother Gregory," Will says upon his approach to Brother Gregory who is stooped over a cucumber patch," I trust you will remember me. We met recently at the home of Humphrey Monmouth."

At the sound of Will's voice, the startled the monk stands and says, "Why of course I remember you. Good morning and may God's blessing be upon you Will Hutchins."

Will feels joy at the broad smile he gets from Brother Gregory. Once they shake hands and exchange a hearty hug, Brother Gregory directs Will to a stone bench in the middle of the lawn in front of the main building.

Once they let the sun warm them as they sit on the stone bench, both are quiet for several minutes taking in the peace and solitude of their surroundings. Then, Will quietly expresses to Brother Gregory, "I must confess that my name is not Will Hutchins. My real name is William Tyndale, I am the nephew of Master William Tyndale who was recently executed for bringing the word of God to England which you may know he had printed in our common language."

Brother Gregory shows no reaction to Will's confession and waits as Will continues to reveal more of who he is and what he is doing in London. When Will is finished Brother Gregory replies, "I have known who you are and why you are here for a long time."

Brother Gregory notices Will's stunned silence and explains, "Humphrey Monmouth has given our religious order much funding over the past nine years. We have been able to use a goodly portion of those funds to help your Uncle in his difficult situation in Europe. We have also helped Monmouth bring your uncle's Bibles back from Europe. However, it is just too dangerous for us to be involved now that Monmouth and your uncle were betrayed. It was fortunate Monmouth has the funds to buy his way out of prison. It saddend me that your uncle was imprisoned for such a long a time. It can't have been easy for him but take heart in this…you uncle never recanted once on his belief he was doing the Lord's work."

"But, why would you give help to my uncle and go against Catholic teaching and dogma," Will exclaims at this new revelation. "And why tell me, especially now?"

"It's a long story, Will, but all English citizenry have seen too much death and destruction at the hands of the King, his paid politicians, papists and English clergy. They seek the privileges of power, social position, and more often fat stipends that come with titles and appointments. Some are simply coveting a neighbor's goods, land, or wife. We Carthusians believe all men are equal under the hand of the Great Father in Heaven and it is only by choice they decide not to be friendly and helpful to each other by going against the Lord's commandments.

Brother Gregory pauses then continues, "Many man-made commandments, such as contained in many English laws, facilitate and perpetuate bad and corrupt behavior. For example, under English Law it is only the eldest son who inherits his father's estate. This leads many sons to be left without a family inheritance and the means to support themselves unless they have a charitable brother. Thus, many sons seek the church as a means to earn their livelihood by collecting tithes and selling indulgences from those too ignorant to ask God for forgiveness on their own."

Gregory continues," We Carthusians have also witnessed how all too often the church draws in people with weak constitutions who use their church position to hide their ungodly behavior, especially predatory behavior . . . of a sexual nature."

Gregory catches his breath then adds, "But not all second sons are lazy, bad people or sit around feeling sorry for themselves. Some decide to work hard by becoming merchants, healers, and tradesmen. Others who are lazy or unskilled decide a life of gambling and crime suits them better than seeking a refuge within the church. This is what, Henry Phillips, the man who betrayed your father did. He took to gambling and sold his soul to betray a good man , as did Judas But never-the-less, today the Catholic Church is afraid of losing power and its stranglehold on people and the riches they collect by offering healing, repentance and salvation."

"Let me add this," says Gregory, "When people read your uncle's translation of the scriptures, they will know what it means to truly be a follower of Christ and how best to follow the ten commandments given to Moses. They will also know that grace and peace are offered to all, and that all can enter heaven when their earthly trials are over based on faith alone. We monks simply exist to help guide others into finding God's graces and his love. We do this by how we live by Christ's example of being kind to one another and forgiving those who trespass against us."

Will feels his head spinning as he tries to absorb what he has just heard. He looks at Brother Gregory and says, "What you have just shared is pretty meaningful. It is also extremely dangerous for you to utter such words in these turbulent times. But since Bibles for the common man already exist in places like Sweden, Germany, France, Spain, Holland, Belgium and some other areas I may not know of, why then do they not exist here in any great abundance or even in this Monastery which has been tasked to spread the word of God ?"

"Will, your questions are appropriate, but the answers are overly complex. But, let me try give you a simple explanation."

Brother Gregory looks into Will eyes then says, "This monastery was built a 100 years ago. The land on which we sit was near a huge hospital, St. Bartholomew's. Behind that hospital is a large graveyard holding victims of the Black Death. Did you notice it? It was created on some of the ground you walked on to come here."

Will shudders at the thought he had walked over a graveyard.

Gregory continues, "Not much has changed since The Black Death to alter men's minds about witchcraft, miasmas, death, and destruction, and especially in understanding God's will. We know now the plague was not caused by God's wrath upon his people but rather spread by dirt and rats.

Will states, I know that".

Gregory again continues in his resonant voice, "However, when you have strong adherents to Church of Rome dogma and ritual that is being espoused by a well-entrenched hierarchy preaching to an almost illiterate population it creates a situation hard to change. We Carthusians pray daily that as new thinking grows in science, medicine, the arts, and humanities, it will do so also in spiritual matters. We pray it happens here more quickly than is occurring in Europe. There is a lot of work to be done and you are truly blessed to be part of helping bring some light into the dark world here at home."

"I can't thank you enough for all that you have just said. Because of you I better understand my role in the important task set before me."

Brother Gregory chuckles a bit as he assesses Will's obvious naivety about worldly matters, but continues, "Will, there are but nine Carthusian houses in all of England, we are but a small group and yet once we had the protection of the local Bishops. Now we live in fear as we have been told we will have to swear a new Oath, one issued by King Henry VIII. It is called the Oath of Supremacy, Submission, and Succession to the Throne. It was crafted by Sir Thomas More as Henry's Lord Chancellor, but it essentially puts more power into both More's and the King's hands."

Gregory pauses then asks Will "Have you heard of it?"

"No, what does it do?" Will asks.

"It is designed to suppress any person who might question authoritarian rule using both secular and religious arguments. For example, some of our Monks have been accused of killing the King's deer but doing so on land we have occupied for years. So now we must pay an exceptionally large assessment or tax on the fruits of our labor on our own productive farms. The truth of who is behind all this is the church. ... the church owns land adjacent lands to ours and covets it. Do you know why the church may want our land?"

"I don't know why, Will responds, so tell me"

"Because they do not know how to increase their farm yields through careful husbandry techniques. Instead they find it easier to bribe the King's well-placed and well-paid aristocrats and bureaucrats to support their self-interests through legislation. They knew we would oppose them, but we are not strong enough to buy support. And so, we have neighbors seeking to confiscate our lands and to do so ...by King's edict."

Will looks at Brother Gregory and says, "Damnation, if that's not plain evil. I had no idea such things were going on. I was raised in a small town isolated from much of such worldly and corrupt affairs."

Will continues, "Please know, Brother Gregory, I am fully committed to get my uncle's bibles into as many English hands as possible. I came to you today as I have had many misgivings about my abilities to carry out a mission for which I had no say in the making. Sadly, I have always procrastinated when it came to making life decisions. After talking with you I find faith in my mission refreshed and my coming here a true blessing. When I return from my journey I trust we can visit each other again."

Brother Gregory looks at Will and says, "I will hold you to that commitment, now would you like for us to pray together?"

As the two close their eyes and bow their heads, Brother Gregory places his hand on Will's shoulder and says, "Most Holy and gracious Lord God look after your servant Will and keep him safe as he brings us your Holy Writ. May he follow Thy commandments and the examples of the saints John the Evangelist and John the Baptist and your son, Jesus Christ. It is in their names we ask your presence, protection, and blessing. Amen."

As Will raises his eyes, he looks solemnly at Brother Gregory at asks, "Thank you for that prayer. But your prayer mentioned the two holy saints named John? Why did you do that?"

"Rather simple, my young friend, besides being kind, righteous, and loving they were men faithful to the trust placed in them."

Will leaves Brother Gregory with an inner peace he has never felt before and with an upbeat confidence towards his mission.

A little later as Will has walked from the Monastery and is nearing the Monmouth estates, he realizes, "*All the questions I formulated on my way to see Brother Gregory were never asked nor answered, Oh well!! They cannot have been all that important anyway.*

A little later Will concludes, *" Every step of the way to Europe and back has been laid out before me. Either by Monmouth or by a man familiar with that same path. I just need to follow the path set before me and if I do so with confidence I just know it will lead to my success."*

-Chapter 13-

The Monmouth Estates, London,

Thursday 4 February 1537

Four days after Will's meeting with Brother Gregory, Humphrey bursts into Will's bedroom to find him lying on his bed resting..

"Have you heard about the Carthusians?" Humphrey inquires.

"No, what has happened? Why are you so excited?"

"Those bastard minions of the King, Thomas More and John Stokely, convinced the King to sign a declaration that the Carthusians be disbanded and that their Monastery be closed. All the Monks have been rounded up, their leader executed, and the others put in prison as heretics.

"Oh God in heaven, "says a startled Will," What will befall them?'

"If they are not burned at the stake they will likely die of starvation No one has been to feed them for fear of being tarred a supporter. There has been no trial date set to plead their case. Everyone knows standing up to the

Catholic Church and asking for reform created this cruel reprisal."

"What of Brother Gregory? Any news of now what has befallen them that this calamity has happened?" Will asks showing more alarm.

"At first it was believed this happened because several refused to sign an oath proclaimed by Henry VIII and which is enforced by sheriffs and bishops throughout England. In essence, the oath is known as the Act of Succession. It prohibits malicious speech against the king and royal family, such speech being prohibited upon pain of death. For example, it would be enforced as an act of treason to call the King a heretic or a tyrant. Thus, it's no longer a question of theology to be called a heretic; it's a matter of loyalty."

Before Will can get another question formed, Monmouth continues, "So, now it is rumored that King Henry is contemplating breaking away from the Catholic Church and making himself Lord Protector of Religion. Many believe Henry wants to suppress opposition from any free-thinking priests, like the Carthusians. What a shame this is happening now".

Monmouth catches his breath then continues, "To make matters worse our mutual friend, Brother Gregory is in prison. And I nor anyone I know have no way of getting him out, especially now as pressure is mounting to stop the Reformation movement here in England."

Will interjects Monmouth by saying, "Oh my God, I never thought such a pious man as Brother Gregory would have such hardship placed upon him for speaking the truth. He understood what God asked through Christ that all men should do…simply to be kind to each other. It would certainly seem Brother Gregory's fears of a conspiracy are well-founded,"

Will pauses to think, then tells Humphrey, "I think it best if we move up my departure to Antwerp a day or two just to be sure I can avoid any church or state officials looking for anybody who visited the Carthusian Charterhouse recently. You never know what spies and other vermin were or are nosing about hoping to curry favor with some church or king's officer."

Humphrey nods his concurrence and says to Will, "I can get you out of here on a ship leaving this Saturday. That gives us less than 48 hours to get ready."

"Not a problem for me," says Will, "I was ready to get on with our mission yesterday. Now that I have witnessed firsthand some of the corruption and abuses of the Church and State I am determined more than ever to be successful in recovering my uncle's Bibles. In fact, since I had my talk with Brother Gregory, I believe full-well you have made me more than prepared. Brother Gregory lit a spark in me that fired up the last bit of confidence I needed to believe I will be successful in our quest."

Two days later Will and Monmouth are in his carriage heading to the London Harbor. There a large merchant sailing ship heading directly to Antwerp awaits. On their way to that ship Will sees a procession of two carts of Carthusian friars being driven through the streets on the road to the Tower of London…" *likely to their execution."* Will thinks.

Then Will shudders and declares silently *"My God in Heaven, thank you for getting me out of this city. I wonder what other cruelty I will see as my mission unfolds. I will pray for all the souls of those poor monks. I have to believe there is more to what has happened to them than just being free-thinking and pious men."*

Monmouth watches Will and knows he is praying, then he diverts Will's thoughts with a question, "Will, please check one more time you have all your documents and funds needed for a successful mission."

Will checks into his shoulder pouch and reviews his identity and travel papers, his admission and registration papers to the Paracelsus lectures, and his charter as a representative of the Honorable Guild of London Apothecaries. He checks to be sure he has the funds necessary to pay customs officials at both ends of his mission and for living and travel expenses. He reads again his directions to meet with George de Bergdorf.

The last thing he checks are the papers and monies given to him by the Apothecaries Guild to pay for the construction and outfitting of the special wagon that will hide his uncle's Bibles. Having never seeing the plans for the wagon's construction he wonders, *"How in the name of all that is holy will the Guild of Apothecaries wagon be able to hide and secure a thousand Tyndale Bibles? I guess I have to trust that better minds than mine have figured it all out."*

A few moments later as Will and Monmouth stand near the gangplank of the vessel that will take him on an overnight trip up the Thames River, around the southern coast of England then across the Channel to Antwerp, Will looks at Monmouth and says, "I truly want to thank you for your continued faith in me to carry out this mission. I am at peace with myself and I have confidence all will go well. Please thank your wife, children, and staff for the time they spent to make my visit enjoyable. But, I can never thank you enough for introducing me to the Guild of Apothecaries."

"When it came to the apothecaries, you should thank Cyril when you return. All that was his doing."

Humphrey leans closer to Will and whispers, "Some folks, like Cyril, like to be in the background of affairs working quietly and without fanfare. Cyril always has said if he remained in the background he would learn more by listening than by being in front and chattering away like a foolish squirrel. Come now Will, it is time to get on board,

Will watched as the mooring lines were taken off. Then says, "Goodbye Mr. Monmouth. Thank You for everything."

Will shakes Monmouth's hand and suddenly stops, steps forward and embraces him with strong, warm, hug and a pat on the back. Monmouth blushes at Will's display of familiarity and says, "You better get on board unless you want to swim across. Goodbye and good luck my dear boy."

As the boat sails up the Thames River the rest of the day, Will finds a place on deck to watch the waves roll by under the ship. Then much later, when the day's light starts to fade, and the ship heads out to cross the English Channel and south to Europe, he goes under deck and finds a small bunk to lie in hoping he can sleep until the ship's arrival in Antwerp.

Lying in a cramped bunk Will eats some cheese and bread and drinks from a flask of wine tucked into in his travelling satchel. Feeling refreshed and with no sense of the ships motion, Will affirms to himself, "*I honestly believe I have found a new and worthy purpose. My decision to leave Hodthorpe was the right one."* The ship's rocking quietly lulls him to sleep.

Will's last waking thought before sleep was, *"If nothing else, I have to believe Brother Gregory's prayer asking for God, the two holy saints John, and Jesus to be on my side. As I go about their work I know they will protect me and get through whatever awaits in Antwerp."*

-Chapter 14-

The Harbor of Antwerp Belgium, and its Market Square: Sunday Morning 7 February 1537

Will wakes early after a calm, overnight journey across the English Channel. As he takes in the sights of Antwerp Harbor he sees it also is a day with lots of sunshine broken only by a few white fluffy clouds passing overhead. As his ship ties up to the dock Will senses a little trace of foreboding by being in a strange city with unfamiliar architecture and with bright colors painted on brick facades. *"But"*, he concludes *"Antwerp looks spotless and without the smells I remember so well of London Harbor"*.

Antwerp harbor is twice that of London's . . . w1ith twice as many people rushing or milling about. Will remembers Monmouth's comment, *"Humphrey told me there were five thousand Englishmen living in Antwerp. Surely they can't all be down here among this throng and at his early hour of the day"*

As Will steps off the ship onto the quay he is jostled by many on the docks by porters, buying and selling merchants, fishermen, and loaders and unloaders of ships, because of his gazing about. Their cacophony of tongues Will decides is like to "the braying and mooing at a cattle market."

Once Will settles down from his initial reaction to being in Antwerp he decides to walk around the massive harbor wondering, "Perhaps I can find the ship carrying the Apothecary Guild's wagon."

Will spends the next hour looking around the harbor and marvels at the size of its estuary on the Scheldt River. He watches personnel go into and out of the Belgium Customs House and recalls Monmouth's explanation, "*it is near where the Scheldt River enters into the harbor and it is where men inspect goods destined for all parts of the world, including London. Inside that Belgium Customs House is where you will pay a tax on the wagon and the medicinals you are bringing back to London. It is also where you will be inspected for contraband.*"

Will locates an area near the Customs House where it appears goods are being quarantined and inspected. They all carry markings indicating they are bound for England. He watches in wonderment at how those wooden crates, boxes, and bales are hoisted onto ships using huge block and tackle pulley systems and tripod cranes. "*I can imagine that one of these will be used to handle my special wagon and load it onto the deck of a ship or into a large cargo hold. I cannot imagine what will become of the horse that pulls the wagon here? I guess Monmouth will have a horse ready to pull it here and then another when I return to*

England. That man certainly thinks of everything. He must have a pretty special group of people who work for him."

When he has finished exploring the harbor, Will walks to the town's market square– Grote Markt van Antwerpen. Once there he finds it silly that the town's largest square is actually a triangle. As he walks into its center, he turns and sees several elaborate guild halls and inns along two sides with the Antwerp city hall taking up the whole third side.

Will looks for the Statue of Silvio Brabo but once he sees it notices that nobody is standing near… just a young woman. Will thinks, *"I must be a bit early and my contact person, George de Bergdorf must be late. Monmouth did tell me what George looked like and I am damn sure he is not that pretty girl sitting on the bench near the statue."*

Will decides to imbed in his mind his vision of the girl with her curly, dark brown hair, slim and curvy build, a turned-up nose, and lips like flower petals. He is too far away to see the color of her eyes, but her image lingers, and he is intrigued.

Next, thinking himself a bit early to meet his contact person, he decides to find the Universiteit Antwerpen… the place where the Paracelsus lectures are to be held. As he crosses the Grote Markt he sees a street entrance with a poster on a wall announcing the lectures in Dutch and English.

Feeling new confidence Will leaves the Grote Markt and enters a side street leading him alongside Antwerp's famous church, The Cathedral of Our Lady, He sees its cornerstone announcing it was built 300 years prior to Will's arrival on earth. He recalls Monmouth warning him that the Cathedral was the seat of Antwerp's Catholic strength. Will feels a cold chill. *"Heaven help me if Henry Phillips is lurking within but even if he was,, how could he recognize me?.*

Will decides he has lingered enough and should get back to the Grote Markt to keep his appointment with George. Again, as he returns to the middle of the market square he sees no one lingering near the statue of Silvius Brabo. As he looks at the statue again he remembers that Monmouth had mentioned Brabo was a mythical soldier who killed a giant and thereby had earned public recognition.

Will sees no one lingering near the statue, nor sitting on a nearby bench. However, his heart does a little flip-flop as he again notices the beautiful girl who was sitting there when he first arrived in the marketplace.

He wonders, *"She seems about my age, perhaps she is a little younger than me. She sure is pretty. Does she speak English?"* Noticing her fidget, he thinks, *"Could she be waiting for someone?"*

Just then she lifts her head and notices Will looking at her. Will flushes in response. *"I've been caught staring at her, now what do I do or say?"*

He is startled when she speaks "Hey Englishman, who are you? What are you doing here?

Will notes her competent English but with hardly any accent but with an endearing lisp but still mesmerized by her beauty, stammers and stutters the only thing he can think of "Uh! Uh! Who are you? why do you want to know who I am?"

Then, as he pauses to compose himself and let the woman answer, he thinks, *"Goodness me, by all the saints what's happening to me? I have never felt like this talking to anyone, especially having spent years talking with folk in the Apothecary back home."*

He instantly regrets what he said to her. *"Now she will think I am a buffoon, village idiot, or at worse a cad. Either that or she will think I have forgotten all propriety and the good manners of a gentleman. I must remember I am a foreigner in a strange land and calm down."*

Will moves closer to her noticing her petite but womanly build, her intense blue eyes, and captivating smile.

He especially admires the curls in her shoulder length dark brown hair.

She again interrupts his thoughts. "I can tell by the cut of your clothes that you are English and like most English I have met, you have rotten manners," she replies curtly.

Taking her words as a challenge Will retorts, "Why do you hold such a large grudge against men? Is it just me? Is it for all men? or is it just for English ones? I take umbrage that your judgment of me has been based on my appearance alone. Hardly what I would expect of someone I hoped would display well-bred manners and hospitality to a stranger."

"Well, I can see you are a pretty smooth talker for one speaking country-bred English. My apologies for my outburst. I do have two good and respectful men in my life, my brother, and my father. The rest of your gender seem to act as pigs, mules, or other ill-mannered animals, especially when rutting around a woman."

"Oh! that's a pretty harsh observation. Look before this conversation gets out of hand; would you know a man by the name of George de Bergdorf? I am hoping to meet him or at least find a way to his print shop."

The woman recoils in shock at the sound of her father's name, then Will notices a pale of sadness on her face as she blurts out. "Oh, my Heavens' above! George de Bergdorf was my father."

"Was?" Will asked.

"He passed away three weeks ago. So why is that you want to meet him? Does he owe some scoundrel like you some money? Have you arrived to pick up a print job he may have finished before he died?"

"No, quite the contrary, I came to pay off a debt. It was left by my Uncle and his friend the English draper, Humphrey Monmouth."

At his mention of Humphrey, the girl's eyes brighten, and her scowl disappears.

"My father was to meet a man sent here by Humphrey Monmouth, I had no idea he would send a boy," she says.

Caught off guard Will retorts, "I will have you know I am a Master Apothecary. I only look young because I have not been tainted or corrupted by the whimsies. musings, and manipulations of any female."

Will hears her scowl, "I guess you will have to do," she responds.

Will sits down on the bench beside her and say's in a low voice *"We had better not look so obvious nor draw attention to ourselves. What has happened?"*

"Since my father passed away, me, my mother, and my brother have had to take over his print shop. Please accept my apologies for not getting word about my father's death to England and to Monmouth sooner than this."

"Are all Monmouth's arrangements still the same?" Will inquires

She continues., Yes, everything is in order as planned. Arrangements have been made for you to lodge in a room atop our print shop. We can't risk you staying at The English House."

She gives a brief pause while she glanced all around, "The English House is that huge Inn by the seaport reserved for English tradesmen, scholars, visitors, and other assorted scoundrels." She smiles at her little joke.

Will remembers Monmouth telling him about The English House; where his uncle lived and from where he had written his translations and treatises. Will shudders, and a wave of dread washes over him. "It is also the place from which Henry Phillips betrayed my uncle" he whispers to the woman..

Will looks into the girl's eyes and asks her, "Can't we start our relationship over? My name is Will Hutchins, what is yours".

She replies, "My name is Elke de Bergdorf, and we have no relationship."

Will rolls his eyes at her rebuke, then smiles.

"We are standing in the square where most Guild Halls in Antwerp are. Behind you is the Guild of Printers. Let us go inside their building so we can discuss what will happen next. I want you to meet my mother… Her name is Margareit," Elke says.

Elke looks around carefully and lowers her voice, "I also want to get us out of this open space. There is a constable roaming around who is a very jealous oaf. He thinks he owns me. If he sees me with any man he will likely club you, stick you with his halberd, or just run you off declaring his claim on me. All of which I find as offensive as I find him ugly."

"Just great!" muses Will, "I find an enchanting girl who could be an angel, but she could also be a devil to deal with, especially if she has a repulsive suitor laying claim to her."

They move inside, and Elke introduces Will to Margareit, a rather petite and slim women – and who could pass for a not-too-much older version of her daughter. She too has dark hair but more of a light brown with a few streaks of grey at the temples, but not as much curl as her daughter. But Margareit has passed on her intense blue eyes to her daughter. Will instantly likes her.

Within a few minutes of quiet conversation Margareit convinces Will their plan will work and that, "The Bibles are still in a safe place. And, the wagon and its medicinal agents are almost ready for you to take them to England."

Will breathes a sigh of relief as Margareit finishes their conversation by adding, "All is prepared to easily get the loaded wagon through Belgium customs and out of the country,"

"Further," Margareit says confidently. "While any tariffs and fees are to be paid on the medicinal agents, certain officials who support your mission will minimize their impact."

"Oh really?"

She continues, "Yes Will, you should know that many officials on the docks support the Reformation. Martin Luther's thoughts are well-regarded throughout this area."

She lets her last thought sink in, then turns to Will and says, "Please pick up your traveling bags and come to our home. We have prepared lodging for you, and you will partake of supper with us tonight. You will also meet our son, Ahren. He has been working hard on preparing your wagon."

Then as Margareit, Elke and Will walk out the door onto the street she turns to Will and says, "We were expecting a much older man than you. You must be pretty special to have earned the confidence of Humphrey Monmouth for this mission."

"Thank you for that nice compliment, Margareit. Yes, I do think a great deal of Humphrey. He has been a friend and benefactor to two uncles for many years."

Margareit changes the subject by saying, "My son, Ahren has been apprenticed as a printer and he has papers as a journeyman. Ahren has taken on a lot more responsibility since my husband's passing. He has helped to ensure the print shop can keep its obligations to the customers we serve. Elke has also been of great help to both of us. We are not sure how long we can keep the shop open as competition for printing work is much fiercer since the invention of the Guttenberg press. But because no print shop in England uses movable type of a Guttenberg Press, we do a lot of printing that is shipped from here to England."

As the three of them walk across Grote Markt and head towards the de Bergdorf home, Will notices Elke pulling her shawl over her face. "It *can't be me she is embarrassed to be seen with, can it?. Perhaps there is more to the relationship between her and that local constable.*"

Wills thoughts continue to ramble s they leave the square and walk into a more residential area lines with small shops. *"I better not ask about Elke's situation until I know more. There is much at stake here, including the safety of a lot of people. I do not want to get in the middle of someone's courtship just to jeopardize my mission. But I am sure I want to spend more time with this girl.*

As they continue to walk along, Will feels the weight of his two travelling valises and thinks, *"I must keep my head clear and my emotions quiet. There is too much time, money, and effort that many good people have invested in my mission to see it blown up because I chased a pretty woman. Perhaps this is what was meant in my Apothecary oath when I promised to subdue irregular passions. What's so irregular about wanting to be a with a pretty girl? Aw! Hell's Bells, why can't life be less complicated."*

-Chapter 15-

The Home and Shop of George de Bergdorf
Later in the day, Sunday 7 February 1537

Will, Elke and Margereit arrive at the DeBergdorf home and print shop situated on Printer's Row. Their building is much like the row homes Will saw in London; the first floor the actual shop with living quarters and either storage space or more living quarters on a second floor. Many have a third floor with either a garret or storage space. The open book etched onto the sign over the front door denotes it as the home of a printer.

Once inside, Elke takes Will to the second floor where a cot, and a wash basin on a small stand, have been prepared for him in a small room. Will also notices a small window for fresh air, or cold air, depending on the weather, slightly above the pillow on his cot. He also notices that this room is at the back of the house away from any noise from the street front.

As Will places his travelling bag on the cot Elke says, "Make yourself comfortable. You can hang your clothes on the wall peg over there. Your travel bag will fit under the bed. Mother will have dinner ready in about thirty minutes. Please come down then and join us. There is water in the jug sitting inside the washbasin. A towel for your use is on your bed. When you come downstairs, I am sure my brother will be home for supper. You're both about the same age and I believe you and he will get along simply fine."

As she pauses, she flashes Will a smile. *"That smile of hers is making my knees shake and loins quake. Damn, I must not be thinking like this!"*

To hide his obvious blush at her smile he stumbles over his reply "Uh, yes, I will see you in half an hour. I look forward to eating with you and your family. I have not eaten since getting off that overnight ship from London."

Then he thinks, *"Well that bumbling remark must have made her think I am a village idiot."*

Left alone Will mulls over the day's events but keeps coming back to how he was instantly attracted to Elke. *"She may have found me attractive, but she is too scared of this constable guy who seems to have laid a claim on her. Seems she is facing an impossible situation. Perhaps she cannot do anything about her true feelings, likely because of being bullied or because it's so soon after her father's death."*

Once Will puts his things away, he wonders, *"I know nothing about this girl. It is stupid of me to think any attraction between us is mutual. I better keep my mind on why I am here. My mission has to remain my number one priority. It would get really fouled up if I got distracted by a girl I hardly know."*

Next, while using the wash basin, Will's thoughts about Elke are interrupted. This time it is her mother shouting up the stair well, "Will, please come down and join us for supper."

"Be right there," he responds.

During supper Will learns more of the father's sudden passing and the disease that took him. He also learns how the mother is keeping their busy print shop going with the help of her two adult children As Will sits across from Ahren, whom he finds very likeable, he also assesses how close this family must have been to the father because of the somber and tearful looks on all three. Will decides to change the subject by stating, "I know you have all been through some very trying times and I trust you are leaning on God to help you through them. Thank you for all you have done and will be doing to help with my Uncle's legacy and especially know that much of that legacy was made possible because of the work and risk undertaken by your husband and father."

The family can only utter a mild, "Thank you" to Will, after which Margareit turns to all and says, "Let us eat but before we do perhaps our guest would like to give a blessing over our humble meal".

The group eat in silence but after they have shared their hot meal of steak and kidney pie, Margareit says to Will, "We are fortunate to get help from some members of our local Printers Guild. While their support these past few weeks is greatly appreciated, the greatest support comes from Elke and Ahren." Margereit looks at her children fondly. "We are blessed to also have a good friend in the same business. His name is Pieter Marten. Pieter can be trusted with helping you with your mission. It is Pieter Marten and Ahren who are finishing the wagon you will be using to secure the Tyndale Bibles. They are making its false floor and secret side panels."

"I can hardly wait to see it," says Will.

"You will and soon," says Ahren.

Elke smiles and says, "It is getting rather late and Master Will has had a long couple of days. I suggest we all retire for the night."

"Good idea," says Margareit, "Let us talk more in the morning. Good night my dear children. It is nice to have you here Will. May you all sleep well and may God protect us all."

When Will retires to his bed he finds it difficult to find sleep. His mind is churning over the day's events.

"Was the steak and kidney pie too rich for me? Could that pie have unsettled my stomach? Perhaps it is just my mind racing about my mission. Or perhaps it's just my being anxious from thinking I have met the girl of my dreams."

Movement downstairs awakens Will from a deep sleep in which he remembers his last thoughts were of Elke. He sits up on his cot, looks around to see where he is, then realizes the deBergdorf family are downstairs having an early breakfast. As he rises to dress he hears a loud knock at the front door, and someone enters the home before anyone says "come in." *"Could it be that local constable? The one called Raemon Gagnon? The one who fancies himself Elke's suitor?"*

Will hurriedly dresses, puts on his boots then clomps down the stairs and announces himself using a bright and cheery" Good Morning everyone, my apologies for sleeping late."

His eyes settle on a surly looking constable in an ill-fitting, wrinkled, uniform. The man is a little over six feet tall and to Will he estimates the man weighs over 220 lbs. but not so much of it muscle but rather "a man of large girth." He has a halberd in one hand as a symbol of his office and eyes that are piercing dark slits. His scruffy mustache looks like an unkempt hedge. The constable stands behind Elke. Will notices she is not looking happy.

The constable turns and scowls at Will's interruption and says, "Who the hell are you?"

Will blurts" Who the hell is asking?"

"I am a Senior Constable Gagnon of Antwerp and I am doing the asking."

To which Will smiles and says, "I am Will Hutchins of London. I am here as a guest of Margareit. while I attend a series of lectures by the famous physician, Paracelsus. He is giving these lectures at your Universitie. Is that satisfactory?

"No," says Gagnon, "Why are you here in this house?"

"Oh that. Well …a generous offer of lodging was made by Madame deBergdorf because many years ago when I was a young pup she and someone in my family were friends. She has offered me that gracious European hospitality folks in this area are known for. Her hospitality is even more appreciated during these times when she should still be mourning her family's loss. My stay here will be short. Once the lectures are over I will be returning promptly to London. Anything else you want to know?"

"Do you have papers to prove who you are and what you are doing here?" Gagnon asks.

"Yes, I do! I am a Master Apothecary. I have papers attesting to my being a trusted agent representing the Worshipful Guild of London Apothecaries."

"When do your lectures at the Universitie start?"

"They start in about an hour, but I overslept as I did not find the voyage here yesterday very relaxing. It made me pretty unsettled when I arrived."

"When are you going back to England?"

"I will be here for three weeks of learning then I return to London."

"See that you do. There are already too many English in this town. They come as merchants, but they stink up the place with their funny ways, bland food, and ale that tastes like horse piss. They have many scurrilous habits and I have found them totally without scruples."

The two pause and just look at each other, then Raemon says, "Walk with me to the door, Will."

When Gagnon reaches the door, he opens it and turns to Will and says, "Get something through your head, I have laid claim to Elke and no English whelp is going to live long if I find him sniffing around her. Do you understand me?"

"Yes sire," Will replies looking down and speaking softly.

Will returns to the table and to the expectant look on the faces of Margareit, Ahren, and Elke wanting to know what Raemon said to him.

"He just wanted me to keep out of trouble and have a good visit at the Universitie," Will lies.

By the look on her face, Will sees that Elke has concluded what Raemon actually said.

Elke then breaks the silence between them and asks Will, "Will, do you know who the Beguines are?"

"Uh, sorry but I do not. That is a word I have not heard before. Just who are they?"

"The Beguines are a group of devout women. They live here in an isolated woman-only community. They do not take any religious vows and consequently are not nuns, nor are they churched laywomen. I would rather live with them than let that oaf of a constable lay his hands on me."

"Oh" Will replies, "Thanks for telling me your true feelings". Then he thinks to himself, *"Now I understand perfectly what's going on here. She would rather be a cloistered nun than let that crude bully touch her."*

Ahren breaks the silence that between the two. "Let us talk about something nicer. Will, your special medicine wagon is nearly complete. You can expect your hidden Tyndale Bibles and the not-so- hidden medications to be stored and ready long before the Paracelsus conference is over. Pieter and I have obtained a horse that will pull the wagon to the docks where it will be loaded onto a ship and you will again travel overnight to London. Once at London's docks some workers have already been paid to unload the wagon using similar block and tackle as us. They will also have a horse ready so you can drive it to the Apothecary Guild Hall for unloading. Do not worry about that constable and do not worry about anything else going wrong. Right now, you need to get to your lectures and learn all you can about the newest medical preparations. You have about a half hour walk from here, so I suggest we do not dally any longer."

"Thank you again for your great hospitality Margereit," Will says and then turns to Ahren, "Since you know the way I will happily follow you. Then tomorrow I will be able to navigate the route on my own."

Finally, Will looks at Elke and with a smile says, "I trust you will be able to rid yourself of that man someday. He comes across as the town bully, always unpredictable and always looking for someone weak to prey on. Seems his type can only stand tall when they stand on someone else's neck."

"I appreciate your understanding of my situation," replies Elke. "I pray your day goes well."

-Chapter 16-

The University of Antwerp (Universiteit Antwerpen)

Monday 8 February 1537

Will and Ahren make their way through the narrow streets of Antwerp. Ahren tells him their world-renowned institute of higher learning is properly called "Universiteit Antwerpen." Ahren says his good-byes at its front gates and as Will enters he finds a main portal off the middle of a narrow street which leads into a large courtyard surrounded on four sides by several two-and three-story buildings. He also sees dormitories for students, a dining hall, a classroom and lecture hall, and a library.

Will notices several dozen students milling about outside the heavy oak doors that lead to the inside of the building he judged to be a lecture hall. He notices most are dressed in a dark blue academic gown with black mortar board hats. They appear to be much younger than he is, most likely in their early teens. *"Is it possible even these young scholars are here to learn from Paracelsus?"*

Will approaches one of the students and asks," Do you speak English? Do any of you know where the Paracelsus lectures are being held?"

"We all learn some English here," a young man responded. "It is the language in which most commerce is conducted. The lectures are being held in the building in front of you. There is a large lecture hall to the right of the entrance, and it is there where everyone will meet. If you have made prior arrangements someone will ask for your credentials before you can be seated."

"Thank you for the information. Are you a student here? Will you and any others be attending these lectures as well?"

"I am. There are about 20 of us attending these lectures as well as about forty-five foreign folk, like yourself. The foreign folk come from all parts of Europe and a couple are from as far away as the Middle East. Paracelsus has a pretty noble reputation."

"Why are so many students attending this series of lectures? Is there a medical college here?"

"Not really. This university is very progressive. It is becoming quite secular in its approach to both student and society needs. As the Reformation Movement spreads it is gradually changing every university curriculum. In the past most students throughout Europe and England went to a university to study theology or the classics. They did so in hopes of finding paid positions handed to them by a King, Lord, civic official or someone within church hierarchy. But as more and more of the population became either sons of the titled gentry or poor waifs without any title, their needs were for a far less theological based education. For example, some students are sons of rich merchants, or sons of professionals like apothecaries or physicians, or landowners. They have needs to better understand how a business operates and how accounts are to be managed if they are to enter the family business or inherit it or strike out on their own.

Will nods.

"Some students are here to learn how to prepare legal documents such as wills and trusts or how to transfer property from one owner to its next," continued the student. "We even have course work here on how to write a proper business letter. Thus, our university is growing in its reputation as an alternative to those who want to live in the past and only offer degrees in divinity."

The student pauses to look at Will. "You seem like a well-informed and educated fellow, so you must see that society is changing from one run by wealthy landowners, the Church of Rome, and those who are paid directly by the King. Today any man who is willing to undertake hard work, persevere, and maintain his integrity, can find that a non-theological education can help him succeed."

Will interrupts, "I can tell you have learned a lot about the world in your young years. Just how old are you?

"I am eighteen, Sir."

"What else can you tell me about life in a changing society?"

"The huge force behind all this started with the Black Death a few generations ago. Folks learned that no man could escape its wrath. They learned how people had to rely upon each other for survival and not just a few handouts from faraway Bishops, Lords, or Kings. High and privileged folks never seemed to help those who made it possible for them to maintain their lofty positions. About that same time movable type was created in Germany making it possible for more and more people to read. Once folk could read scripture in their common language, they realized that to enter the Lord's Kingdom all they had to do was have faith and to follow God's simple commandments. And be kind to each other."

"My apologies for holding you up, Sir, but since you seemed inquisitive, I just needed to tell you what I know to be true," the student says.

"You are not holding me up. Thank you for sharing your thoughts with me. They are in harmony with my own, but I have been unable to articulate them as well as you. I believe you will be successful at whatever you decide to do with your life. Will I see you inside?

"Without a doubt" says the young student, "I too am here to learn. Paracelsus is as much a philosopher and astrologer as he is a physician."

Will enters the stone building in front of him and makes his way through a central hallway to a large tiered lecture hall. Outside the lecture hall's doors, two Fellows of the University sit at a table. As Will approaches them one asks for his credentials. Will opens his pouch and hands his papers to the man who examine then then says, "Please go inside Master Hutchins and find a seat wherever you want. The good doctor Paracelsus will start his lectures in about ten minutes."

Will is so startled at being called Will Hutchins, instead of Will Tyndall, he nearly corrects the man. But after a gulp of air, it is all he can do to say a simple, "Thank you."

Will enters the stepped lecture room, finds a seat about the center of its curved middle. *"If I sit squarely in front of the lectern, I will have a direct view of Paracelsus and will be able to hear him more clearly. Already I can see we have about 50 people here as the great Paracelsus is about to start his lectures. I am so excited to be here."*

A few moments later the famous German physician enters the room and all in the room rise and give him a hearty round of applause. Once introductions are made by the Proctor of the University Paracelsus says," I am going to lecture in English, but it will be with a thick German accent, which I hope you won't have too much trouble with."

The audience smiles at this comment and Will is delighted as he hears Paracelsus continue, "In a few days I will deliver my notes on a substance known as Theriac."

Will's excitement rises again because he knows of Theriac and remembers the day Cyril Blackham taught him the first formula for Theriac. The five-ingredient potion created by the ancient Greeks was revered as a cure-all for fevers brought on by bites…of serpents, mad dogs, and beasts. Cyril had taught him how Theriac became a mainstay of Galenic Medicine as a universal cure-all.

Will marvels at his luck at being in front of Paracelsus "*I know today Theriac may contain between 33 and 100 substances depending on its intended use as an antidote for poison. It will be great to see what Paracelsus has to say about it and what his formula consists of.*"

Will's attention returns to the lecture as he recalls what his mentor taught him. "*But, whatever its use today I Theriac gained immense popularity as a treatment during the times of the Black Death. It is genuinely great to be here*

and to learn how this ancient medicine has been revised by
this great man and healer. So much of what Cyril and I do
are "simples" using just a few herbal or plant ingredients
either ingested raw or made into teas."

Will spends the morning listening to how Paracelsus created new formulations using processes such as distillation which removed impurities and non-essential elements making medicines more potent. The attendees break at high twelve for a small luncheon served in the dining hall in the building across the courtyard. Will runs into the same student he had talked with earlier that morning, but Will had not noticed he was sitting in the back of the lecture room intently listening to Paracelsus.

Will approaches the student and introduces himself again by saying, "Hello, thank you for talking with me earlier today. My name is Will Hutchins. I am an Apothecary from London representing the London Guild of Apothecaries. May I inquire about you and what you are doing?"

"Uh!, My name is Geoffrey Pierson. I am here to help me decide what it is I should be doing for the rest of my life."

"I did not know what I wanted to do with my life until I was seventeen. It was then I chose to become an

Apothecary and started my seven-year apprenticeship and I have loved every moment of that decision."

"At what point were you sure you had made the right decision?"

"Once I decided to become an Apothecary I discovered the joy in its intellectual challenges and also the satisfaction it brought in of helping people. Are you interested in the use of medicines? Why did you take time from your studies to attend these Paracelsus lectures?"

"It's a long story but I have studied all the reasons about how and why people have diseases and the only prevailing reason I can find is there are just several theories, the most prevalent being centered on one of the four humors being out of balance. When black bile, yellow bile, phlegm, and blood are in disorder, disease appears. Good health requires balance. Too me that seems too simplistic. Other causes of disease we are told to believe are elves, fairies, witchcraft, the devil, or God's wrath on sinners. I cannot accept that. I have read the Bible in my own language and I do believe there is a lot we do not know but I am convinced that paying alms to a priest is not a means to a cure nor is blood-letting by draining bad humors."   Geoffrey was clearly passionate about his subject.

"Seems to me you have a surprisingly good thinking and curious mind. Listen intently to what Paracelsus has to say then make up your own mind. Paracelsus is a strong advocate for observation and the use of science. Perhaps you might want to seek him out after our classes for some personal advice about your pathway forward. I imagine Paracelsus would be honored to talk with you. Perhaps he may know how you can apprentice one of the healing professions."

"What a great idea! Thank you. I will do that. I am truly glad that we have met Mr. Hutchins."

Will notices its time to return to the classroom. He chastises himself for forgetting, even for a few minutes, why he is in Antwerp. He says goodbye to Geoffrey and thinks, *"Lord keep me steadfast on my reason for being here so I do not stray due to thoughts I have of that fair damsel Elke. Amen."*

-Chapter 17-

Inside the Green Dragon Tavern

Friday evening, 12 February 1537

The Green Dragon Tavern was strategically situated in the waterfront district of Antwerp. It was the first building on the dock by the estuary of the Scheldt River and beside the Antwerp Customs House. Green Dragon patrons were mostly sailors and shore-men. Over its front door was a large wooden sign depicting a fire breathing dragon drinking ale from a tankard. The patrons loved it.

At a secluded table near the back of the tavern Raemon Gagnon sat with his boyhood compatriot Jaxon DeKlerk. Both government officials, they are rather large, with large egos and mean-spirited behavior. It is clear they believe they can do whatever they want because of the perceived authority that comes with their long-held city positions.

Because Jaxson works as a custom official and Raemon as a constable, they use their positions to conduct nefarious schemes that net them the occasional hefty purse; seizing merchandise from a foreign merchant they knew would never get a fair hearing in a local court, or by overcharging a gullible merchant who had no idea of the true exit taxes levied on cargo leaving Antwerp. Most of their schemes involved one of them using their positions to find a likely target and then using that knowledge to extract a "penalty" or "surcharge" or "tax" which later the two of them would split failing to report the income to the city treasurer.

After ordering a second round of ale, Raemon turns to Jaxson. "Have you heard anything about a wagon full of medicines being readied to go to London?"

"NO, should I? I have heard talk that those attending the series of Paracelsus lectures at the university are physicians, surgeons, apothecaries, astronomers, philosophers, and local students. Perhaps some medical men are taking supplies back to their homes once these lectures are over. I would also assume few would have the means to pay for a wagon load. Do you have information there may be some way we can take a few coins from one of them?" Jaxson is always alert to a fresh scheme.

"Not sure. I have met an arrogant apothecary from England. He has papers saying he is an agent of the London Guild of Apothecaries. He also mentioned he was returning to London with a large amount of medicines for use by that specific group of apothecaries."

"What's your interest in him?" Jaxson asked.

"He is an arrogant young dog who I believe may be sniffing around my woman, Elke. I do not like him. He is also staying at her home. If there is some way we can trip him up and take a few coins while we are at it, I am favorably disposed to do so."

"Uh, I see. Do you know his name?"

"Will Hutchins of London. He has the title of Master Apothecary on his papers which also show he is a registered and trusted agent of the Worshipful Society of London Apothecaries."

"Perhaps I can check this fellow out for you as I know a physician attending those Paracelsus lectures. I also have a connection inside The English House. Perhaps someone living there would know what this Hutchins fellow might be up to."

"Well, it would be great to inspect whatever cargo he will be leaving with. We could extract a big fine if we find anything amiss and especially if he has any contraband."

"You seem pretty agitated by his presence," Jaxson says after another huge swig of his ale.

"I do not like his good looks and his high-brow mannerisms. He could be a possible influence on Elke. I would love to pin his ears back, but I need a good reason to do so. This town thrives on having visitors and merchants bring trade and coin to swell its treasury so we must be subtle about how we go about treating men like Hutchins. "

Jaxson interrupts Raemon, "There is a scurrilous fellow I know who hangs around The English House. Henry Phillips. Perhaps he can report to us on this Hutchins fellow. Since Phillips is educated and English, he may be able to get into the lectures at the University and not be noticed. What do you think about starting with him?"

Raemon hesitates, then replies, "I am not comfortable using anyone but us in any scheme, but when it comes to this Will fellow, there is something about him that just does not seem right. So, getting a third person involved in our plan may be best. Let us hope some good for us comes out of it... and perhaps some bad for Hutchins. Even if we toss Phillips a few coins, it would be worth it to me to have that brash monkey sent the hell away from here with an empty purse and no cargo for his friends in England."

"Glad you agree," nods Jaxson. "Now let's finish our Ale, perhaps have another, and while we drink you can tell me more about how you plan to bed this Elke who has you so vexed."

-Chapter 18-

Inside the deBergdorf Print Shop

Saturday February 13, 1537

It has been almost three weeks since Will arrived in Antwerp. With each passing day he grows fonder of Elke and her family. On this sunny but cool morning Will is alone in his room in the deBergdorf home. He is sitting quietly but having trouble organizing his notes; constantly distracted by thoughts of Elke and the happiness he feels seeing her every day. His confidence in their budding relationship, and his commitment to retrieve his uncle's Bibles, has been rising but he is also struggling with his conflicting priorities… and the knowledge he will soon leave for England.

If he must leave Antwerp he will find a way to come back and pursue a relationship with Elke. However, on some days he thinks a life with Elke is just wishful thinking and he fears rotting away in some foreign dungeon. Other days he believes himself to be fortunate to be alive and to have such a privileged position of attending the Paracelsus lectures which have validated so much of what he believes about being an Apothecary.

As Will is musing over what will come during next week's lectures, his anxiety rises in tempo with his ruminating over the mission. However, these thoughts do little to stop Will also thinking about Elke, and how God has intervened to bring her to him. Then as Will puts his notes into a satchel, he thinks, *I am glad that I have had no recent run-ins with Raemon Gagnon."*

The previous weekend the relationship between Will and Elke blossomed when she took him on a walking tour of her city. Will noticed she stayed away from crowds and any place the constable might find them. And he noticed their closeness. *"Why am I feeling such joy at just being with a girl I barely know? Is she the girl of my dreams? Is she an angel sent from heaven to guard me on my mission? Why does my heartbeat flutter whenever she smiles at me?"*

Such thoughts cause Will to realize how much he misses his family, his friends, and his life back in Hodthorpe. He prays to himself. *"Thank You God for the blessing and gift of Cyril Blackham especially his teaching, guidance, and patience these past seven years. I know that all good gifts and mercies come from you. I thank you also for giving me supportive friends, my loving family, as well as the trust placed in me by Henry Monmouth and the Worshipful Apothecary Guild of London. I know dear God that it is by your grace and some divine mystery I would have never been able to earn the trust of so many and to possibly earn the love of Elke, one of your wonderful servants and an angel here on earth."*

Will's pensive and solitary thoughts are interrupted by the sound of footsteps approaching his room. He sits up, somewhat startled, and then hears Elke's voice. *"Hello, Will, since today is Saturday and you do not have lectures to go to I thought perhaps I could show you some more sights around Antwerp. Would you like to do that? Perhaps I can pack a mid-day meal. We could walk through some of Antwerp's parks and find a nice place to sit and eat it. Would that interest you?"*

Will's pulse quickens., "Uh! yes, let us do just that. I love this city and would love to learn more about it. Especially with you as my guide."

Elke smiles back at him, "Well, then its settled. I would love to squire you about and teach you more about this great city and the folks who live here."

Several hours later the two are walking along the banks of the Scheldt River in a small park from which folks can watch boats and ships going up and down this massive water highway. As promised, Elke has packed a wicker basket with some fresh bread, smoked sausage, cheeses, and some wine. They find a secluded spot to sit on a blanket and as they eat their conversation meanders from the mundane to the more personal until Elke asks, "What are you going to do when you return back to England, Will? Do you have a special girl that you will settle down with? Will you start your own Apothecary in London? Will you go back to a small town in middle England and settle down there?"

Before Will can answer Elke barrages him with more questions, "I notice how you look at me. Are you truly shy and afraid to approach a woman and state your feelings? Is there something you particularly want in a relationship with a woman and do not have the courage to say it? Will, you can be honest with me. So, what is this special attraction that is growing between us?"

"Good God in heaven, before I say anything more, please know I love your straightforward talk. I am surprised you have thoughts about me as much as I have thoughts about you. There is so much more I would like to know about you. But we live in times where courtship is a much-prescribed ritual and it involves both sets of families and friends. Courtship often lasts a long-time and time is something we have little of."

Will pauses and moves closer to Elke. "My reason for being here is important to many. It is so important I have been afraid to say how I feel about you. Time is not on our side. You know as well as I that soon I must depart for England."

"Will, while I do care about traditions, family involvement and courtship rules sometimes when two people truly care about each other, are honest and respectful of all that, should they be denied the opportunity to be with each other?"

"That may be a bit too simplistic, Elke. What about Gagnon. He has declared he is the only one who has a claim on you. You can only hide behind the mourning period of your father for so long then he will demand you submit to him. If that situation is never resolved in his favor, he will torment you and your family forever. He is not the type to forgive being slighted. I do think him a danger to you and your family. He is not to be trifled with."

"Are you afraid of him?"

"Not really, but I have thought of what he can do to you when I am not with you."

By now their need to speak a quieter conversation has closed the physical space between them. With this new closeness Will can smell the fragrance of soap in her hair. He looks into her clear blue eyes. He reaches out his arms to her and she fold into his chest, lifts her head and they embrace. After a few moments of intimacy, they pull back from their happy reverie remembering they are in a public place where any public show of affection is quite taboo.

Somewhat embarrassed, Elke says, "We better go home, Will, before we forget ourselves and someone catches us. I think you are correct we truly must not anger Gagnon right now. That man would harm my family and our business if he put a mind to it. I believe I can hold him off for a while. I also believe the two of us can find a means for us to be together. Know this, I am not giving up on us."

"Nor am I," Elke responds

On their way back to the deBergdorf home they walk past the Universiteit. As they pass its entrance Will says to Elke, "Look over there. On the right. That building has the lecture hall where I go to hear Paracelsus, the famous visiting physician."

As they both gaze across the lawn a student approach from behind saying, "Hi, Master Hutchins, remember me? I have been sitting in with you at the Paracelsus lectures. His lectures make me think I may like to go to medical school. Who is this pretty girl/'"?

Will manages to compose himself and says, "This is Mistress Elke the daughter of the family I am staying with."

As they continue talking Will notices a plain man of slim build, rather unkempt dark hair, and who appears out of place among the students entering the large wooden doors of the lecture hall. "Who is that fellow?" Will asks. "Is he faculty?"

"Uh, NO! That man is Henry Phillips. He hangs out at the English House where most of your conferees are staying."

"Uh, is he an Apothecary or a physician?"

"Neither. He has a reputation of being a scoundrel and not trustworthy, He is always hanging around, yet we do not know how he supports himself. He is not faculty, nor any kind of tradesman. I have told my mates it best if none of us associate with him as he always seems to be wanting to pry information out of them."

Will feels nauseated. "*What if Phillips looks over the list of registrants and sees my name on that list? Would he recognize it as the surname my uncle used at Oxford? Damn. This could not have happened at a worse time. In another week, these lectures will be over, and I can head for home. Must I do something now to keep from being detected by that hateful man? Would he be the type to be in cahoots with that dumb oaf constable chasing after Elke. Perhaps it is time to create alternative plans just in case things go awry.*"

-Chapter 19-

Once Will and Elke return to her parents' home Elke notices Will has assumed a rather quite mood. After querying him about his mood Will tells Elke about Henry Phillips and his suspicions that Phillips might be up to no good.

"If you want to know anything about anyone and all the goings on in this town, both good and bad, the best place is The White Horse Tavern," Elke says. "It is across the street from The English House."

"Well, I think no matter what, it would be worth the risk to check out what he may be up to. He once knew my uncle and because of him my uncle is dead. Do you think we may be able to ferret out something useful?"

"Ahren thinks a lot of you and I am sure if he believes it would be helpful, he will go along with you. I would suggest you both wear clothes like you belong. The more you appear as a pair of middle-class merchants the less chance you will be challenged."

Two nights later Will and Ahren enter the White Horse Tavern and dressed as merchants just as Elke suggested. Once Will sees Henry Phillips in the middle of the tavern; they ease into an empty side booth where they can observe who is coming and who is going. They also can overhear the loud conversation between Phillips and his cronies. Will and Ahren sit opposite each other and appear engaged in a private conversation

Will wears a hat Elke retrieved from her father's closet. The hat hides Will's eyes. He also wears a well-made overcoat from the same closet. Ahren has on his father's best "church-going" cloak and looks the part of a well-groomed merchant.   Will thinks *"I sure hope my dress and manner hide who I truly am…. especially should any lecture hall attendees walk into here or that bully Gagnon."*

Ahren sees the consternation on Will's face and leans into him. He speaks with a low voice, "Will, I can tell you look anxious about something. Everything will be fine. Let us get a couple tankards of ale from the barmaid. For heaven's sake, learn to relax and behave as if we are having a good time or else you will draw attention. Remember we are dressed as merchants and must behave as such."

Will agrees and tries to calm down.

As the night progresses and after several rounds of ale, they hear Phillips' voice get louder. Now Phillips starts to brag to his tablemates about how he shares bribes and extortions with a corrupt Antwerp custom official, Jaxson de Klerk.

Phillips continues his drinking then blurts out to his companions that he and town constable, Raymon Gagnon have also become friends. "This relationship, I am proud as a peacock to say, affords me some official protection on several business dealings that Raymond, Jaxson and I are engaged in."

After a few more swigs of his ale, Phillips continues his bragging, "Gagnon and I look out for each other. We find opportunities to fatten our purses by collecting bribes and acting on tips that help Gagnon and deKlerck collect money from those shipping contraband or foreign goods. They charge less that what the taxes would be, and the merchants are happy to get away with avoiding those tariffs and taxes."

At this latest revelation, Ahren reaches across the table and puts his hand on Will's arm to restrain him from confronting Phillips.

But as the group across from Will and Ahren drink more ale, Phillips prattles on with more swagger and braggadocio saying, "Soon I am going to go to Rome where

I will be welcomed as a hero by the Pope for my helping the Catholic Church fight the Protestant Reformation."

"What did you do to help the church?" one of his drinking companions slurs.

"Why, you should know it was me that hunted down and turned that heretic William Tyndale over to the Catholic authorities. For which I was handsomely rewarded."

"Did you do that all by yourself?"

"Yes, I had known the man when we were both students at Oxford so when I recognized him living across the street from here in The English House, my Catholic upbringing guided my decision to alert the authorities. Tyndale's warrant had already been issued on behalf of the King of England through his Lord Constable. The arrest itself was easy. I took Tyndale out for dinner one night, and the fool even paid for it. Then, when the constables came along, and because they knew me, I just had to point out to them that poor hapless Tyndale. Now I am going to Rome in a few weeks because I know I can be of further help to the Pope."

"Pretty impressive," says one of the companions, "Usually doing good works for the church will enable you to get your reward when you get to heaven. But since you earned some coinage to spend here on earth, perhaps with such largesse you can pay tonight's tavern bill. In fact, betraying someone after an evening meal reminds me of what Judas did to Christ."

"Oh, I would love to pay for tonight's refreshment. But as I reach for my purse, I find my purse has been left back at my lodgings. Perhaps we can all equally share tonight's fare and if someone picks up my portion, I can bring him coin for that kind gesture tomorrow."

Will has heard enough, and his temper starts to rise. Ahren notices Will's nostrils flare. "Come on Will, you have heard enough, let us get the hell out of here before we are discovered. We both would love to see that scoundrel get his just deserts but a confrontation here in this very public place is not the best place to extract revenge. Besides revenge is like much of the food served here, it is a meal best served cold."

Ahren sees Wills hesitation and reaches across the table and places his hand on Will's forearm. Ahren then leans into Will and says, "We should leave now. Let us do so quickly before one of those fellows figures out we have been listening to their conversation. So, stop thinking about what we have heard and let us just pay our bill and get out of here. Is that all right with you?"

Will nods his concurrence.

"Besides, we have learned two pieces of valuable information by our being here, the first is that Gagnon is a crook and thus more dangerous than a bully and second you have heard confirmation of who and how your uncle was betrayed. I just know Phillips trial before God is just around the corner."

After a second pause, Ahren again leans towards Will. "You heard that bastard Phillips say he believes he is going to get a reward from the Pope. I do not think he will. The church is like any military organization, always demanding loyalty from the bottom to the top. It is the only way for it to survive. Phillips' integrity and loyalty are compromised. Should he ever get an audience with the Pope it will likely be one in which he is told his services are no longer needed. They already know he will betray a friend for money and thus he is likely to betray anyone else having dealings with him. His search for redemption and church favor is going to be as futile as it was for Judas."

Will looks downcast and starts to think about what they should do next. Finally, he says to Ahren, "You are right about Phillips. Let us just go."

As the two exit the tavern they continue to walk a gait as if they had they had been drinking inside the White Horse Tavern for several hours. But, once they cross out of the town square Will again expresses his misgivings about his ability to complete his mission.

-Chapter 20-

In an alley near the White Horse Tavern

Monday night late, February 15, 1537

Once the pair have crossed Antwerp's Grote Markt, they head down several narrow streets towards the deBergdorf home. After a few blocks they enter a narrow street joining Grote Markt to a smaller square and see their exit blocked by a man. He looks to be alone but they sense something amiss and ominous. Together, they turn to go back the way they came. It is then they notice a second man blocking their way back to Grote Markt.

"I think we are going to have a problem," says Ahren.

"Aye, I feel it too."

Just then, a voice calls out, "Hey, you two ugly Englishmen, hand over your purses or you will get the beating of your life."

Before either Ahren or Will can answer they notice a third man steps up beside the man in front, making for three likely ruffians. And they fear there could be more.

Ahren whispers, "We have to get out of here. Perhaps we can go back and push the guy behind us aside, holler like crazy, and hope someone will come and help us."

Before Ahren gets an answer, Will leaps forward and heads towards the man a few steps ahead of him.

"What in the name of the Holy Saints are you up too? Have you gone berserk?" shouts Ahren wide-eyed and with a high-pitched shriek." Come back here!"

The three ruffians wear dumfounded expressions as Will runs headlong towards the one in front of him. As he draws closer the lead ruffian lifts a truncheon and readies it to swing at Will. Once Will is within two step of the ruffian the man swings the truncheon down across the front of Will hoping to strike him on the head. But Will anticipates the man's move and suddenly turns sideways. The truncheon whooshes as it hits only air.

Will ducks and grabs the man's right arm. Using the force behind the man's swing Will is able to give his assailant a mighty shove smashing his face into the brick wall in front of him.

Will hears him gasp for air and as he doubles over to cup his face Will puts a well-placed kick to the side of the ruffian's his head. This second jolt makes the man fall unconscious onto the cobblestones. His nose is bleeding profusely.

The second man shouts. "You should not have done that 'cause now things are going to get ugly."

The second man lunges at Will pulling a dagger from under his coat, and quickly closing the distance between them. Will picks up the dropped truncheon and as the man raises the dagger to strike, Will hits him across his forearm with the truncheon and he drops the dagger with a cry of pain.

Will swings the truncheon back the other way and it cracks against the second robber's cheek, who howls and spits out a mouthful of blood and a tooth. "You broke some of my teeth you bastard and now my friend is going to give you what you deserve," he mumbles through swollen lip.

While he is talking, Will is able to swing the truncheon back against the man's knee. They all hear a loud crack as the kneecap breaks, which sends the man howling even louder and rolling onto the ground.

Then Will turns his attention to the man running after Ahren and who is catching up to him. Will drops the truncheon and runs to catch up to both. Just as the robber reaches out to grab Ahren by his shoulders to force him onto the ground, Will rushes up to the two struggling men and pulls a dirk from inside his boot top and sticks it into the would-be robber's arm. Will pulls the dirk back and jabs it into the robber's thigh. However, Will's forward motion causes all three to fall onto the ground.

As the third ruffian winces in pain, he rolls off to the side where he sees his two companions, one unconscious and the second one groggy and bleeding from the nose and mouth. Before the third man can get up, Will jumps up and leans over the wounded man and puts his knee into the small of his back. The man turns his head and Will threatens to give him another jab with his dirk.

Will shouts "Who sent you to rob us? Was it Phillips? Was it Gagnon? Come on speak up before I put another hole in you. Your two friends are in no shape to help you."

The man stutters and cowers on the ground. Then he rolls into a fetal position and grabs his thigh. "We work alone, no one sent us," he stammers. "You are crazy if you think someone hired us to harm you or to steal your purses. You looked like rich Englishmen who must have money. We saw you exit the Tavern where only wealthy travelers or merchants are patrons. Now leave us alone as we need help for our bleeding wounds. Soon our brothers will be looking for you to even the score."

Will ignores the warning, grabs Ahren by his coat and says to him, "Let us get the hell out of here before any more friends of these scoundrels come along. Imagine that third guy asking me for mercy, most men would have killed him on the spot. I am sure those robbers would have cut our throats had we not acted first and took them by surprise."

"What surprise?" says Ahren, "And what do you mean by "we." It was all you. The only surprising thing I saw was you tearing into those guys like a man possessed. My heart was beating faster than it has ever done. I can still feel it thumping in my chest."

"I guess I just was so angry at what we heard from Phillips. What a braggart and such a rotten scoundrel. I have also been angry for days at Gagnon for how he treats Elke. When those robbers tried to stop us, I just exploded without thinking. I have not been in a street fight since I was a kid. I learned early in life that bullies and cowards are unpredictable, especially when challenged. I just knew I had to make the first move not knowing how much harm they might inflict.

Will adds, "Underneath all this, I guess I just had enough of being anxious about all the reasons why I am here. I just exploded at the thought my mission here might end because of a senseless robbery or some entanglement with folk like Phillips or Gagnon."

Will pauses to catch his breath and as he looks at Ahren standing quietly by he continues, "My pent-up anger caused me to over-react. It seemed like the right thing to do when I snapped. It's an odd thing that criminals like these never seem to learn from their mistakes."

As Will puts his knife away, and straightens his clothing, he leans over to Ahren and says, "Years ago I found out that when someone rushes you it's possible to use their weight and momentum against them. Most people just stand their ground and then lose a fight because standing still makes it easier to get hit or hurt. I learned as a kid to look your assailant in the eye then assess what his target is, then slightly shift out of harm's way when he starts taking a swing at you. If you can react quickly, they will invariable miss their intended target."

"I understand you better now," Ahren says.

Will continues, "Ahren, if I handed my purse over to one of them I would not have been able to pay the tariffs or fees required for the successful completion of my mission. That would have been worse than being hurt or cut given all the trust placed on me to see our mission through."

Will adds, "Besides, there was no promise that we would have been left alone once these scoundrels had our coins. So, it worked out for the best that I went on the offensive and surprised them."

"Holy Mother! Will, what you did was frightening. I have never seen anyone act with such fury. And it was all over so quickly," says Ahren realizing he can hardly speak after all the excitement.

"Let's go home and clean up," Will implores. Lord help me but I never ever thought I would use my dirk on a man. Oh well, he asked for it and he got to taste its business end. We should just leave now and let these ruffians fend for themselves. They deserve no better. Besides, someone may have heard the fight and raised an alarm. Also, I do not want to deal with any city constables this close to my departure from your fair city and its much fairer daughter, your sister. So, is your mind clear? Can you walk us out of here?"

"Yea, I am good. No lumps, bumps, or cuts. I am just like you... a little dirty from rolling on the ground."

"Go pick up that ruffian's dagger and his truncheon. We can drop both into the river. That will prevent them from being used again to harm or threaten some poor innocent wayfarer or merchant."

Just then the ruffian Will slammed into the wall stands up and stumbles his way back through the narrow passageway leaving his two companions on the ground. As he bursts out of the narrow street, into the large square, he starts shouting, "Help, help, Good God Almighty help us. We are being attacked. It is bloody murder. I need help now. Call the constables. Thieves want to rob us blind. Help, help, help, For God's sake we need help."

Will sees doors and windows opening. A few people come out into the square. He turns to Ahren and says "We have no time to dally. We must get out of here now and do so quickly. We cannot go back the way we came. Can you direct us home without our being seen? Whoever it is that comes to his aid will likely help those two writhing on the ground. It would be best for us if we were not seen by anyone who could identify us. We cannot risk being turned into the constabulary. After all you are a local citizen and will be known my many. So, let us get going with great haste."

Ahren and Will run ahead into the square that they originally planned to enter but now Ahren leads them onto a side street from which they can take a different, but longer, route back to the deBergdorf home. Once they feel safe and are sure that no one has followed them, they slow their pace and breathe easier.

"Will, you could have killed any one of those guys and it would have been justified, why didn't you?" Ahren says.

"I don't really know why I didn't. Perhaps I was more worried about stopping them and getting us out of there. Besides, I do not think we needed to explain a corpse to any law official. Dead citizens killed in a street fight would have been bad for the tourist and merchant trade." Will laughs.

"Jesus, Mary and Joseph, Will, how can you joke at a time like this?"

"I guess it eases the tension."

"Uh, by the way, why did you say something a moment ago, something about …my fair city and my much fairer sister. What prompted that remark? Were you thinking of my sister during a street fight?

"I will talk to you later about that, I believe its best we just walk quietly but keep on going so you can get us home as quickly as possible."

A few minutes later they arrive at Ahren's home. Once inside they quietly try make their way through the kitchen.. But Ahren's mother, as most mothers do when they wait for their sons to come safely home had waited patiently for their safe return. Upon hearing their muffled entry and hearing them take off their boots, she gets up, throws on a robe, then greets her son and guest before either can leave the downstairs rooms.

Startled by their unkempt appearance, she blurts: "What happened to you? I cannot imagine either of you falling into the street from too much ale. Tell me what happened."

"Not to worry, Mother," says Ahren. We met up with a couple of ruffians, but Will scared them off. Please go back to bed and we will give you details in the morning. I love you Mother but too much happened tonight to talk about now. We are both safe and that is all that really matters. So, let us all get some sleep. Will, thank you for a most interesting evening."

The two young men walk upstairs and crawl into their beds. Will ruminates over the enormity of the nights events and the impact it could have on his mission. "I *think I better start making a secondary plan or I might find myself unable to leave this town except by casket, or worse be locked up in the same prison as my uncle. Damnation why is God throwing so many obstacles into what should have been an easy path to tread. Mother told me it would be honorable, but she never said it would be difficult.*"

Will's next thoughts were of Elke and especially what it would have done to their relationship if he had not been able to protect Ahren "*I need to give thanks to the Lord for protecting both of us tonight. I think also I need his intervention to help get me out of here as quickly and safely as possible. Perhaps the best words for me to call on Him and thank him are those he taught us so long ago...Our Father which art . . .* "

-Chapter 21-

At the home of Margareit de Bergdorf
early morning, Tuesday 16 February 1537

The morning following the street incident, Will
awakens. Fear, anger, and desperation haunt him as he
wonders what might happen if he and Ahren are discovered
as the men who sent three of Antwerp's citizens to seek
medical help. It will not matter that they were ruffians. Will
dresses in clean cloths and then joins the family for
breakfast in the kitchen. As he walks in with a not so
sincere cheery "Good Morning" he finds Ahren telling his
mother and sister of their encounter which Ahren
embellishes as to how Will dispatched the ruffians and
literally saved their lives. As he finishes his story a knock at
the door startles them. A hush fills the room, followed by an
audible sigh of relief as Pieter Marten comes in and tells
them the wagon and its cargo are ready to leave whenever
they are ready.

Pieter says, "I have arranged a horse to pull the
wagon to the docks. I have also arranged for five dock
workers to help hoist the wagon onto the deck of a ship
going to London. Such ships usually leave late in the day,
sail across the English Channel and up the Thames River

estuary. This ship will take Will and his cargo straight to the London docks for unloading early the next morning."

Will fills Pieter in on the previous night's events saying, "I believe it would be best for me to leave Antwerp either tonight or tomorrow morning at the latest. This will be at least three or four days earlier than Monmouth planned and much before he had arranged passage on a different ship to England. Because of what happened last night I believe all his and our planning is in jeopardy. It is also possible city constables, or other authorities, may have been alerted to look for two men who beat up three fine local citizens… no matter how well they deserved it. These men also are likely to be using their own street thugs to find us and extract revenge."

After a few nods and some pauses, Ahren speaks up, "I agree with Will. It would be better for him to leave Antwerp as soon as possible. However, rather than leave on a ship out of Antwerp on Saturday, or tomorrow, he should travel overland and go south. French cities such as Calais, Dunkerque, Dieppe or Caen offer suitable ports and ships on which he can gain passage for himself and the Apothecary wagon."

Pieter interrupts Ahren and says with some exuberance "That's good thinking, Ahren, and if I can add to it … Will…your finding passage to England in one of those four towns would be quite easy. Additionally, they are towns with a large contingent of Protestant supporters. Thus, you may find folks helpful in getting you and your precious wagon out of their country."

They all nod their agreement that travelling to France offers Will the safest route from Antwerp.

Then Margareit chimes in. "I would like to suggest we find a merchant caravan travelling south. Rather than have him travel alone his being part of a merchant caravan would offer protection from bandits, robbers, and highwaymen. These scoundrels are known to travel on the same roads that Will would be on and they will be looking for easy prey such as a lone traveler. Many a lone traveler has been found in a ditch because he met with and likely resisted a gang of bandits."

"What a great idea" says Will, "Can we find such a caravan? Can we do this by tomorrow?"

"I will use today, and tomorrow if need be, to find you a suitable caravan," says Ahren. "I know where several assemble to start their journey south to French ports. This may make us delay Will's departure by a day or two. But perhaps another quiet day or two having Will at the Paracelsus lectures could also be helpful."

"Please explain yourself, Ahren," says Pieter "I thought our plans were pretty much set."

"What new mischief are you thinking about?" Will asks.

Ahren responds calmly, "Until all the details are in place I believe it would be best if Will behaves as if nothing is wrong. Leaving before the lectures are over may attract attention to him as would leaving much later. Will may also be able to pick up some useful news if he keeps attending the Paracelsus lectures. Besides this will give us all the time we need to complete the details for his trip."

Seeing their nods of understanding, Ahren continues. "Because several attendees stay at The English House, Will may hear something more about the street fight and the investigation by any constabulary. We also may learn more about that scurrilous fellow, Phillips, and what he may be up to. Finally, most caravans leave on Saturday. They use the weekend to travel and they are typically twice or thrice the size of those leaving mid-week. If we can hold off sending Will from here until Saturday, Will can attach himself to a safer and larger caravan and thus avoid the Antwerp docks where he may find a lot more scrutiny than usual."

Will, Pieter, Margareit, Elke and Ahren look at each other then again nod agreement at Ahren's reasoning.

Will then speaks, "I fully support the idea of joining a caravan idea. I will depart this Saturday and continue with the Paracelsus lectures. That will help keep up appearances but more especially it will afford me the opportunity to listen for any gossip or news that could hinder my mission and the safety of everyone in this room."

"Let's finish our breakfasts so Ahren can go look for a safe and suitable caravan," Margareit says. "Will, you need to get off to your Paracelsus lectures. Elke and I have some laundry to do and we will have a nice supper ready for you boys this evening"

Ahren looks at his mother and says, "We are not boys dear Mother. We are grown men on a dangerous mission."

Margareit stares at him and then with a set jaw that could stop a dog in its tracks, hugs her son. "As long as you live in my house you are still my boy."

That evening, they all sit down to a hearty meal of lamb stew cooked over the hearth in an iron pot and served on a trencher with warm fresh bread. They wash down the meal with a local red wine.

Will quietly waits until the supper table is being cleared by the two women. Once he is sure they are out of earshot he leans over and talks softly to Ahren, "During my time here with you and your family I have come to think of you as a brother. I cannot thank you and your mother enough for the hospitality and risk you both have taken on my behalf.

Will pauses then continues looking Ahren in the eye, and says, "Now that you have assumed the mantle as male head of this family, I must ask your blessing on a personal matter. It is my intent, once I get that wagon full of Bibles and medicines into England, to return here so I may court your sister. This is not something I ask lightly, As Elke and I are in love, would you be comfortable with my returning and becoming your brother-in law?"

"Good God man. That is damn nice, and most proper, that you should ask. Why of course I would be comfortable with you being part of our family. Nothing else would make me happier. In the short time that you and I have known each other we have become good and trusting, friends."

Ahren's jovial manner changes and now he continues with a serious look., "We both know Elke is being pursued by Raemon Gagnon. I hate that Gagnon is crude, rude and a bully. He is a self-serving oaf and causes me to worry about my sister's safety whenever I see him near her. His behavior reminds me of a lecherous seaman who after a six-month voyage is looking to scratch an itch that won't go away."

Will smiles at Ahren's metaphor then Ahren continues, "Gagnon does not know what love and tenderness are. He just wants to possess women as a farmer possesses a sheep … chattel to be used. I am convinced once he has taken her virtue any interest he has to deepen the relationship would be gone as he would then tire of her as quickly as a child does with a new plaything. I know Elke could never love a man like him. I also know he could never see a strong, smart, and funny woman as his equal. Thus, she would soon be treated like dirt beneath his feet."

Ahren then looks directly into Will's eyes and adds, "What I also believe is this. I have seen you in action, observed your intelligence, integrity, and work ethic. I see how you have earned the trust of the likes of Monmouth. I truly do support your petition to have me as a brother-in law.."

Ahren pauses, smiles, then looks into Will's gaze. "I have seen Elke look at you with moon eyes. Besides she has already said in front of you, me, and her mother that she would rather be an old maid, joint a convent, or join the beguines rather than see her life and happiness tied to the whims and fancies of someone like Gagnon. So, Will, you have my blessing and if it is all right with you, I will share your intentions with my Mother. I know she will be as pleased as I am that you had the good manners to declare your intentions. But tell me, have you made your intentions known to Elke?"

Immediately Will feels a sinking feeling in his stomach," Uh, No, well maybe, perhaps, just a little, why do you ask?"

"Well, it would seem you both are in love. However, she would not have any idea if her feelings are reciprocated unless you take some initiative and tell her.. My sister is not the type to fall in love with a man who would treat her harshly. But because she is so intelligent and sensitive, she easily hides her true feelings behind a little humor and playful teasing, but like all women she does need someone to show her tenderness and let her know she is cared for."

"Ahren, I will confess that I enjoy our little teasing and her wry humor. We have made a good beginning at building our relationship. Moreover, I get a little flushed and weak in the knees whenever I think of her or am with her."

Will pauses and after running his fingers through his hair he says, "I am not good at expressing my feelings. When I am with her, I just seem to stumble along like some country bumpkin. I know my mission here is too important that it should not be distracted by an affair of the heart, but truthfully since I have met your sister, I just cannot seem to remain as focused as I should. The past two Saturdays we have toured the city together. While it has been great being with her I know she has been wary of taking me to places where we could run into Gagnon. However, last Saturday as we were walking along the Scheldt River, we did talk a little about having a future with each other. But we were careful to be away from public view."

"As her brother, I can tell you that Elke has been a lot quieter these many days that you have been here," Ahren says. It started the day you arrived. She seems deep in thought more so than usual. I can only say that if you do not know how she truly feels towards you then she does not know exactly how you feel towards her. You say you feel like a country bumpkin when you are around her, well I think you both have been stumbling around like two addled country bumkins. Until you get up the courage to tell her what's in your heart you will leave here in a couple of days and you both will be blind to whatever lies ahead as your future."

"God bless you for saying that Ahren. I am having trouble thinking about any future with Elke, especially since this whole mission of ours has so deviated from Monmouth's original plan. This is troublesome for me since you and your whole family are also involved. I do not want to see you or anyone else in jeopardy because of me and so I have been doing my best to keep my head clear and my mind focused on my mission."

Ahren sighs in exasperation "Damn it, Man. You will have a clearer head if you take time to talk to my sister. Women are much different than men when it comes to expressing matters of the heart. If nothing else, a good frank talk between you will open both of your eyes. So, before you get out of town make the time to talk to Elke and tell her what you really feel and see how she responds. You know, for a very smart man and one who has had lots of experiences helping people with their ills and problems, you are naïve when it comes to dealing with your own problems. So again, I ask you, please go, talk to Elke, and get at least one more problem solved before you get out of town. If you can't do that perhaps I shall have to conclude that you are a poor candidate for her hand."

The two men shake hands, and Will says "Ahren, I expect you to keep close watch over your sister and Mother until my return. "

"Not a problem, I already look after them both and I am proud to do it for you as well."

"Now I can go to bed and be happy knowing that I have your blessing. I promise you I will talk with Elke before my departure."

Once Will has left the room and is in his sleeping quarters, Elke enters the room Will had just left. She pulls up a chair beside her brother, looks at him and says in a low voice, "I overheard the conversation between you and Will. I am pleased that he took the initiative to talk with you about our relationship. I am in love with him and know that we will build a good life together. Whether we live here or in England remains to be seen. But I know my relationship with Will is bound to infuriate Gagnon. He may take it out on you and Mother"

Elke then reaches over the table, takes her brother's hand and then continues, "I just cannot stand to be near Gagnon. I know with father gone we must be nice to everyone for the sake of the business, but I do not want to become a possession of Gagnon's and then be used or abused as he sees fit. The day would likely come when I would fear him worse than I do now."

Elke pauses then looks into her brother's eyes saying, "I have never felt this way about anybody. Since Will has been in our home I have talked with him on quite a few occasions and twice we have gone walking alone. I do believe he is gentle and kind. Will makes me laugh, he is smart, and certainly his profession will provide a level of comfort in which we could raise some nieces and nephews for you. Now, before you say no to this request, just listen, I have been thinking that when Will leaves Antwerp in two days I should go with him to France."

Ahren looks aghast at her suggestion, but before he can speak, his sister stops him "Do not interrupt me until I finish telling you why I want to do this. First, I speak the dialect south of here and Will does not. Second, I know I would be safe with him. Third, we both would be safe travelling together, and besides that, we would be watched over by the caravan's leader. Fourth, once Will leaves for England, I can easily get a merchant ship to return me back to home.

Elke gives her brother's hand a squeeze and adds, " But last and most importantly, as Will has declared himself to be my suitor it would also give me a chance to learn more about him, his family, his ambitions, and his true heart before he returns here again. I know I have similar feelings for him and am willing to endure any wait till he returns."

Now Elke takes her eyes away from her brother, drops his hand, and continues in a soft but firm voice, "My dear brother, what do you think about this idea? Oh! in case you are wondering, you should also know I have shared my feelings for Will, and my plans to go with him, with our mother. You will not have to put me off by saying… let us go ask mother. Mother   has already given me her approval. She knows full well how important it is for Will to get that wagon back to England. She believes Monmouth would never have sent a man he did not believe would be successful. Mother also believes Will is a man with enough integrity not to trifle with a maiden's feelings or her virtue."

Then after another short pause, Elke says, "All right brother, you can speak now."

Ahren grimaces and replies, "Well if mother believes this is the right thing for you to be doing, then it has my blessing. I know how unhappy you have been with Gagnon's poking around here. Besides Gagnon would never let any other man court you and if one did he would run him off. The best thing now for you would be to pack your bags for at least a ten-day journey away from here."

The brother and sister hug and she let Ahren kiss her forehead. HE then steps back then he adds, "Tomorrow I will search for a merchant caravan going to France that can hide both of you within its ranks. I know a few caravan masters who have taken some of our father's printings to France, so I trust one of them will be helpful in remembrance of him."

Oh!, he says a little more emphatically, "You can plan to leave here early in the morning on Friday or Saturday. So, pack now so you will be ready to go when we are sure of the day. But do not tell Will of the decision for you to travel with him. I believe he cares for you so much that he will likely talk you out of going with him. He will put your safety and your comfort above his own. Secondly, he must also appear at the Paracelsus lectures as if there is nothing amiss as he is the kind of man who finds it hard to cover up his emotions. If he appears to be anything but a scholar he will likely give himself away because it's so easy to read his feelings."

"Oh Ahren, I do love you so. Thank you for believing in me and supporting me. I pray the day will soon come when you have the same feelings for someone as I do for Will." Elke hugs her brother again. Then, with a light step she slips away to her bed chamber.

Upstairs Will is lying in his bed but is wide awake looking for holes in their new plan. He can feel his heart racing as he reviews what may lie before him in the next few weeks. But his central thoughts center around questions such as, *"No matter how well I was trained by Monmouth and how much effort went into his planning was put together, neither he nor I counted on my being distracted by falling in love with Elke."*

Will breaths deep. *"I never thought Ahren and his mother would support my courting Elke. Now what do I do? Am I wrong or just being arrogant in believing this poor apothecary has a chance of a future with Elke? I should not be ruining the certainty of her stable life here where she is really needed to help run the print shop. Perhaps God has a plan for us both but if he does, I sure hope He reveals it to us soon as I am going crazy thinking about what's next."*

Later in the night Will is still awake, restless, and continues to think this is the longest night he has ever experienced as the eerie silence of the middle of the night in a large town is almost deafening to him. Just as the sun is about to rise he finally falls into a light sleep but not before concluding, *"Is this tossing and turning what love does? Ahren is right, I just need to find the right words to express my feelings to Elke. But what happens if I fully express myself and she rejects me and joins that local band of holy women.*

A dog barking at a passing drunk pulls Will from his slight, light sleep which now causes Will to be tangled in his bedclothes. This causes him once again to contemplate his situation by searching for means to satisfy his thinking over thoughts such as, *"How best should I declare my intentions to Elke? Do I utterly understand my own true feelings and what I must do to win her heart?? Is she safe, especially with that cur of a fellow sniffing around all the time? Why did Ahren so readily support me pressing forward with my intentions towards Elke? Does he know something I do not know?*

Finally, Will looks out his window at the stars he can see and concludes, *"I better just stick to why I came here in the first place and put any notions of love aside, at least until I accomplish my reason for coming here. I believe it best if I put this whole matter into God's hands"*

A moment later as Will continues to look up to the stars, he asks. *"Heavenly father you have you brought me to a place where I do not know what your plan for me is. You have guided me to new people. You have caused me to fight ruffians which has left me a hunted man in a strange city. You have fueled my passions for medical knowledge by seeing that I attend the lectures of the great Paracelsus's lectures. You have introduced me to a constable who would rather knock my head off than engage in decent and polite conversation, and lastly Dear Lord, you have introduced me to a fair and lovely women who befuddles me when I should be clear thinking and confident. I pray that you soon reveal to me to what end all this has happened and what it is that I must do that would be pleasing to your eye and prove I am in service to your glory and Holy Name."*

His prayer quiets Will's racing mind after which he quickly falls asleep.

-Chapter 22-

On a street outside the Universitie Antwerpen.

Wednesday 17 February 1536.

Still sleepy Will wakes early. After breakfast he walks the cobblestone streets towards the Universitie Antwerpen. This is the second to last day of the Paracelsus lectures. He is deep in thought going over every detail of the new plan to leave Antwerp by caravan. He cannot shake the nagging possibility he is to blame for all these new decisions. *"No matter what happens to me or my mission, I will definitely come back to Antwerp and court the fair Elke, tell her how I feel, and ask if she would like to marry and become be the mother of our children."*

Will's thoughts of Elke are suddenly interrupted by a gruff voice shouting, "Where are

you are going Englishman?"

"Huh," says the startled Will turning towards the voice and sees Raemon Gagnon with a snarl and piercing stare aimed directly at him.

The startled Will sneers back, "You know bloody well where I am going. I must arrive at the Paracelsus lectures in a few minutes or else I will be late. What is it you want now?"

"When are you leaving our great city, you English cur?'

"My plans have not changed. I have told you before when I was leaving and again yesterday…which is …I will be leaving this coming Saturday. That is… if the ship is ready to leave port and if the seas are not too rough."

"Well, why don't I walk along with you just to be sure you get to your lectures safely. Did you know three ruffians were savagely beaten a few days ago? They were bloodied and cut badly in what appears to be an unprovoked attack. This all occurred near the English House in an alley off Grote Markt."

"I know nothing about such matters."

"I thought you may have heard something from your English friends attending the University lectures. I do believe several of them are lodging at The English House."

"I pretty much stick to myself since I have been in your fair city. Besides, I do not have the resources to spend money in your fine ale houses. Neither do I have the coin to afford lodging at The English House."

After a quick pause Will looks at Raemon and adds, "Besides, you called these three... ruffians. Perhaps they got what they deserved."

After more stares between the two, Gagnon continues, "Well one ruffian was cut pretty bad. He said the fellow cut him with a dirk, which makes me think it was an Englishman. These men stated they were leaving a side street near Grote Mark't when they were jumped on by five or six possible Englishman looking for trouble."

"Did your ruffians ever tell you who it was that attacked them?"

"Yeah, they said they could identify them. One said they were English bastards and that he could identify the dirk."

"Well, good luck with that. A dirk is as common as flowers in the spring.

"You may be right, but I still think it was some English bastards who beat and cut our fine citizens and they should not get away with it."

"Well, good luck finding whoever it was. Now this is where I enter the University to obtain more learning from that great physician, Paracelsus."

As Will turns to leave Raemon grabs his sleeve and turns Will toward him saying, "I am cautioning you is to stay away from Elke. My intention is to have that girl and to have her soon. Your being in her home is a distraction as is the loss of her Father. Once you are gone from her and her family, and her period of mourning passes. I will find clear sailing into her heart and bed."

Will ignores Raemon's warning. He steps through the portal of the University turns and says, "Good luck finding a Scotsman with a missing dirk."

As Will enters the University's common grounds he shudders at the thought of that fat, ugly man, putting his hands-on Elke. "*I pray the day comes soon when that poor excuse for a human gets his comeuppance.*"

-Chapter 23-

The Green Dragon Inn
Wednesday February 17, 1536

Having had their meager supper washed down with
several tankards of ale, Raemon Gagnon and Jaxson de
Klerk discuss the day's events. Jaxson regards Raemon.
"You look a little worse for wear. Did you have a bad day?
Did something happen to spoil our plans?"

"Aw! It is just that damn Will Hutchins. He really
gets my backside up. I wish I could pin some sort of crime
on him. Earlier this morning I met him on a street in front of
the Universiteit. I was pretty nice to him. I also warned him
calmly that he is not to play with the affections of Elke. I
tried to be nice to him, but he just seemed not to want to
listen. Let us not dwell on that English cur, how has you day
gone?"

"Down on the docks it was business as usual. Tell
me more about Hutchins."

"Other than him being a brash horse's rear, he did
offer a piece of advice about a dirk being an exclusive
weapon of a Scotsman. So, I have been nosing around by
the docks where many of them hang out to see if I can pick

up on anything that might unravel why three of our citizens were brutally attacked."

"Well, enough of your troubles." says Jaxson taking another swig from his tankard. "What I learned from having Henry Phillips nose around the German doctor's lectures is that they are over this coming Friday. He says almost everyone from out of town is leaving on Saturday. My friend at the shipyards says there is a manifest showing Will Hutchins as a passenger on a ship sailing Saturday morning for London. He also says if the weather turns bad the ship may sail on Sunday…and you know how rough the seas can get going across to England. Philips also says that he is convinced Hutchins is not related to the man he once knew in England. He also said, Hutchins is popular family name in England. Phillips believes the man is who he says he is and truly is a master apothecary representing the Worshipful London Guild of Apothecaries. He affirmed that having talked to several delegates who had conversations with Hutchins and found he could speak fluently the language of a healer. Phillips also said the staff found Hutchins' credential papers absolutely legitimate."

"Well I guess all that's good news…for Hutchins. I wish he were a fraud and up to something we could catch him at. I would like to see that cocky Englishman sitting in one of our local cells and kept away from Elke. Anything else?"

"Oh, I nearly forgot, it seems on his booking to leave on Saturday there is a notation he will need help loading some medicines bound for London's Guild of Apothecaries. He will pay import taxes when he arrives at London. But we can collect export taxes here if he has drugs, plants and mineral found in Europe."

"Maybe that's how I can pin his ears back. Let us be sure that whatever he brings aboard is thoroughly inspected for any contraband and then we levy heavy taxes and keep a portion. What do you think of that? Would it not be fun for us to see his inspection take so much time he misses his sailing time?"

"Raemon, you really are a devilish man." Jaxson says then adds, "I will be sure I am working this Saturday, and on Sunday if need be. I will put myself in a position where I can watch for Hutchins to come to the Customs House. I will make sure a thorough search is conducted. If you so ask, I can cause him to miss his sailing time. Should hold up his leaving?"

"No, upon thinking this through again, I believe the faster he gets out of this city the better I will feel about him being unable to influence Elke."

"What should we do about Henry Phillips?" says Jaxson after taking another draught of his ale.

"Well, let us give him five silver coins and send him on his way. I do not trust that scoundrel. I do not like him and do not want him any more involved than he already is. He would back-stab anybody and might sell us out as easily as he did that Oxford priest Tyndale."

"I agree, Raemon, he has shown no honor among Antwerp's thieves. He told me he is saving as much coin as he can to pay for a trip to Rome. He wants to meet with the Pope. He is hoping for redemption both for his gambling habit and his betrayal of the scholar Master Tyndale. He believes he can do even greater work for the Church of Rome because he has developed a relationship with its high-ranking officials in England."

"Methinks the man a fool. If he betrayed a friend, as he betrayed Master Tyndale, the prelates in Rome will ask at what point in time would Phillips betray one of them. His reputation as a liar and cheat will not endear him to church authority. I agree, we give him a few coins to help send him out of our town. I will be more comfortable knowing Hutchins and Phillips are both out of my sight."

-Chapter 24-

Early Evening at a secluded warehouse on the edge of Antwerp.

After a supper of leftover meat, boiled vegetables, and whole-grain bread, the deBergdorf family and Will, leave their home and walk for an hour. They arrive at a large warehouse owned by Pieter Marten who arranged for Will to meet-up with a merchant caravan early on Saturday morning.

"How far will I be travelling with this caravan?" Will asks. "I have no idea of the French countryside, what is it like? This whole affair has me feeling somewhat overwhelmed with what could go wrong."

"Folks in the caravan are good and honest merchants, Pieter says. "Most are going as far as Calais which has the shortest distance between France and England and offers the most common port to cross the English Channel. Leaving from Calais can be a pretty rough passage should strong winds howl in from the north. But Calais remains a popular port for many ships not only go to England but head south to ports in Spain or the other side of the Pillars of Hercules. You will lose most of the caravan at

Calais, stripping away the protection that comes from having large numbers of travelers."

Pieter pauses to let that last remark sink in then turns to Will, "Will, you will have to decide when you get to Calais whether or not you will need to push on to either Dunkerque or Dieppe or go as far as Caen. If you decide to go to one of those three towns it will add another few days to your journey. There are possibilities for a ship at either Dunkerque or Dieppe because they have suitable harbors to get your wagon loaded onto one of the few ships that cross the channel. I suggest Caen, it is more hospitable. From Caen you will have a longer water voyage and one likely to either Brighton or Southampton. From either one you will need another few days of overland travel to London. That will require securing another horse to pull your wagon unless you are able to take the one from here."

Pieter takes a breath then continues, "One benefit of Caen is it should be easy to find a ship to bring Elke back to Antwerp. They also have larger ships, large enough to carry both a horse and your wagon. Finally, in Caen you are on French soil and the French are better at understanding commerce than the Belgians. You should also find a savings on any taxes they might impose compared to Antwerp."

Will interrupts, stammering, "What? Did I hear you correctly? What did you mean by …when Elke and I get to Caen? When was it decided she was going on this dangerous trip?

"Oh, I guess we forgot to tell you," Ahren chimes in, "Or else you must have stepped out of the room when that was decided. We all have agreed, Elke too, that going with you increases the chance of you completing your mission."

"Why was I not consulted? I should be happy about this change in events, but I resent not being told. Are there any other surprises I should know about?"

"Will, it was Elke who first suggested she travel with you. Mother and I agreed she would add greatly to your success. As you know folks in Belgium speak three languages, Dutch or Flemish in the North, French in the south, and German in the east. Most have mastered some English because of the heavy presence of Englishmen. In the south they speak a French dialect known as "Walloon" in which Elke is quite proficient. You would be lost without someone helping interpret for you."

They all look around the room, waiting for Will's reply. "I guess its settled as I am outnumbered," Will says. "Tomorrow is the last day of the Paracelsus lectures, I believe it only proper I should say goodbye to some of the attendees and students. This should help keep up appearances and to avoid suspicion."

Ahren interrupts Will saying, "We have all agreed it best you don't leave from Antwerp's harbor. But I must remind your being in Antwerp could be compromised if Gagnon and Phillips keep snooping about. Second, you have responsibility for Elke's safety."

Ahren gives Will a moment to let his comments sink in, "The Reformation movement is growing in Europe, yet it has only the support of about 20 percent of Antwerpians. Even less in rural areas.. Spies and ne'er-do-wells exist in abundance and most would burn your uncle's books with you and Elke along with them. Thus, think about her safety as much as you think about your mission."

"On that score you have my assurance. I understand my need to protect the Bibles, but Elke's safety rises above that. My uncle's Bibles can always be replaced at another time."

Will, looking somewhat embarrassed at being reminded of his priorities, shifts his gaze onto Margareit. "If anything, bad were to happen to Elke I know I would be as devastated, as would you, and Ahren. Know this as my solemn pledge, I will devote every inch of my being to protect and look after her." Ahren and Margareit nod and give him an understanding smile.

"Now speaking of travelling with a female, let me introduce you to another one," Pieter says.

Pieter walks over to a make-shift stable and says, "This here is Betsy, she is the lucky mare that will be pulling your wagon. She is very gentle, easy to handle and strong. It should be easy for you to manage her. I have acquired the latest leather harnessing. This harness is designed to take advantage of her broad and strong shoulders so she should not tire easily. Will, what experience do you have with horses?"

"Quite a bit actually. I was raised on an English farm and we have always kept one or two horses."

"Have you ever used one to pull a buggy, wagon, or farm cart?

"Yes, but not much since I turned seventeen. I gave up farming when I started my apprenticeship seven years ago. In truth, it is been a long time since I held any reins. But for a few days each year I help my father with planting and harvesting."

"Well, this time it will be much like driving a farm cart, only this one is bigger. You will notice this wagon has two large wheels. Its drawers and cargo have been placed so the mare can pull straight ahead without the poles pulling up on her. Betsy will not feel much weight on her even with two passengers."

Will responds, "The workmanship is magnificent. The wagon has been well designed, and all details thought out. An exceptionally talented man must have labored hard to rig such a wonderful harness."

"The wagon has been constructed like the pieces of a wooden Chinese puzzle. Here, let me show you," Pieter says.

As Pieter pulls a couple of drawers from their casements he comments, "Much of the wagon's sides and floor are hollow. See how they fit together with interlocking pieces? These pieces must be slid aside and removed in a sequence if you want access to what is hidden behind them. Now in front of these hidden side and floor panels are these separate yet easily accessible storage drawers giving access to the many agents and substances you are delivering to the London Guild of Apothecaries."

Pieter continues, "With your uncle's Bibles securely hidden it should also deter robbers, brigands, and custom house officials as only you know how the drawers interlock and open. Additionally, should ever a need arise for you to demonstrate you are a real Apothecary you can easily reach the items you need to prove you know what you are doing."

Will smiles at Pieter, "What a remarkable piece of craftmanship."

Once Will finishes running his hands over its fine wooden finish and looking over and into its many drawers he turns and says to Pieter, "I don't think a wagon full of drugs would be attractive to a thief with no knowledge of what they are. But I am beginning to think the horse and this wagon itself would have great appeal to some nefarious scoundrel."

Pieter continues to demonstrate the wagon's capabilities. "Please notice only the center of the wagon is lined with drawers and these drawers face inside the center aisle. They can only be reached by someone inside the wagon. This is because the wagon was also designed to accommodate the Guild of Apothecary's wishes for a working, mobile apothecary. There is a folding table also to accommodate compounding medicines away from public view. Thus, the wagon will be able to go from town-to-town with fewer worries about thievery. Additionally, that center aisle has room enough for one or two to bed down for the night. close the back tailgate, place a drape from the front seat over the top, and feel secure from the elements when sleeping within."

Will looks over the wagon again and exclaims, "I cannot imagine the time and skill that it took to create the wagon. The idea of it also being a giant Chinese puzzle box is brilliant. I am honored at being the first to take it on the road."

"Speaking of being on the road," Ahren says. "Let me give us something else to think about. We know Caen is the furthest away of the four likely ports and that Will should expect to travel about 7 days to reach it. However, what could lengthen that trip will be the endurance of the mare to walk all day and for Will to give it several stops for feed, water and rest."

Will asks, "What exactly are you trying to say?"

"Joining a merchant caravan for safety reasons is a great idea," Ahren continues. "However, they do not travel as far and a fast as one man could by travelling alone. This is because it takes more time for a group to gather, travel, rest, eat, and set-up for the night. Thus, the slowest member in any group will always lengthen any trip. If one wagon in a caravan breaks down, they do not leave that wagon behind, the wagon-master will stop the whole caravan until they all pitch in to help and resume travel together."

There is a collective sigh.

Oh my," Elke says to her brother as he continues, "I want you both to think about how an occasional band of brigands stalk and then hit a straggler from a caravan if he decides to strike out on his own or is left behind.. Brigands also steal from a caravan during the night… then hurry to a port city to sell their stolen goods. They like port cities because they know merchants are about to leave the country. These brigands and thieves are also fond of stealing food and anything else of value they can use. Unfortunately, more than one hapless soul has been found dead beside the road because resisting the demands of ruthless and desperate men."

"Good God in heaven! "exclaims Will." This is getting to be a much more dangerous situation than I ever bargained for. What you have just said is that Elke and I will be facing risks all the way by either by being part of a caravan or by travelling alone. Did I hear that right?"

Ahren responds, "It is my opinion that the caravan is the safer option. However, a caravan does reduce travel time. The caravan we found is quite large and reduces the appeal to any band of brigands."

Ahren sees Will's mouth agape and says with a half-smile, "Just be totally aware of your surroundings and the people around you at all times. This is especially important because it has my sister who is travelling with you and her virtue and safety are more at stake than your special cargo. She is more valuable to us than any cargo and especially a cargo that could be replaced if it had to be. However, my sister can't be replaced."

"Thanks for showing brotherly love and concern, Ahren. I really do understand your message. I will be nervous, alert, and jumpy all the way to wherever it is we find passage across the channel. And what am I to do with the horse once the wagon is loaded onto a ship? Do I need to sell Betsy? Just let her run loose. Take her with me? Pieter speaks up, "You can sell Betsy on this side of the channel for good money. If the ship you contract with is large, they usually have a hold in which a horse can be stabled, or they may have a pen for it to be stabled on an open deck. Horses do not like a water voyages as it agitates them terribly when they feel the ship's movement beneath their feet. especially if the sea is rough."

The room falls silent. After a few looks about the room and at each other Pieter breaks the silence saying, "Let us review the distance involved here. This is what I think. Calais offers the shortest distance between it and England. Also, Calais is where most of the caravan will break off. Calais to Dover is about 21 of your English miles. That is if you can take the trip from Cape Gris Nez near the Calais port. A second option may be to go from Calais to Southampton rather than Dover as Southampton is the largest and busiest port in England. Southampton is also where you will be charged import taxes on many of the foreign drugs contained in this wagon. I hope you have the necessary coin to pay for this?"

Will nods.

Pieter continues, "Dover is a port more suitable for passengers and travelers, so you may have an issue if you wind up there. But either way you can expect the better part of a day to cross from France to one of those English ports. Do you understand all this? It is important that you do because once you leave here you and Elke will be on your own. "

"Yes, I do understand and thanks for sharing these details." says Will.

Pieter continues, "Now Will, if you do decide to go to Caen remember it is further south and twice the distance from here to Calais. You will not be riding a mounted horse but rather using a horse pulling a wagon and that will double your travel time As fit as Betsy is you will be constrained by the ability of the caravan horses, wagons that break, and drivers who stop for water, feed, and rest breaks. The wagon master will do his best to help keep everyone moving to make a 25-30 mile a day goal but do expect one or two delays at a minimum,. The caravan will likely not make that daily goal as it only goes as fast as its slowest member. I think you should plan on being on the road for 10 days once you depart from here."

What about provisions? "asks Will. "How do I feed and water both Elke and me as well as a horse?"

"You cannot take enough food for that many days. The wagon-master will have arranged lodging at inns along the way. There you can replenish food, or any other supplies, or find help, such as a blacksmith, should that need arise. However, inns do attract a certain unsavory element at night so if you are inside an inn you may not have the right security to protect this wagon outside. Do you and Elke both understand what I am implying?"

Will nods that he understands, and Elke just looks down and quietly says, "Yes, you are being very thorough. We may find ourselves sleeping in the cold wagon at night in order to protect it."

"Now then, I can put oats and hay on the wagon for five days, but I cannot provide that much water for both you and the horse for the entire trip. Since your first few days will be with a caravan of merchants, they will prepare for watering the horses. You may be able to stretch out what I give you.

"Oh, lest I forget, there is one advantage of pushing on to Caen. It has a large French protestant community. Should you need help someone may be willing and able to help you with contacts to get across the Channel to either Brighton or Southampton. However, to either of those towns its five times the distance from Calais to Dover which would put you on rough seas for a much longer time than if you left from Calais."

"Jesus, Mary, and Joseph," exclaims Will, "Is there nothing easy about this whole mess?"

"Will," Ahren implores, "You have to think clearly and calmly. Monmouth's original plan has gone to hell in a handbasket. It is now up to us to see it through, and yes, we know it is burdensome on you. However, since Monmouth is not here to advise us as an experienced smuggler, it seems to me a five-day trip to Calais, and its shorter crossing of the Channel, would be the preferable route."

Will says, "What do you think Pieter?"

Pieter responds "Calais has fewer conditions for your success but personally, I favor the safer but longer road trip to Caen. But that takes Elke further away from home. While Caen presents a much longer passage across the channel, it could likely get you into a safe port for disembarkation. At least you have some options that can only be played out as the mix of things unfold after you leave Antwerp."

Will nods and says, "Yes, I understand what you all have been saying. I truly have to assess my situation as I go along and have confidence in my ability to make the right decisions."

Ahren looks at Will and calmly says, "Will this is no time for you to fall back on your habit of ruminating and procrastinating. Your head, heart and belly need to be in tune with each decision."

The two men look at each other as Ahren continues "I know you to be a smart and practical man but let me also point out that this is that time when all your clear-thinking and intelligence are going to be muddled with your responsibility of traveling with Elke. You must see her as a resource, one that adds to your success. You must maintain the appearance of being a couple travelling together. If you two cannot do that, she will be vulnerable. Since she knows the languages of both countries you have to travel as a team trusting each other as equals."

Will then turns from Ahren to Pieter and asks him, "How confident are you that this whole scheme will work?"

"Will, I am damn confident! But, let me state that your success relies just as much on Betsy. So remember this… a well-conditioned and good-sized horse pulling a well-made and well-balanced wagon with two adults, and which makes a few stops for rest, water, grazing or eating hay, is capable of pulling your wagon for 6–8 hours per day, 4–5 days per week without any ill effects. So, currently I am extremely confident about Betsy and her capabilities. Additionally, since your wagon is so well made, I have confidence that Betsy and the wagon will not break down. Finally, I have known Elke since she was a baby, so I am confident in her abilities. However, I am not so confident in the horse's driver nor in some of the unknowns about what might happen on the road."

Will grimaces at this obvious jab.

Adopting a serious visage, Pieter again looks at Will and says, " You will not have the luxury of changing horses during the day, like some coach lines do , in order to get passengers longer travel days or longer distances per day to reach an inn. Thus, your caravan will likely have its travelers sleeping under the stars, under or in their wagons. Caravans do this, so they can guard their cargo and quickly move out in the morning. Thus, again I have to believe it will take you four to five days to reach Calais and four to five more if you go on to Caen, but either will cause you to be tired if you're not sleeping in a warm bed in an inn.."

"God willing, I hope sleeping under, or in that wagon, with Elke next to me, will be the only exciting thing that happens to us on this trip. Maybe that's what was meant when the Apothecary oath said I should subdue my "irregular passions"."

Will again turns to Pieter and asks, "What kind of people like to travel in merchant caravans?"

"Most are only plain hard-working folks. Many are families who travel with their wives and children. But mostly they are hardworking people who stay to themselves but prefer travel in numbers because of the safety it affords. If they are a successful merchant, they will have made many such trips. Thus, many folks know each other because they have traveled with each other. So, Will, it really is safe doing so but from time-to-time you may find a scurrilous twit comes along and upsets peace and order."

Seeing Will frown at Pieter's last comment, Pieter continues, "Usually when some man exhibits unseemly or bad behavior other caravan members dissuade that behavior with a beating. Also, anyone labeled a disturber of the peace is typically sent off by a tribunal charged with enforcing all agreements of travel, or by the strong arm of the wagon-master. This happens rarely but when does it is occasioned by someone who has had too much to drink."

"Will, look at it this way," interrupts Ahren before Pieter can finish, "You come from a small town. A caravan is just like a small town but only it is a town-on-wheels. Most of its inhabitants are merchants who are successful and honest men. These men know who is travelling with them, and, as it is in any small town, they treat each kindly and as neighbors they trust. Without expectation, they look out for each other. I would think they would accept you as the newest person to move into their town. However, because you are travelling with a woman it typically increases their comfort having a couple in their midst rather than a single male."

"Thanks, Ahren, that's exceptionally good information. I really do see myself having three missions. The second is to protect the wagon, the third is to get passage for it to England, but the first and most important is Elke and seeing that nothing untoward befalls her. Rest assuredly that I want nothing more than her safe return to her family."

"Before you leave France for England be sure Elke has quick passage back to us. There are many merchant ships that carry small numbers of passengers. Elke will be quite safe on such a ship as a ship's captain takes pride in protecting his paying passengers," Ahren says.

"I do respect your confidence in all this, Ahren," Will says. I now believe that nothing will go wrong. So, with our plans being set let us get on with their execution and trust that God adds his presence and protection as we bring his word to England."

Margareit ends their conversation by adding, "Elke and I have put together supplies and food for your journey. We also put blankets in the cart for warmth and bedding. We filled a new pallyass with fresh straw and put it on the floor of the wagon should you have need of a mattress. But again, I caution you, Will, be sure your last day at the University appears as normal as any other day during the weeks you have been here. If any suspicions are raised that something is afoot, it might get back to that rotten dog, Raemon Gagnon. It is he who could spoil all we have worked so hard to accomplish. It's going to be tough enough to explain to him why Elke is missing at the same time Will left town."

Margareit pauses as she sees the grim faces all around her at the mention of Gagnon. She continues, "Should Gagnon show up either tomorrow or the next day I think it best to say Elke was called away to help her aunt and uncle on their dairy farm in Belgium. He knows her aunt needs help recovering from her recent childbirth. Does anyone not think he will accept this? Can we agree on saying Elke will return in three weeks to keep him from looking for her?"

"Yes, Let's do that" they all say or nod, and Ahren adds, "Gagnon may be an oaf when it comes to women's issues but he will pick up on any inconsistencies we have as he does when he interrogates some poor hapless soul."

"Well then, that's that" says Margareit," Let us all go home and get some rest. The upcoming days are going to be quite stressful. Saturday especially so."

-Chapter 25-

The de Bergdorf home in Antwerp
Friday, 19 February 1537

Following a great dinner of a meat pie washed down with some fresh mead, Ahren reports to his mother, Elke and Will, "Today I have been talking with a few friends who work at the Antwerp Harbor. It seems they have noticed security measures are a bit stronger than ever. To them this seemed odd and especially so as the weekend coming is not the busiest day for merchant departures. Some dock workers believe an informant tipped off the Harbor Master or one or more of his customs officials that someone is trying to take contraband out of the country and avoid taxes on goods going to a foreign land."

"Oh, my goodness," exclaims Margareit, "Do you think somehow someone, has found out about us?"

"Yes, Will, what do you think about this new information?" asks Elke.

"Do not panic," Will says.. "We are not leaving here by ship. But just to be safe we can leave the city by a circuitous route and avoid harbor officials, tax folk, and any constables who should be lurking about. Secondly, I have said my goodbyes to those I met at the Paracelsus lectures.

As I said my farewells I discovered many attendees are also leaving on Saturday and so I am not surprised that several have drawn the attention of harbor officials. They could be targeted as possibly leaving with contraband, after all there were many countries represented in that group."

Before Will can say more Ahren interrupts "I am happy to also tell you that while I heard rumblings about the added security at the Antwerp Harbor , I also found a trusted friend who was leaving today on a merchant ship bound for London. He has agreed to take a sealed letter to Humphrey Monmouth telling him of our change in his plans."

"Excellent," Will says. "Monmouth will now know to look for me to arrive a few days later than planned and also using an overland route. I hope he does not worry unnecessarily. But I am sure if I am quite a bit late, because something has gone wrong, he will have the presence of mind to send someone out to look for me should I and the wagon's arrival be behind schedule."

"Yes, I am sure he would come looking for you as the Bibles and the wagon full of medications are both important to his causes and his reputation. Monmouth certainly does have a lot riding on your skills as well," says Ahren.

"Well, Elke and I, are going to make a wonderful team and be successful at what we accomplish. We do not want to disappoint Henry," says Will emphatically.

"Are all the details in place to meet up with the caravan?' asks Elke.

"Yes, they are," her brother responds," We will meet the merchant caravan early on Saturday morning. The departure time is sunrise and they will assemble outside the western gate of the city. That should present no problem unless we are late. By that I mean they do move promptly once they are in line and ready to go. So, we should plan on being there just at sun-up."

After their hearty dinner and a bit more rehash of the plans Elke, Margareit, Will and Ahren return to the warehouse to make one last and final check on their horse Betsy, their wagon, their money for food and money for lodging along the way, and money to secure passage across the English Channel. They then load their limited food and supplies plus some oats, hay, and water for the horse.

Satisfied they are as ready as they ever will be, they return to the deBergdorf home for a good-night's sleep. But before they retire Margareit asks them to join hands around the kitchen table "Heavenly Father," Margareit implores,, "We know all good gifts, graces, and blessings come from Thee. We gather now to ask that you keep Will and my daughter safe on their journey of helping others know your words of love. May You provide good weather for their travels. Please see that they return safely to our outstretched and loving arms. We ask this in your name and in those of your son and the Holy Spirit. Amen."

Once they have all retired, they find sleep does not come easy. They all remain silent in their beds awaiting the day ahead, anxious about the unknowns to come.

-Chapter 26-

Early Morning, The deBergdorf Home
Saturday 20 February 1537

Ahren, Elke, and Will awaken to the sounds of someone in the kitchen. It is still dark outside. After dressing quickly, they meet each other on the stairs leading down to the second floor. They notice a light in the kitchen, and as they enter they smell something cooking. It is in a skillet propped on a tripod placed in the open hearth.

"What are you doing up so early?" exclaims Elke as she recognizes her mother.

"I would never send my daughter and my house guest on a long trip if I did not let them have a hearty meal to start their day. In any case I have been awake most all the night. As I could not sleep, I thought it best to get up and do something useful."

"Mother, you really should be sainted. What can I do to help?"

"Elke, please set the table. Use our good plates and mugs." Margareit then turns to the men and asks, "Do you want to get the horse and wagon now or would you rather eat?"

The two men look at each other, smile, then in unison, chant, "Let us eat first. We do have time."

After a full meal of oatmeal porridge, fried eggs, and ham, washed down with the last of some wine and ale Ahren jokes, "I am too stuffed to even move. Will you are on your own to get that horse and wagon and then let us get you and Elke out of here."

Elke retorts, "Well, my brother, I will be gone soon enough. I hope you are ready to help our mother with all the kitchen chores I have had to endure for years."

"Enough of that," chimes Margareit, "You both know darn well you are going to miss each other. Have the guts to say so instead of banter and horseplay. This is a profoundly serious business we are about to undertake with real serious consequences if we are caught."

"You are right Mother. This is important work and I do take it seriously. I also realize my brother will miss me, but likely not as much as I will miss the two of you," Elke says with a smirk.

"Now that our breakfast of sausage and fried potatoes is cooked and we have drink ,let us eat and once we are done the boys can go fetch the horse and wagon while we do the last bit of packing and clean up. We can say our goodbyes when they return."

"Yes, Mother. We cannot sit and banter all day, that caravan will leave without us if we do. Its departure time is exact. Come on Will," says Ahren, "Let us go get the horse and wagon. We can pick up Elke afterward as we will pass by here on our way to the town gates."

Will and Ahren leave the deBergdorf home and return about an hour later with the horse and wagon. On the cobblestone walk outside the deBergdorf home they pack in Elke's carpet satchel which contains clothing for the trip and some food items prepared by Margareit. Ahren sits on the wagon seat between Will and Elke all three having said tearful and emotional goodbyes to Margareit. As the horse trots away, Will glances at Margareit and the last image he has of her is her crossing herself, face awash in tears.

Ahren guides Will to the departure gate. As they pull along outside the gate Will finds about 20 wagons of many sizes and descriptions making last preparations. Each wagon is being pulled by either one or two horses. Once ready each driver steers his wagon into a straight line behind one ahead. A few drivers look as if they had been there since the day before as a few cooking fires are being extinguished.

Ahren directs Will to a wagon that is at the front of the line. As they approach it, Ahren jumps of their wagon and rushes up to the man shouting orders for how he wants the caravan to assemble.

"This is the wagon master, Denis deWitt," says Ahren turning to Will and Elke "Let me introduce you to my brother and sister. You do remember our arrangement? Your job is to get them and their wagon safely into France."

"Yes, how do you do," replies Denis with a cheery smile. "It's great to finally meet you both. What I would like for you to do is pull your horse and wagon into a spot I have reserved for you right behind mine. I see you have a sturdy horse and a well-crafted wagon. They should do you both good service and not delay our caravan. If you pull into that spot I have reserved for you I can keep an eye out for you. Also being there will offer a lot less dust, dirt, and muck than if I put you at the end of the line.

"That is nice of you Mr. deWitt," says Will." We are looking forward to our time with you"

"Well, the trip has not begun yet. But please, all my friends call me Denis."

"Do you see the light in the sky? that's the sun coming up. As soon as it shines on the city gate we pull out of here. We will travel a long while today as most in the caravan expect it. Ahren tells me this is your first caravan trip. Well, stick close by and I will do my best to keep us all moving ahead.

About a half hour later Will and Elke are more relaxed Their conversation remains light as Elke and her brother continue their loving banter. Then the sun lights up a spot on the city gate and the wagon master waves his right arm in a huge circle.

Ahren jumps off the wagon and looks at his sister and says, "Well, my dear sister it's time for me to go. I believe Will is most capable to keep you safe. I will do my best to keep our Mother from worrying about you. You both know what is expected. I cannot wait to hear many tales when you both returns. May God keep you both safe. Always remember this dear sister, I love you and so does the man who sits next to you."

At that last comment, Elke reaches over and kisses her brother on both cheeks, then with a halting voice and tear in her eye says "Goodbye, I love you as well."

Will reaches across to shake Ahren's hand, and says," I am aware of the precious cargo I have been entrusted with and I promise I will not let that trust falter."

The lead wagon moves out. Will speaks to Betsy and she responds by following the lead. Soon they are well past the city gates and the walled city of Antwerp. The sounds of the city quickly fade, and Will suddenly notices how quiet it is and the softer clip-clop of his horse on dirt roads as opposed to the city's cobblestone streets.

Soon Will is entranced by the pastoral scenes in front and beside him and say's to Elke, "I am finding it hard to keep my eyes on the road. This countryside is absolutely beautiful. I can see several farms where agriculture is important and several with grapes growing in what appears to be gravelly soil."

"You are right about that, Elke responds, "The gravel you see is the erosion of a lot of limestone. Limestone is mined to help make the blocks of which many of the houses around her are made. Also, limestone imparts a unique taste to the wine made from the grapes harvested along our way".

The day passes quickly for Will as he takes in all he can see, reminding him of how much he misses his home village back in England, especially his friends and family. From time to time their road rises up and over a rocky hill. From it top Will and Elke sit silently as they see the landscape spread before them under a deep blue sky with either a small village ahead having winding streets and limestone houses , some with pastel pained façades, or picturesque farms with sheds of yellow, brown, or red tiled cottages often with whitewashed walls.

The caravan moves all day, making two stops for watering the horses and one stop as a break from everyone sitting on hard wooden wagon benches. Betsy seems to have no problem pulling the wagon, its cargo, and its two passengers.

Will notices, "*She can keep up with the caravan's walking pace and does not tire easily. My horse has been fortunate. She has a well- balanced wagon and is benefitting from the skill of the leather maker who made her harness..*"

It is late afternoon when the wagon master calls a halt to the day's journey as at this time of the year nightfall is early. Once their horse is tethered, fed, and watered from supplies in the wagon Will and Elke make a campfire and heat a meat pie for their dinner.

Soon after nightfall Will notices the assemblage of drivers, wives, and a few children are quiet and remarks to Elke. "Do you think a long day on the road and sitting on a wagon's seat, has made so many people tired? It is pretty quiet around this campsite."

Elke responds, "I believe you are right. While looking at the beautiful countryside is interesting, looking over the rear end of a horse all day cannot be a lot of fun for everyone... including you. Perhaps folks are plain tired and that is why the camp is quiet. Ahren did tell me that many on this caravan have made this trip many, many, times. To them it is just business. While they can appreciate the notion of having safety in numbers they just don't get too excited about travel in a caravan."

"Well, I believe you have the nub of it. Perhaps we better turn in as well and get rested up for another early start tomorrow. What do you think?"

"You are right, Will, It's a bit chilly tonight. Perhaps it is best if we lie down on the straw-filled pallyass in the center of the wagon. There is a nice blanket and a quilt my mother gave to me to bring on this trip. We can both lie under them and keep warm."

"You are right again," Will says. "The past few nights have not been restful. First, however, go inside the wagon. I will tidy up the fire and put away the things we have outside. I will lock the rear gate and be sure the wind does not blow any of the canvas roof off. Then I will climb in through the driver's seat and we should be safe and secure until we hear the wagon master blow his whistle in the morning."

After a few chores to secure the horse and wagon for the night are done Will climbs into the wagon and lies next to Elke. But the wagon floor is small and does not have a lot of wiggle room for two people. Elke says, "You must be exhausted after such a long day and by worrying about us both being so far away from friends and family."

Yes,. I am absolutly wrung out" replies Will

A few seconds later Elke leans over and gives Will a kiss on his cheek and Will feels the warmth of her lips on his face. But for both it seems like only minutes later they hear the wagon masters first whistle, and his loud shouting, "Everybody up. You have only an hour to make ready."

Will sits up and says, "Elke, I thank the Lord, I thought to get our wagon ready to move last night. Once we climbed into bed. I am not sure I got much sleep.

"I did not sleep much either, I hope my restlessness did not disturb you," replies Elke.

"No, not at all, But I do have feelings for you. Since the day we met in front of that statue in Grote Markt. I have done nothing but think about you every day. At one point I wished I could abandon my mission and just spend the rest of my days with you."

"I bet you say that to all the girls."

"Don't tease me, Elke, no girl has excited me as you have. I cannot believe how quickly we have become comfortable being with each other. It is like we have known each other all lives. Because of you I now know how it feels to love another person.'

"Oh Will, I do know what you mean. I know also that I love you. Secretly, I have wanted to be with you since the day we met but I never thought that possible because of so much happening in my life, especially having to fend off that oaf, Gagnon."

"Promise me you will not bring his name up while we are on this mission.. I know if I ever run into him again, I will do more than insult him. I will likely bloody his nose."

"That would be amusing. And yes, I will not bring his name up while we are together. I also know you will do whatever it takes to come back to me when this trip is over.".

"You're damn right I will. Now, let us get ourselves something cold to eat to start the day. There is not enough time before the caravan leaves to cook anything. I am surprisingly well- rested, but this morning I am starving. We can talk more as the wagon train keeps heading south towards France, I can only assume this will be another long day, but it will pass quickly with you sitting beside me knowing we have a future together."

A few minutes later the wagon-master's whistle gives notice they have fifteen minutes to be ready or be left behind. With her new harness, Will has Betsy ready with time to spare and regain his position behind the wagon-master. Once the caravan starts out Elke hands Will a piece of bread with some sliced summer sausage and cheese on it. They both nibble on it as the caravan starts its journey towards the French border.

Later that morning the sun comes out and warms their chilled bodies Will looks at Elke and finds her in a pensive mood and asks. "Why are you so deep in thought?"

"Would it be safe if I were to read one of the Bibles in this wagon?"

"I see no reason not to. Are there question you need answering that only God's words will provide answers for? I see that the wagons are about to stop for a rest. When they do I will retrieve a Bible from one of the hidden compartments. Are you sure you are alright? You seem to have a faraway look in your eyes."

Yes, I am, I just want to read a few passages.

Will enters the central area of the wagon and after a few manipulations of the woodwork is able to retrieve a Bible and then he hands it to Elke

Elke looks directly at Will and says, "I want to read what God has said about love. Do we really need clergy to bless our relationship? What I am wondering about is are we feeling love or just the excitement and danger surrounding your mission."

"My dear Elke, I have read my Uncle's Bible and found God's message repeated over and over….God wants us to love one another, to forgive those who trespass against us, and to be kind to our neighbors, There is no better way to show Him that we love him than by living a life based on us following his commandments.

"Will, I could never be with someone like Gagnon as I do not love him. I know many girls marry for family expectations or for many other reasons,. But I know I could not share myself with someone who did not love me."

Suddenly, they are distracted by loud shouting. A wheel has broken off on one of the nearby wagons. As it tipped it threw a passenger off the seat and into the ditch causing the man to cut his scalp on a tree stump. Will says to Elke, "I can help that wounded man with some of the materials I have here in the wagon. "

As Will readies some herbs and bandages to help dress the man's wound, Elke says to him, "I know now what you are trying to say about God asking us all to be kind to each other. You are helping someone without hesitation and without asking for any reward. The world would be a better place if more people believed they should be doing the same."

"I well remember what my uncle said about all that. Yes, the world would be better if we were all kinder to each other, but we do not get to heaven by doing good and kind deeds, we get there by having faith in God's promise for us."

-Chapter 27-

Tuesday February 23, 1537

At an Inn, a short distance from the city of Calais

Four days after leaving Antwerp Elke and Will drive their wagon into a large courtyard. Earlier that morning the caravan master told them, "Late this afternoon, a little before mealtime we will stop. We will be but a short distance from the road that takes us into the City of Calais. We will be at a safe place overlooking the Calais Harbor. Tomorrow many will leave for the Calais Harbor, a short distance of about two miles."

"What are my chances of making passage across the English Channel with this wagon?" Will asks Wagonmaster Denis.

"I would say chances of finding help are rather good. Calais remains the last bastion of English influence near here. The King of England and the King of France are still discussing, in peaceful terms, whose country should possess Calais. Each has advisors, councilors, and bishops run back and forth to discuss the matter as neither king has the funds to wage war. As many Englishmen have taken up residence in Calais you should find it quite simple to ferret out the help you need. "

"Does this place have a name?" asks Will as Elke looks on a little bewildered.

"Yes, it is called The Vale of Ardres and once was decorated with pavilions, towers, artificial lakes, and fountains that were gushing beer and wine. Those who gathered here knew important treaties between France and England and were the real reason for the gathering. Thus, many distractions were held, such as jousts, wrestling matches, dancing and feasting as negotiations settled the fate of this area and likely two countries. King Henry wanted to claim this area as part of his birthright thus he ordered more pomp and entertainment to show his power and not his friendship to France.

"Whatever happened to end all this?" asked Elke

"Well, young miss, as expected, all the secret dealings finally faded as money and time wore on. The two sides finally parted when rumors of the King's infidelities began, and which caused Henry to return to London. As he was a loyal son of the catholic church his presence was needed to ferret out those guilty of lust or who were reformers. Reformers believed Christianity was being buried beneath meaningless ritual and blind devotion. But ahh! I speak too much, please forgive me."

"Thank you for all you have done to get us here safely. I will let you know of our plans… once I think a little more on what they should be."

Will spends the rest of the day pondering whether or not it would be wise for them to look around Calais Harbor and secure a means for him and the wagon to find passage to London. If he can do than what should be done with Betsy? He also spends time ruminating over how to arrange passage back to Antwerp for Elke." *I don't have enough information, perhaps tomorrow will bring an opportunity to check out this harbor and perhaps find a willing soul to help with my mission."*

"What are you thinking about?" Elke says as she wakes from a small nap. "The wagon-master has indicated we will be staying in this area for the night, but I am not sure if this timber-framed building before us is a tavern or if it is an inn. It seems too small for a tavern and not big enough to be an inn."

"What is the difference?"

"Well a tavern is not a nice place for a young lady to spend a lot of time. They are not safe places for a woman to be staying in overnight, unless there is a large group of them. If a tavern has any accommodations, they are usually used by rowdy drunks unable to go home. They then line up and sleep on the floor or four or so to a bed.

Elke looks wide-eyed, the Will continues, "Additionally, taverns serve best as a gathering place for local townsfolk and because of that they encourage gaming, card playing, and dice games. The maids who work in taverns also make extra money by engaging in the world's oldest profession. It is also well-known that tavern owners often accept dubiously obtained goods in order to cancel a patron's bills and many of them serve as moneylenders.

"Oh, my goodness", exclaims Elke," Might we not be safe here?"

"Well, it might be safe, and we might be left alone if our wagon-master has been here many times before. But because taverns are favorite places of local townspeople, we would be strangers and viewed with suspicion. But if this place is well-known among many in our caravan, we may not be labeled as suspicious characters. We will just have to see what happens next however, because it is a tavern we will be able to get food and drink, but I am not sure about secure sleeping rooms"

Will pauses for a moment then instructs Elke, "Please see if you can recognize a sort of stable and garden beyond the courtyard,. I am going to steer our wagon under that oak tree over there just in case we have to stay overnight in the wagon. From where I sit, I cannot see any sign that tells us what this place is, but its signage may be on the other side of the building facing the street. Most locals would be using that street rather than the road we just travelled on."

As Elke takes a good look around, Will tends to the horse and wagon. She returns to Will and says, "I did see a sign facing the front street and it indicates we have come to an inn."

"That's good to hear," sighs Will, "It means they will have quarters upstairs for a few overnight travelers, especially those on a long-distance stagecoach. But I cannot imagine there being enough space inside for the entire lot of us. I do think many will be sleeping around a campfire or in our wagons."

"Either option is fine with me. I know I will be safe with you, "says Elke as she gives Will's arm a squeeze.

Then as Elke turns her attention to the building once again, she shouts, "Oh look, Will, over there, I see a door with some branches and leaves hanging over the top of it. What does that mean?"

"What that means is that wine as well as beer and ale are served inside."

Will finishes securing the wagon and unhitches Betsy. He ties her to the tree in front of them and prepares to feed and water her. He then turns to Elke and says, "When I finish with the horse I am going to see if I can purchase some food for our supper. It is been a long day of travel and neither of us needs to prepare a meal when tomorrow may be longer and busier. Will you be alright if I leave you for a short time?

"Yes, Will, I will be all right. You will not be far away. I have Betsy here to keep me company.".

"Oh! That is comforting," Will says with a smirk, "Can you speak to the horse in Dutch, French and Flemish like you do to customers at your family's print shop?"

"Look Will, I know I will be safe. Then, after we share supper, I am looking forward to staying warm all night cuddled up under our shared blanket."

"Well then, I shall hold onto that nice thought," says Will as he gives Elke a kiss on the cheek and heads toward the inn.

Elke busies herself tiding up their campsite and preparing the wagon for an early night sleep…knowing she will be lying beside the man she loves.

Her thoughts of Will are interrupted by a voice that comes from behind her. The words are in French *"Bonjour jolie fille, comment alley vous cete belle journee?"* which she quickly interprets as "Hello pretty girl, how are you this fine day?"

Elke turns to face a man she has seen before. He is a driver of one of the wagons in the caravan, but he has not spoken to her the entire trip. He is rather portly and with a mustache that looks like a caterpillar lying across his upper lip. His eyes are dark and seem foreboding and sinister. Not wanting to offend or create a scene Elke decides to see what he wants, so she asks him in French, "*Que voulez-vous? puis je vous aider?*" thinking it best to ask, "what do you want? and may I be of help?"

The man draws closer as Elke smells ale on his breath. He stares at her saying, I have been watching you since leaving Antwerp and now you and I are alone, how about you give me a little kiss and le\t me feel your luscious body. If you want you can run your hands over my codpiece."

Elke is so startled at his words, lewd gestures, and menacing demeanor that she backs away. As she does she bumps up against the wagon allowing the man to press in closer and put his hand on her breast.

"Please! Do not touch me. She cries in English, then repeats it in French using a determined voice "*S'il te plait ne me touché pas.*'

As the man presses his advantage over the frightened Elke she closes her eyes, afraid of what might happen next. As she does she hears a thud which causes her to open her eyes and see the man slump to the ground. Then she sees Will standing over the man with a wooden trencher in his hand and food slopped all over the man. Will has put one foot on the man's chest as the man's draws his hands to the back of his head obviously writhing in pain.

"Are you alright?" Will asks. "I will hold this devil here. Run and get the caravan master. I just saw him about ten wagon lengths away.. up on the left. Can you do that?"

"Yes, I can do that "

Will then presses his foot harder on the dazed man's chest and shouts at him, "Don't move."

A few seconds later the wagon master comes running up to Will with a few other members of the caravan and Elke, and asks "What going on here?"

"This man tried to force himself onto the fair Elke" shouts Will.

"Well, we do not tolerate such behavior. You have a choice of sending this man to a constable, allowing him to remain in the caravan until tomorrow, or asking us to expel him from our group... right now."

"Is he going to leave from the harbor in Calais tomorrow morning? asks Will

"Yes. That is his plan"

"Well, I suggest we allow eject him from our caravan and send him down to the harbor NOW. I also want that he should pay for our spilled supper. You will notice that half of our supper is on his clothes the rest is on the ground."

"That's fair by me. If this happened to my lady, I would have run him through with a sword. He is getting off pretty lightly I would say." At that point, the wagon master reaches into the man's purse hanging from his belt and extracts a few coins.

"Here Master Will is enough to pay for a nice supper and a few drinks to wash it down. I will take this man away and have him move his wagon to the end of the line. I will also make sure he and his wagon are gone within the half hour."

The man on the ground has been cowering through all this conversation and with Will's foot upon his chest seems too afraid to speak seeing the rage in Will's face. As Will takes his foot off the man he says, "Listen, you son of a cockroach, if I ever see you near Elke again, I will drill a sword through your miserable heart. Nod if you understand what I have just said."

The man gives a feeble nod, rolls to the side, stands, and sheepishly walks away with the wagon master following behind.

Will turns to Elke and as he puts his arm around her and says," I am sure you are happy that incident is done with. I am also happy that I arrived in time to give that awful man a good clout on the side of his head with the trencher. But I was not happy to see our meal go flying all over the place. He sure looked scared when I whacked him, but he was pretty quiet on the ground as that wooden trencher almost knocked him senseless."

Will gives Elke a hug then adds "I am relieved you could get the wagon master so quickly. By the way, the wagon master handed us more coin that needed to replace the meal. Now we can eat well tonight and do the same tomorrow. Just listen to me prattle on, I really do hope he did not hurt you. Are you really all right? I am sure you are quite safe now."

"Yes, Will. I am perfectly fine. You were wonderful and your timing impeccable. I cannot imagine what might have befallen me if you had not come along. The man seemed harmless at first but once I saw into his eyes I was frightened."

"Well, again just know you are safe and let us put this incident behind us. It has however caused me to decide our next course of action. I believe it best that we avoid Calais Harbor and push on to Caen. It will add a few days to our journey, and it will take longer to cross the English Channel. But I think it wise to avoid Calais' larger crowds and the possibility of that oaf having friends there whom he could muster against us."

"Yes, Will, going to Caen seems the right course of action. Besides, it has the added benefit of being able to sleep together in the wagon for a few more nights."

Will notices the cute smile on Elke and says to her, "Elke, you really are bewitching. I am happy to see you have your sense of humor back. Now let us walk together over to that inn and purchase another fine meal courtesy of your erstwhile suitor."

"Don't be funny Will, the only suitor I want, and need, is you. Come to think of that there is something have been wanting to tell you all day but did not have the courage to do so. Now that I have seen you defend my honor I am inspired to say what I am feeling".

"What is that?"

"Will, I do love you."

"Oh my, my dear Elke, you should know that I love you and have done so since the day we met. You have made my heart flutter and race whenever you are near. I believe even more deeply you and I are meant to be together.

They hold hands and walk into the inn. As Will returns the trencher to the innkeeper he asks, "Could I please have two more of these wonderful meals and two tankards of ale. I have been working all day and I am famished."

The innkeeper says, "You must be famished, you just left here a moment ago and now return wanting another two meals. Young people really do have voracious appetites."

"You don't know the half of it," smiles Will as the innkeeper walks way to replenish their meals.

Elke also smiles as the innkeeper goes into the kitchen to retrieve the meals and says, "Will you can be such a tease. He must think you have the appetite of a horse and can eat three meals at one sitting. Are you not going to tell him what happened to the first dinner?"

"No, I let him think what he wants."

Once the innkeeper returns with two plates of food and two tankards of ale he looks at Will and says, "Is this all for you or are you going to share some with the fair lass here?"

"Yes, the lass will share, but I would like to ask you a question? Do you know if ships are sailing out of Calais on the morning tide?"

"I've heard talk of storms blowing in from the North Sea. The harbormaster has closed all shipping for two days.

It will likely be one or two days after that before the backlog is cleared for new cargo heading to England."

Will thanks the innkeeper as he lays down coins for the meal.

Will turns to Elke and asks, "Would you like to eat here or take the food back to our wagon?"

"Will, I would just as soon eat here. It is still a bit early before the nightl crowd comes in. We can go back to the wagon after eating and get a good night's rest."

"That's fine with me, but I am hoping we can do more than have a long rest."

Elke smiles at Will "I too am hopeful that we do more than just rest and do so without interruptions."

-Chapter 28-

Thursday February 25, 1537

A short distance from the city of Caen

Will and Elke have been travelling alone for two days. As they agreed when they left Calais they would press Betsy south along the coastline leaving early ahead of the few caravanners also heading south. The rough event steeled their resolve to leave at daybreak and before any aroma from early morning fires awakened other travelers.

Though they were cuddled together on the straw pallyass and under a warm blanket, neither slept soundly. All both could think about was what might happen should Elke's intruder decide on a reprisal or any other confrontation with him especially if he was backed up with surly friends. They finally came to an understanding the second night that they could sleep by both agreeing their priority had to be the contents of their wagon and the safety of each other demanded they be refreshed and alert. On the second day they were able to relax and chat almost the whole time. They also found their feelings for each other growing so much that by the end of the day they could almost finish each other's sentences.

Late in the afternoon Elke asked Will, "Tell me why you think Henry VIII, the King of England had you uncle persecuted?

"He was not persecuted because of his translating the Bible into English, as many believe. Henry VIIII wanted to divorce his latest wife and marry another. He was fanatic about his need for a male heir and Catholicism and Pope Paul III prevented his divorce. My uncle wrote a treatise condemning the King's desires. At one time Henry curried much favor with Pope Paul III by his writing a rebuttal to the writings of Martin Luther. But now the Pope does not agree with Henry. Additionally, Henry saw how Catholic idolatry and a lack of piety can make even the clergy rich and powerful, thus Henry's self-interests rose to where he believes as a King he is equal in power and influence as any Pope.

"Do you believe the Bibles we are transporting will make a difference to the reformation movement?"

"Most definitely. For over a thousand years the church has been the arbiter and source of authority over how people should behave. It has been especially convincing of those who do not behave into buying indulgences or giving gifts of penance to assure their ascension into heaven. In England, and as it has happened in other countries, the past few decades have seen a swell in how democratic governments write laws which replace the church on matters of how citizens are to behave. Thus, when people break earthy laws they are subject to earthy punishments, especially collection of fines. This secular momentum has diminished greatly the power of priests and bishops as dispensers of justice. For example, The Bible says thou shall not steal and yet when someone does steal, he is told by a priest all is forgiven if you repent, say a certain number of prayers, contribute to the parish, or undertake some other form of penance. But your local sheriff says if you steal you hand will be cut off or you might spend a year in prison. Thus, societies' laws have greater impact today on the behavior of the common man than does the church. Losing power after more than twelve centuries is causing the church to fight back. I really believe it will snow in July or Hell will freeze over, before the Catholic church relents on anything that would weakens its influence and power, especially by having anything to do with the Protestant reformation. Recognizing Protestants, in a formal way, would make it possible for two or more sects of Christianity to rise up. Since the Catholic church is bigger and richer than any Protestant movement the Catholic church can fight back with unlimited means. However, it does not mean the Protestants are any less correct in their beliefs and faith."

"Goodness Gracious Will, I never thought of it like that."

Yes, that is why the church is fighting back very vigorously, they do not want to lose, nor share, any of their power with anybody.

Elke was enthralled with his knowledge of political power and faith.

"Interestingly, King Henry VIII believes himself to be as good as any Bishop or Pope," Will says. "And I believe someday he will appoint himself head of the church, at least in England, if he does not get his way. It's well rumored he is annoyed at sending chests of money to Rome which he would rather see used to support his interests at home."

"Will, I never cease to be amazed at your insights. How do you know so much? Why are you so wise at such an early age?"

"I am not so smart, but I am well- read, and I talk with many people every day especially those from outside my small hometown of Hodthorpe. When I am in the Apothecary people tell me many things in confidence, which I have vowed never to break. Also, I have the pleasure of working with a very learned and wise mentor, Cyril Blackham. He caused me to read every scrap of paper and book that came along. He believed reading prevents ignorance and besides reading is how I learned so much about medicines and herbs so I could become the best apothecary that I was able."

"Oh, look Will, there is small stream up ahead. It is incredibly beautiful over there. We could camp there for the night and go into Caen tomorrow. Have we come far enough today that we could do that? Besides, I am not sure I want to stay at an inn, I do like the comfort of our wagon and its very comforting to have you so close beside me. Would that be a satisfactory arrangement with you?"

"That is a great idea, Elke. We can camp there if it affords us a source of fresh water and some wood for making a fire. Tomorrow we can arrive refreshed and then seek passage for the wagon. We must just trust that God has a plan to see the wagon safely to England. I am not sure what will happen next, but we have come so far that things just have to go right for us."

A few hours later they have unhitched their horse, fed the horse and themselves. The

wagon has been prepared for the two of them to go to sleep early in contemplation of the next day being long and likely arduous.

Then Will says to Elke, "I think I will walk over to the river and wash our dinner trencher and pot so it will be done before tomorrow morning. The walk will clear my head and let me think more on what we may encounter tomorrow. You should be fine sitting here."

"Thanks for washing up, I think I will just sit here by the campfire and await your return"

Will is gone all of five minutes when Elke hears a gruff, but familiar voice behind her. Startled she jumps up and almost falls off the log she and Will were sitting on a few minutes before. As she turns to face an intruder, she gazes directly into the face of Raemon Gagnon.

Before Elke can speak Gagnon moves closer and rudely states, "Ah ha, I see you are alone, and where is that bastard Will Hutchins? I have come all this way to arrest him. I am going to take him back to Antwerp for charges against him. He stabbed, cut, and maimed three of our fine citizens and I am going to make an example out of that pompous Englishman. Who does he is that he can come into our country and behave with impunity?

"But why, Raemon?" says Elke, now thinking if she talks in a more personal manner he may reveal his real motive for undertaking such a long journey and also perhaps Will will appear and help her deal with Gagnon. After she pauses she goes on, "You are good at being a constable so you know Will has done nothing wrong."

"Do you really think I am a good constable?"

"Why yes, of course I do. You have influence everywhere in Antwerp".

"Well if I could just speak to Will, perhaps that would be enough and then he could go on his way and then you could come back to Antwerp with me".

"Will has gone ahead to an inn about a mile up the road, we need some repairs done to the axel on this wagon and he hopes they have the parts he needs," she lied but in hope Gagnon would not bother looking for Will.

Suddenly there was a cold glint in Gagnon's eyes." How about we do this, I will take you back to Antwerp with me. We can ride double on my fast and sturdy horse. Will can take care of himself and continue on his journey to wherever it is that he is going."

As Elke looked incredulously at Gagnon, he reached forward and ran his fingers through her hair, "Look Elke, if you look after me a little bit, I will look after you, and we will keep this matter between the two of us."

"What!, What!, Whatever do you mean?' Elke blurts and stutters, but in her mind she knows what Gagnon's intentions are.

"Elke, Let's start our friendship anew by you showing me what it is you keep under that pretty skirt and bodice," Gagnon says as he lurches forward and pushes Elke up against a tree. His hands now move from her hair to her breasts. She smells his fetid breath, the strong scent of ale. The foulness brings on nausea. "Stop it!" she cries out as she tries to push his hand away but his grip on one breast and another grip on her waist hold her firm.

"What is that you think I am? I am not one of those ladies of the evening you are so quick to arrest and then let go with a few silver coins as a fine or do you trade their freedom for a short burst of pleasure?"

Started by Elke's rebuke Gagnon released his hold a little giving Elke a chance to struggle free of him. As she twirls to her right, she is able to continue turning around until she is centered on Gagnon and able to bring her right knee up with a sharp flick connecting it into Gagnon's groin.

Gagnon unable to keep up his groping as he gasps for air releases his grip on Elke. "You damnable wench, here I am trying to save you and your reputation from whispers and scandal by your running off with that horse's ass of an Englishman and this is how you show your gratitude? Just you wait till I get my hands on you again.".

Gagnon reaches out and grabs her hair. Elke claws at him as if she were a cat. Her nails rake over his face but Gagnon, being the stronger, pushes her back up against the tree and then up onto the side of the wagon. Once she is pinned with his left arm across her throat he reaches down with his right hand and lifts her skirt.

As she squirms, and he fumbles, they struggle until she slides down onto the ground with him standing over her. She looks up to see him tearing at the belt holding up his breeches and at the buttons keeping his cod piece closed.

"Now I have you where I have always wanted you. Now you will behave like any proper wife of mine and you will like it".

He leans over and grabs a goatskin bag filled with wine and takes a huge swig. Now he is breathing hard and staring lasciviously at Elke who is still lying on her back with her dress pulled up is exposing her legs and stomach. Gagnon raises his wine-bag and taunts her saying, "Would you like to have some wine. I am sure it will lift your spirits as I lift your maidenhood."

Elke looks at him in horror realizing what he will do to her. Any tears she might have shed are gone. All she can feel is contempt and anger at not being able to defend herself. *This son of a bitch can damage and possess my body, but never can he possess who I am, nor my soul, and nor my love for Will."*

As Gagnon kneels before her, her mind drifts into memories of fields of tulips blooming outside her parent's home. Gagnon's snorting and heavy breathing has been lulled into a sound she cannot hear. As her anger and her mind shut down, she is left with one feeling ...pure hate for the man and the evil deed he is about to put her through.

As she quiets Gagnon notices this and he jostles her and taunts her saying "Just you wait, I know you are going to like this."

Gagnon takes another gulp of his wine, "You women are all the same," he shouts, "You need a strong man to teach you some manners and show you who is in charge. I know that the more chaste you are the more you hunger for a man like me to show you the joy from laying together. It's really a shame I had to travel such a distance to find you."

Gagnon looks at the helpless Elke pinned beneath him. With spittle dripping from his mouth he says, "You know I have always liked you. There is something so wild and exciting about a beautiful, smart, and strong woman such as you. Most women I have known are boringly submissive, but I knew a good chase was on the first time I laid eyes on you. I just knew that with patience you would be nine...and then you went and spoiled all this by running off with that bastard of an Englishman. By the way, where is he?"

"Raemon," she whispers as her first audible word since he attacked her.

"Yes, my dear one," he said leaning closer to her.

"I want to tell you a secret. I have always been looking forward to my first time with a man, but I know it will not be with you. As for Will Hutchins," she looks directly into Gagnon's eyes," He is right behind you and I have been saving myself for him." Then with a deep breath she spits in his face.

Oh yea, you are a witch, let us see about that," and with a hard-handed fist he hits her in the jaw and renders her almost unconscious. But she rolls to one side and bangs her head on a flat rock.

"Well now that rock sure got you quiet. And now I will enjoy even more the pleasure of

your body, Gagnon says.

Just as he drops his trousers and is about to mount her, a searing pain on the back of his head causes him to roll off Elke. Gagnon looks up almost glassy-eyed and with a look of wonder he sees Will standing over him clutching a tree limb he had picked up for firewood.

Will pounces on Gagnon and tries hitting him again with the tree limb. This time Gagnon is clipped behind the ear and rolls forward onto Elke crushing the breath out her semi- conscious body. It is then Will notices Gagnon still has his fly open and with Elke's dress askew and the thought she might be hurt, or worse, refuels his resolve to stop Gagnon.

"You don't deserve to live you arrogant and evil bastard," Will shouts as he moves forward to strike Gagnon again. But Gagnon is a product of the streets and instinctively rolls to the left side again and narrowly misses being hit by Will's incoming blow.

Gagnon continues to roll and then stumbles a few steps away, arises and faces Will with raised fists.

"You two have no idea what I am capable of. I am the one with authority here. I can do whatever I want. You two are under my authority. It my command that you two are now under arrest," Gagnon shouts

"Why in hell should I obey you?" shouts Will stepping over the dazed Elke in order to protect her by putting himself between her and Gagnon, "As I see it, I am acting in self-defense by protecting myself and this girl from a man who snuck up on her with the intent of committing a most heinous criminal act. However, you have no authority over common decency. You really are a rotten son of an ugly dog."

Gagnon looks at Will incredulously and then he hears Will say, "Before you do or say anything else, and attempt to show authority over me or Elke, you better cover up your little manhood."

Aghast at being exposed behind his open codpiece, Gagnon reaches down to tidy up his clothing. Will hopes this is the distraction he needs to go on the attack. But Gagnon is a wily man and uses that moment to reach not his trousers but rather to reach down into his boot and pull out a long thin stiletto. Reacting in response, Will reaches into his boot and pull out the small dirk he had used earlier on the Antwerp ruffians.

The two men square off ready to fight. As they circle each other, both are looking for an advantage. But Will knows Gagnon, being bigger, with longer arms, and with a longer knife, has the advantage. Gagnon feigns a few swings and as he draws closer his unhitched britches falter and hinder his steps as they tighten about his knees. This gives Will a chance to duck underneath Gagnon's swing and he nicks Gagnon's ribs and swings away unscathed.

Gagnon feels the stabbing pain and his eyes fill with fury, "I will get you now, you English dog for what you have taken away from me. I will give you a lesson on what it's like to cut an official constable."

"You're not a constable out here in the woods, You're just a bumbling idiot. You have no authority outside the Antwerp city limits," Elke yells.

Gagnon again rushes forward and hits Will straight in the chest. His forward momentum and bulk cause both men to fall to the ground. However, the impact of hitting the ground also causes both men to drop their weapons. Finding himself without a weapon and in pain, Gagnon starts pounding on Will's head and face with his bare hands. This mad pummeling draws blood from Will's nose and cheeks. Will raises both hands in a defensive move as his eyes start to puff shut.

Will next feels Gagnon fall on top of him and hears a raspy voice behind him saying, "Take that you rotten excuse for a man."

Before he can see who the voice belongs to, Will next hears the same voice stutter "Holy Mother of God, what have I done."

Will feels Gagnon try to get up off him but Gagnon cannot rise fully, and he staggers backward in order to roll off Will and then he flops onto his back next to Will. Will, with half-open eyes and his head spinning hears a death rattle in Gagnon's throat. Then as Will focuses on Gagnon, he watches Gagnon draw his last breath. It is then Will sees Gagnon's dropped stiletto handle is sticking out of his back and the point of it protruding from his chest.

"Oh Will, what have I done?" Elke screams.

She rushes to his side and kneels beside him, she asks, "Are you badly hurt?"

"I don't think I'm hurt awfully bad. But my face and body will have a few cuts and bruises that will need tending. Fortunately, we can both use any needed medical supplies in the wagon to tend to our needs."

After a short pause to catch his breath, Will turns to Elke and says, "You were absolutely magnificent to have done what you did. I can't imagine what terror you must have gone through with that man about to assault you."

"I was not sure where you were or how far away you were. But I knew in my heart you were nearby and would come to my rescue."

"Well, if truth be told, in the end it was I who needed rescuing. When he pulled out that stiletto, I was sure both of us would not see the light of another day. I knew I could not survive without you in my life and that gave me great resolve."

Elke looks at Will calmly and says," I know God commands us not to kill and I believe that to be a very well-intentioned commandment. However, after what happened tonight and the rage and evil we both saw in Gagnon, sometimes your survival depends on doing things that might be considered wrong, I also believe now, more than ever, that God wants us to survive, continue to love each other, and deliver His words written in your uncle's Bibles."

After another moment of silence, and some additional time to clear their heads and slow their racing pulses, Elke says to Will, "I remember vividly the last thing Gagnon said to me. He called me a witch. What do you think of that? Could he have dragged me back to Antwerp and declare that he had caught a witch?"

"Well, my understanding that witchcraft is it is punishable by burning, dunking, or imprisonment... if the witch does not recant. But for 50 years Pope Innocent VII's declaration of December 1484 defined what makes a witch and his declaration has been used ever since for today's popular habit of which hunting both in your country and in mine, and wherever Catholicism has spread. But I can truthfully say you are not a witch., However, I do find your feminine charms very bewitching.... and that, my dear lady does not qualify as meeting the test of any religious or civil offense. Think of the mess that would ensue if every man who has ever loved anyone as much as I love you would be in if he could not love a woman whose feminine charms cast a spell on him.".

Elke tosses Will a smirk and wistful smile.

"I do know that a charge of witchcraft has been used as a mean-spirited and petty way to press a case of jealousy, envy, and just about anything ignorant people use to explain diseases, people they can't understand, and people they dislike."

The two continue clinging to each other for another hour or so and then Will says to Elke," I have two more thoughts on this matter. The first is, Gagnon's obsession with exerting power over you was caused by a devil-inspired mind. If he had not found us, he would have returned to hurt your family in Antwerp. My second thought is Gagnon was a bully and as everyone knows the behavior of a bully is entirely unpredictable but so is the behavior of a courageous and determined woman, a woman like you. I really must thank you for saving my life."

"Will, sometimes you just think too much. It was kind of you to say that, and I love you for it, but I never thought of myself as courageous or unpredictable. Maybe I am a wee bit stubborn. But it bothers me to think I had to kill a man for us to live and carry on together."

"Well, let us just figure out what we do next. It's hard to know what to do next when you have been in the middle of chaos."

"Will"

"Yes, my dear or should I say, "mon Cherie?"

"Will this is profoundly serious.... What are we going to do with Gagnon's body?"

"We are going to give him a burial right here in this idyllic place. I think we should bury him with his belongings. We will take his horse and use it to spell off

Betsy. Using two horses we can make better time and get away from here as fast as we can. Maybe we can sell one of the horses later, or both if need be. We may need extra money to pay for the longer passage over to England.

"Will"

"Yes, Elke"

"I just heard you say we; did you mean that?"

"Yes, I meant it. I never want to be in a situation where the thought of losing you rises again. I want to always watch over you and… be your husband. So…Elke, will you marry me?"

"Oh Will, I certainly will. I do love you and with all my heart. I am so happy we have found each other."

Feeling quite secure in each other's arms, the two huddle under a blanket to ward off any chill but keep warm by waiting for the sun to rise and both wondering what new adventures lie ahead of them.

Elke awakens early and finds Will gone from beside her. Startled at his absence she peers out of the wagon and sees him getting Betsy ready for her harness and traces. She also notices the saddle and gear on Gagnon's horse has been removed and their extra halter tied to the horse's head.

"How long have you been up?" she shouts at Will

"I have not been up long. I thought it best to take care of Gagnon and his effects in such a manner that you would not have to see him or anything else reminding you about last night."

"Good God in Heaven, I was so relaxed after such a sleep I almost put last night's events out of my mind. But to put your mind at rest, *je vais bien, merci…* which you must know means, I am well thank you.".

Will smiles again, then Elke quips, "With your poor French accent why don't we keep speaking English?"

"I will, if you will " grins Will, "but truthfully, it was an unpleasant task but I did it knowing that while his actions earned him a place in the ground, the memory of what he was about to do will likely reside in us for a long time. But I was strengthened by knowing his spirit has left his earthly body, his soul is now before God awaiting final judgement. It up to Gagnon now to settle whatever accounts God and His angels tallied against his time here on earth and to decide his final judgement."

"Will, you have a special way with words. I believe what you have said is the only way of putting it."

"Thank you. I earnestly believe it. Now let us do our best to put this matter behind us and look forward to finishing our mission to get this wagon to where it belongs.

Perhaps along the way we can find some of the happiness we created by the love we carry for each other."

"Thanks, Will, for putting the ugliness of yesterday into such a nice a way of looking at it. Your attitude and what you have said makes me comfortable with what happened between us and Gagnon. However, I'll be even more at ease when we leave this place."

Elke looks at Will pensively "Will, if you don't mind my asking, would you let me read one of your uncle's Bibles once we start along the road? I do have a good command of written English and would like to read a few passages of scripture and perhaps it will bring me additional comfort"

"That's not going to be a problem. I will retrieve one from a hiding place once we have left this area and are the road.to Caen. However, be sure to hide the Bible should any strangers come along."

A little while later, after eating some cold food for breakfast, the wagon was finally loaded. With Betsy in her harness, and Gagnon's horse tethered behind the wagon, Will then requests of Elke, "Please, Elke let's just store the last of our belongings, fold up the palyass, and get as far away from here as possible."

A few minutes later Will, with Elke on the seat beside him, shouts at Betsy to "walk on. "He then drives the wagon out of their quiet place onto the road leading them towards Caen. They remain quiet for several hours but, it being a chilly morning, they wrap one of their blankets around their shoulders and another one over their laps. Cuddled up on the wagon's seat they wait for the sun to reach its zenith so they can warm themselves by its rays.

It is almost noon before they speak again and Elke says, "I am feeling much better about all that has happened. If you do not mind, I think I will read a little more scripture."

"Please go ahead. Once we get a little closer to Caen I will let you know so you can put it away just in case we meet any suspicious characters."

"Thanks, Will"

Will then retrieves the Tyndale Bible that Elke had been reading earlier from its hidden compartments in the wagon and gives it to her. Elke assumes a lost-in-thought intensity as she starts to read. Will sees no reason to interrupt her and so he focuses onto driving them down the road towards Caen.

-Chapter 29-

Friday 26 February 1537

the city of Caen

Will and Elke do not stop for their mid-day meal. Rather they push across a wide plain with lush, green, well-kept farmland. As Will leans over to read a sign Elke notices his shift in posture and lifts her head from reading. Together they see a sign. It says they are near the Orne River.

"Are we close to Caen?" Elke asks?

"Not quite so. Once we cross the Orne River it will be just a short distance, perhaps nine or so miles into the city. We are in the French province of Normandy known as Calvados. The city of Caen has some lovely churches and if we have time to see any of them we should do so. We may never pass this way again."

"I think that would be nice. Perhaps in that church we could offer up a prayer for old' Gagnon, God rest his damaged mind and soul."

Will decides to say nothing more about the Caen churches. He then looks at Elke, "While Caen is inland on an estuary it is but a short distance from the English Channel. It has a good port to either access the English

Channel or to go down river to many trading cities of Europe."

"I never noticed till now that Caen is a walled city," says Elke

"It has been a walled city since the times when Vikings raided here. As capital city of this region it provides many benefits to the merchants, industries, and farm folk along the 100 miles of the Orne River. Denis told me the Orne River is so well established with many heavy commercial ships we should have no problem finding a ship for our wagon and perhaps even Betsy. I believe we might be better off here than back at Calais."

"Why? Will, tell me your reasoning, especially since you have never been here before."

"I know that a lot people here have English ties. This city was once important to the Normans who conquered it in the 10th and 11th Century. But then the English captured Caen in 1346 and did so again just a few years ago in 1417. Therefore, I am hopeful that a goodly number of English leaning folk either remain here or come here to do business…just like in Antwerp. Perhaps one of them has the means and the methods to help us."

"Is there anything else that tickles your fancy about a place you have never been to?"

"That's a funny way of putting it. I believe we will find the Protestant movement strong here. That should work in our favor if we need like-minded people to help us. Finally, just five years ago, Henry VI started a University here in Caen Perhaps we might have to call on a learned man to help us,…unless we discover they are all Papists."

"Will" asks Elke

"Oui, *ma Cherie*, what is it?

"How come you know so much?"

"I was given a lot of information about Europe by my English benefactor Monmouth. I spent several weeks with him before he would let me come to Antwerp. He genuinely wanted to be sure I was prepared for every contingency. But there were two things that he did not prepare me for."

"Which are?"

"How such a venture like this would test me as a person. Also, he never prepared me for what would happen should I be fortunate enough to fall in love."

"Oh Will, you are such a tease, Oh! Look over there. I can see we are coming closer to being inside that stone-walled town. Look again, I can see the spires of a cathedral. Any idea what those spires belong to?"

"Yes, my dear. Those spires likely belong to the Abbaye-aux Hommes where William the Conqueror is buried. I was told he is in front of its High Alter. His wife, Matilda, is also buried near where the choir used to sit. Those two austere towers you see are 90 meters tall or about 295 of our English feet. That's about all I can remember."

Will then takes his eyes off the road and turns to look at Elke and says, "Perhaps if we have to wait a day or two to catch a boat for either of us, we could go look at that church and see its spires close-up. Would you like that?"

"Will, that would be wonderful," says Elke as she takes his hand and sits closer to him.

"Oh, I know that limestone is quarried here and shipped to England. I know it was used to build Norwich Cathedral So if they have ships that haul the heavy weight of limestone across the channel, then certainly one such ship will be able to take our wagon across and perhaps one or both horses."

"I have never heard of Norwich Cathedral," asks Elke, "What is it and where is it?'

"I know it's a huge cathedral in Norwich, the second largest city in England. Its cathedral is considered the largest building in all of East Anglia. It is devoted to the Holy and Undivided Trinity and is faced with a cream-colored limestone shipped over from Caen. It was completed about four hundred years ago, just around 1135

AD. Its spire is the tallest in all of England and it has over one thousand painted and carved stone bosses.

"What's a boss?" Elke asks.

"It's the keystone that intersects a ribbed vaulted ceiling. I have never been to Norwich. But people who come into the Apothecary where I used to work have been there and they have described it to me as being magnificent. I hope someday to go there and now perhaps the day will come when we will get to do that."

"You stated Norwich was in East Anglia, just what is that? I thought that island we called England is all one country."

"Well, that is so today but way back, maybe ten centuries ago, East Anglia was the home country of the Anglo-Saxons. Their Kingdom consisted of north people, those in Norwich and south people, those in Suffolk and all the people in between."

"Will, I am so impressed, you really have knowledge about a lot of things. To look at you when you are quiet it is hard for me not to think of you as being either bored, hard of hearing, or off somewhere with a mind either bewitched or in a trance."

"I do apologize if I sometimes seem aloof or distracted. I am not being centered on myself, but I tend to ruminate. Unfortunately, I don't always notice when I am doing it."

"I will try and be better at sharing what is on my mind and especially with you. You have your work cut out for you if you want to shape a man like me into the kind of husband you truly deserve," Will says.

"Will! I have already determined our life together is going to be a challenge, but it will be interesting. Earlier today I read in the Bible, I believe it was Peter who said… above all things be earnest in your love among yourselves, because love covers a multitude of sins."

Yes, as I have seen with my parents, when two people love each other they work together and get through anything that comes their way."

They kiss and then Elke again curls herself around Will's arm. A few minutes later as they are close to Caen Will nudges Elke and says: "Well, my dearest, isn't this area very pretty? The little pastures and farms we are passing seem so restful. It is a lot greener here than back in Hodthorpe. I saw a sign that said this little green area is called Prairie St. Gilles. Would it not be nice if today did not end and we just travelled and talked with each other without anything or anyone to disturb us?"

"Are you getting worried about going through the city gates and finding trouble?"

"No, I was just thinking about home".

Elke smiles and turns her face Will saying, "Just keep your eyes on the road and our horse from wandering off it or we may have trouble neither of us thought of."

Elke returns to reading her Bible. Feeling spiritually awakened she distracts Will with questions about some words and passages caused when her English falters. As the two discuss the meaning of some of Tyndall's translations they find they share similar insights and feelings both about their faith and the church's role in their lives. Before too long they reach the town of Caen, as both realize their love has truly blossomed.

Seeing the walled city before them Elke looks at Will and says, "Will, whatever lies ahead for us in Caen, I do not want it to end with me going back to Antwerp. What I want is to stay with you and go to England."

"Well Elke, there is nothing I would like more than us staying together. but we must be sure we are clear of anything that might befall us. There are ruffians and brigands also in England. But know this, I had a long talk with your brother when we were back in Antwerp. He assured me I have his and your mother's blessings to court you. They expect me to return you safely to Antwerp, as I promised. However, if you do come to England, I suggest we do two things. First, we send them a letter saying our plans have changed and, secondly, we should get married in Caen and include that news in the letter."

"What a great idea! We should get married," says Elke with a smile that stretches from ear to ear, "Then we can travel as husband and wife and avoid issues that may arise by our traveling as brother and sister."

"Very well then, we agree, let us see what we can do about getting married. Then, if there are any problems with our marriage being recognized either here or in your country, we can do it all over again either in London or by returning to Antwerp.'

Elke pauses then turns and looks demurely at Will, "Since you confessed that you had talked with my brother and had his approval to court me, I must tell you that I talked with my Mother   as well. It was she who approved my coming with you knowing my feelings for you. She is a wise woman and could see from the first the day you arrived there was an attraction between us. She saw it as God's blessing we both deserved.."

"I suspected something as she watched over us like a mother duck watches her hatchlings. As for us I want that we should have no secrets between us. My pledge to you is I will work hard at keeping you happy?"

"I pledge to always be totally honest and work to keep us both happy ... my dear Lord and Master," she says with a smirk.

"Don't smirk. You did make a splendid idea about restating our vows in England. We can have my sisters and parents, aunts and uncles, and some friends, Cyril Blackham, and perhaps even Humphrey Monmouth as celebrants. Humphrey especially would be nice and so would Cyril Blackham. They have been the two greatest influences on my life. Besides, I know once my family meet you they will love you as much as I do."

After a short pause Will continues, "Elke know this. I believe it with all my heart. I believe God is watching over us. And as He is the giver of all good things and graces, He has brought me the greatest blessing…to love and to be loved. We are also being blessed by undertaking the transport of His words as written in my uncle's Bibles. They will not only help glorify His holy name, but they will allow people to learn of His commandments and show them His rewards by loving and caring for one another."

"Will, how do you know so much about God's words?. Have you read the Bible and studied it? Is not studying the Bible heresy for which your uncle was killed?" asks Elke with a bewildered look.

"I have not studied it well nor often, but I do remember several pieces of scripture. Here let me show you something in that Bible next to you.."

"Here Elke, are the words of God as written in Ephesians Chapter 4, Verse 23. It says, 'be kind to each other, tenderhearted, forgiving one another just as God through Christ has forgiven you.'"

"Hummn, I see," says Elke, "I remember reading the Book of Galatians a while ago and…Here give it to me and I will look it up, I remember there were nine things….. Here it is", she said with a little excitement, "It says, the fruit of the Spirit is love, joy, peace, forbearance, tenderness, goodness, faithfulness, gentleness, and self-control, against such things there is no law.'"

"Do you understand what that means?" asks Will," especially the part about the fruit of the spirit."

"Yes, I think God is telling us if we follow his commandment to love one another it will cause Him to bring the nine manifestations of the Spirit into our lives. God's love is immense even when some people are unlovable, such as Gagnon, and this is why he allowed his son to die for the sins of all mankind."

"Now you understand why getting these Bibles back to England is important and why folks like my uncle and Martin Luther and others worked so hard to get God's word to every man, woman, and child…so they can understand God's words in their own language."

After a short pause Will continues, "These Bibles, and others in different languages, allow people to realize on their own that they can find salvation by how they live and behave and not by having some prelate dictate that you buy your way into heaven by paying the church to get a family member out of purgatory. God wants us to look after each other not build a layer upon layer of prelates laden with gold, social privilege, and huge cathedrals to intimidate the poor."

After Will's little outburst Elke sits silent until the wagon goes through the gates of Caen Once inside the town they notice they are being scrutinized by an odd-looking town constable. Elke offers him a warm smile while Will keeps his eyes on the cobblestone street ahead, as he drives their wagon into the city's center area and market square. They see it as a bustling area of merchants in stalls and start assessing how they should approach someone for help.

Suddenly, Will spots a familiar sign. It is placed over the door of an Apothecary. The sign is a yard square, "That's rather large" thinks Will, "Larger than any I have seen."

The sign's distinctive gold mortar and pestle is painted on slatted wooden boards surrounded by an Acacia wreath. It is hanging about a foot higher than the top of the front door. The sign is hinged so it sways whenever the wind picks up a little strength. In the front window are two glass show globes sitting upright in iron stands of three-legs each. One has about a gallon of a green liquid the other holds about the same but with a red liquid. Will knows they are in the window to do more than attract passersby, for as he learned sunshine acts as a natural preservative to keep whatever concoction is inside them from spoiling.

After a small discussion Will and Elke agree that they should go inside and determine if the apothecary would help them, if Will can earn his trust as a fellow apothecary. By the smells they also conclude that the town square is not the center of the city and that they must be close to Caen's harbor. This gives them hope the Apothecary might also serve seafaring men with knowledge of how they can board a ship bound for England.

Will pulls the wagon up to a hitching post in front of the Apothecary. But since the wagon is drawing some attention from passersby, he asks Elke, "Please remain outside and hold onto the reins. You will need to keep the two horses quiet while I go inside to introduce myself. I will not be long. But I will be more relaxed knowing our wagon is attended to."

Once inside Will finds the local apothecary hard at work making suppositories. approaches the grey-haired, short, and stocky man. He wears a distinctive bushy moustache and a monocle. He also wears a leather apron over breeches and a cream-colored rough linen shirt. Will coughs as the man looks up to see who has intruded upon his work.

Will says, "pardonnez-moi monsieur apothrcaire." "Oui?" the man says as Will breaks the man's concentration. He looks at Will with one steely blue eye, but Will is not sure of the other eye's color because of the monocle, so Will continues with "*Pardonnez mois monsieur, mon nom est William, ne cous parley anglaise?*"

Now the man looks a little puzzled and gives Will a quizzical look, so Will asks him another question, in his best use of French, and talking very slowly, "*Est-ce que vous comprenez ce que je veux dire?*" Will now speaks a little louder and slower and asks the man if he speaks English.

The man changes his quizzical expression, smiles, gives Will a friendly grin and says in perfect English, "You're damn right I do."

"Oh! my goodness," blurts out Will, "*Je ne parle pas encore tres bien le francis*" letting him know that he does not speak French very well.

"Don't worry mate", says the man now in a well recognizable London accent, "*Votre francais est preque aussi mauvais que mon anglaise*".

"I think you just said your English is just as bad as my French, is that what I think I heard?"

"Yes," he says with a bit of a laugh, "I do not get to use my English as much as I would like to, but one never forgets it. But French is hard to learn as there are many dialects, especially among the various regions and especially among country folk."

"Well, I will let you practice your English then," Will says, also with a smile and extending his hand across the worktable to shake it, adds, "How did you come to be living here as an apothecary?"

"It's not a long story but it is a happy one. Some years back, and having apprenticed for seven years, I was received into the London Society of Apothecaries. Then, while working one day in an Apothecary in Brighton, I fell in love with a French lady. She was a customer but had come to England as a school mistress. After we were married, and she with child, she longed to return home. Since I was raised in an orphanage I did not care where I lived. Lucky for me many English families live here either as merchants or tradesmen. So, to me it did not seem I was going to a foreign country. Please excuse me, I forget to introduce myself, my name is Bruce Siefert."

"My name is Will Hutchins and you may call me Will. If it is alright with you, may I call you Bruce? I hope it would not be too much of an imposition, but I would like to fall on the good graces of a fellow apothecary and ask for your help."

"Well Will, like it is with most requests my answer has to be…it depends. So, tell me what are you doing here in Caen? What can I do to help?"

Bruce looks incredulous as Will gives the fake account of his mission. "The Guild officers want this wagon to help promote the Guild," Will explains, "To help find young lads interested in taking up our profession and the membership see it as compounding and making medicines for the poor and those with no access to a local apothecary."

"That all sounds very altruistic, so what is it that I can do to help?"

"Please know that while I am responsible for getting this wagon to London on behalf of the Guild of Apothecaries, I myself am an apothecary. This past year I finished my seven years of apprenticeship. Then, like you, I too was inducted into the London Society of Apothecaries. Thus, as we both are Master Apothecaries and fraternal brothers, I really need your help to get that wagon to London."

"Where did you obtain that wagon?

"Actually, it was custom made by craftsmen who by all accounts are quite a distance from here…in Belgium, in Antwerp actually."

"Heavenly Days my man. What possessed you to drive all the way down here to Caen? Why did you not cross the English Channel from Antwerp or at least Calais?"

"The answer to that is overly complicated. Suffice it to say that the lady travelling with me, and I, faced some personal issues that forced us to travel away from both of those cities."

"Is that your "travelling lady" sitting outside on that wagon parked in front of my shop?"

"Yes, that's her. We are "hand-fasted" with plans to be married as soon as we can… even sooner if we can deliver the wagon without any more delays. But first, we must find passage from here across the channel to Brighton or some other English port. As a stranger in town I just do not know how to best accomplish that but I have all the legitimate and necessary papers confirming the wagon as being commissioned by the London Society of Apothecaries and that I am authorized as their emissary to bring it to them."

As an afterthought, and still hoping to convince a fellow apothecary to help him, Will says, "I am an active member of the society. I have papers showing my trip to

Antwerp was to attend a series of lectures by the renowned physician Paracelsus and that I am bringing his new knowledge back to London to benefit the advancement of our profession.".

Will still thinking Bruce need convincing adds, "Additionally, the London Guild has given me the necessary coinage I might need to pay any tariffs, duties and passage fees. Or if need be a few coins for bribes and help."

"I find you plight very interesting, which makes me dare to ask …does your wagon contain any processed poppy plants?"

"Why do you ask?"

"I get a lot of sailors and dock workers to tend to. They seek me out when they have a broken arm, hand, finger, foot, leg, gash or knock on the head causing them great pain. Many lose fingers loading and unloading cargo and a finger gets caught in a winch. The pain they suffer is quite agonizing. Some cannot sleep as the pain is so bad.

Bruce notices Will wince and continues, "I learned about this special plant extract when I met a physician travelling from the middle east. It has powerful pain killing properties when I make it into tincture using 10 percent denatured spirits. My Jewish friends here in Caen say the Talmud refers to cultured poppy plants as "opyon", Have you ever heard of it?"

"What do you mean, the Talmud, or Opyon?"

As Bruce smiles at Will's quick wit, Will responds with "Yes, I know of what you speak, and yes, I do have a small amount of its resin in a locked drawer inside my wagon."

"If you could spare but a few ounces I would be most grateful. I am also prepared to buy some of it from you."

"If you can help me get across to England, I will gladly give you some."

"What about your two horses?"

"If the ship we travel on has room, I believe one should come with us to pull the wagon from the English harbor to London. Our horse has a specially made harness that allows it to travel long periods without tiring. I would be happy to sell the spare horse you saw tied up at the back of our wagon…. Perhaps… I may find a worthy gentleman to give it to….as a gift…. for his helping out a brother apothecary."

"Thanks, but I have no need of a horse, but I do know many others who do. Perhaps I can find a buyer for you before you leave. But since you mentioned that you want to marry that girl sitting on your wagon seat, would you like to do that here in Caen.?

"Oh, my goodness, yes!" says Will showing his exuberance. He quickly calms and says, "but only if she consents and only if the marriage would be recognized in England. Can you help with such a thing?"

"I have a brother-in law who is a local cleric. But, before I talk to him you must tell me, are you Papists? Or are you Reformists?

With some hesitation Will responds, "We are both quite... proud... to call ourselves.... supporters of the Protestant Movement."

"You're not one of those Anabaptists are you? Tell me you are not running away from their most recent prosecution and executions."

"Heavens, no! I do not believe like they do that only people who have been re-baptized as adults can be true Christians. Their idea that infant baptism is to be denied is off-putting. While I was attending the recent Paracelsus lectures in Antwerp, some German apothecaries told me of how, in the city of Munster, about two years ago, the Anabaptists seized the city hall. Then, these new ruling leaders declared everyone inside their city limits is an equal but only if they conform to their religious beliefs. They secured that conformity by being re-baptized, as an adult, fully clothed, and immersed into a large vessel of water. I even heard the Anabaptists renamed the city of Munster 'New Jerusalem.'

"I'm glad you know something about them. Yesterday several sailors arrived here in Caen and they revealed two days prior the last Anabaptist leaders were executed. Their executions were done to quell their rebellion against Catholicism However cruel the Anabaptists were to their fellow man, and however cruel the catholic Bishop who ordered their execution, it seems to me that tolerance should have existed on both sides. A few of the Anabaptists have escaped and have come here to Caen, seeking sanctuary."

"How awful for those people. It must be terrible to live in such fear or be forced to adopt a new way to worship the one God that gave us life and whose Son died to give us salvation."

"Since we are on this topic, are you a devout Catholic or are you part of the Reformed Church of France whose members are seeking greater religious freedom?" Will asks.

"We should not be talking like this. Caen is a city not very tolerant of non-Catholics. I and my family are members of the Reformed Church of France. As French protestants we are better known as Huguenots. We are growing in numbers, but we have many facing scurrilous hostility and persecution. However, as most of our leaders are either from the royal houses, such as those of Navarre. Many of us Huguenots are officers in the military or well placed in the professions, or high society. We are trying hard to grow our members and more openly practice y our faith.

"How are you doing? Can you grow your members? "asks Will,

"Despite our many efforts many are deciding that becoming an émigré to a foreign land is preferable to putting up with persecution. Two such places offering tolerant refuge for Protestants are the new American lands of Carolina and further north in Catholic Quebec. My guess is if the Catholic church keeps up its resistance to Protestantism that it will ultimately be squashed in spite of the contributions made by aristocrats, merchants, professionals and intellectuals supporting the Reformation in all its forms and not only religion."

"I find that all very interesting and perhaps someday we can talk more about it, but first, can I count on you for help in getting my Apothecary wagon to England?"

"Yes, you can count on me to help you. But first I would like to have a look at your wagon and engage in some talk with your soon-to-be-wife. After that I will see about some lodging and arrangements for getting you both across the Channel."

Will and Bruce step outside the Apothecary and Will introduces Bruce to Elke. She has been sitting patiently on the wagon, but she also has been gathering stares and quizzical looks from folks passing by.

"My dear Elke, I would like you to meet Bruce Seifert. He is an apothecary and owns this fine establishment. He is an Englishman and a member of the London Society of Apothecaries. He has agreed to help us cross the English Channel. He also has a connection that may help us as a couple."

Elke looks down from her perch to see a friendly looking man of about 40, rather short and a bit stout. She also notices his bushy moustache. She notices his bright eyes and laugh lines at each corner of his mouth. She is immediately drawn to his warmth when Bruce reaches his hand to shake hers. She responds with a firm grip and a smile when she hears his friendly voice.

"My Goodness, you are a pretty lass. Will tells me you are to be married. He has also told me you have come a great distance… from Antwerp no less."

As their handshake lingers Elke says, "It's a pleasure to meet you Monsieur Seifert. It is so nice that Will has found a fellow apothecary to talk with. Thank you for wanting to help us get to England."

"I am going to do what I can, fair lady."

"I can tell by your accent you are not French. How is it that you have an Apothecary shop here in a very French city?"

"It is a long story and I hope my wife will share it with you later when you meet her. I do belong to the same Society of Apothecaries as Will and am thus pledged to help you. But first know this. It may take a day or two to complete arrangements to get you and Will across the Channel. Would you and Will avail yourselves of the hospitality of my home? We have extra rooms and a stable to put up your horses and wagon. My wife and I live in a large place handed down through her family over several generations. It would be a lot safer there than having you camp outside the city walls or roaming the streets of Caen."

"That is a generous offer. It makes good sense to get this wagon off the streets and into a place of safety. Yes, we will do that if Will agrees to it as well."

"Yes, Elke, I do think that's a wise decision."

Bruce then looks directly into Elke's eyes and asks her, "Now that is settled, I will close up my shop in a few minutes and we can drive to my home together. This is so you do not get lost and so I can introduce you to my wife, Rachael.

"Now for my second question, and this one is just for the wee lady. As it might take several days to get you passage over to England and as Will has indicated the two of you wish to marry, would you like for me to arrange a marriage here in Caen so you can arrive in England as man and wife.?

"You can do that? And you would do that?" Elke asks.

"Oh yes, on both counts. I would be happy to do it. You know the French love any excuse to hold a party... especially my Rachael. We are members in the local Protestant group of Huguenots. I have a brother- in-law who is ordained as one of our clergy. We could hold the ceremony in the cathedral you passed as you entered through the city gates. Of course, church bans would have to be expedited but your marriage would be recognized in the eyes of God and church officials. You would also have a certificate that authenticates it before any laity. What do you think about that?"

Elke breaks into a wide grin, leans over and hugs Bruce with both arms tight around his neck. As she pulls him to her, her excitement shows and she blurts, "I would love being married in that cathedral. I do so love Will most dearly. I do want to be his wife, I love the idea that from here we can travel together as man and wife, and I love you for making all that happen'. Thank you, *merci beaucoup*."

" Elke, as Bruce and his family are members of the French Protestant Movement, would being married in a Protestant church be bothersome?".

"No, it would not," she replies, "We have had a number of French Protestants in Antwerp. Several have been customers in my father's print shop. A lot of them live in the Dutch lowlands where they settled after being severely persecuted and forced to convert back to Catholicism. At one time the King of France issued a government policy called the dragonnades. This was a system designed to intimidate Huguenot families into either leaving France or converting back to Catholicism. What the dragonnades did was allow the billeting of the worst soldiers in the French Dragoons in Protestant households. This was done after empowering these ill-mannered ruffians with permission to abuse those in Huguenot households and even destroy or steal their property or possessions.

"Well, then, now you know who I and my family are. Even though we have survived a half-century of persecution I think the time may come when even I will leave France for somewhere else. However, enough of all that. Now its settled," says Bruce as he steps back from Elke's enthusiastic hug, "Let me go back inside to finish up some work then we shall be on our way to meet Rachael and my family. You will love them all once you get to know them."

A little while later Bruce, Elke and Will are sitting on the driver's seat and Will heads the horse-drawn apothecary away from the market square. As they near the town gates Will looks at Bruce and says, "May I ask you a question?"

"Please do.".

"From whence does the name Huguenot derive?"

"You know, truthfully I do not know. But many believe when both John Calvin and Besacon Hughes lived in Geneva they met. It was then Hughes adopted many of Calvin's reformist views. Hughes was also a Catholic, but he believed an alliance between the city State of Geneva and the republican State of Switzerland should exist to keep Geneva from being ruled by a Duke. The source of the name Huguenot has never been proven. I suppose we will never know as Hughes died four years ago."

After the cart ambled along a narrow country dirt road for about an hour, its three passengers arrived at a pebbled driveway in front of a two-story lime-stone estate house. Once they drew close all three started to smile as they could hear a cacophony of children running about the yard laughing and yelling. A tall brunette woman with slight aquiline nose, dressed in a modest floor length dress with a wimple stood at the door to great them. Elke knew her wimple addressed the cultural stigma of married women being labeled as "unseemly" if they showed their hair. The woman's full-length over-apron started to fly up as she rushed down the front doorsteps. Once she was close all three could see her large deep blue eyes and rosy cheeks.

Before Bruce could wave or shout anything, she shouted to him in a husky but friendly voice, "Well now, My Dear Husband. What have we here? Did you bring home some more strays needing feeding and lodging?"

"Love of my life and dearest mother of my children. These two are Elke deBergdorf and Will Hutchins. Elke is from Antwerp and Will is from London. He is a member of the London Society of Apothecaries and that makes he and I fraternal brothers. They will be staying with us for a few days until I can arrange two things."

"And what might that be, dear husband?" she says looking somewhat skeptical as if she had doubts about her husband and his intentions.

"My dear Rachael, I am going to arrange passage for them to England and we are going to arrange to have them married, if we can, before they leave."

Rachael replies, "Well are you not generous and a most clever man? A marriage ceremony is always a good excuse for a gathering of family and friends. I will help you with that in any way I can, But, as for passage to England, that is an expense we surely can do without. They are not runaways or elopers, are they? Or worse yet, could they be Catholic spies looking for heretics? And what is this fancy wagon all about? Why do they have two horses?"

"All will be revealed soon my dear lady. But first, let us all go inside and share an evening meal. There are too many prying eyes out here by the road. Once inside I assure you all your questions will be answered."

Once Elke alights Bruce turns to him and asks," Will please drive your wagon into the courtyard in the back of the house. There is a stable behind there where Rachael's family used to keep cows and horses. It will be a safe place for both the wagon and your horses.

Bruce steps down and turns to Elke saying, "Elke, please go with Racheal and take whatever you need from the wagon for a few days stay with us. Racheal, please show Elke to the guest room on the second floor where she can wash up and rest a bit before supper. Thank you, mon Cherie."

As Elke steps down from the wagon, Racheal gives her a warm smile and embrace. "Welcome to our home. Sometimes, Bruce surprises me with his good deeds, many of which cause great consternation and some upheaval in our household. But I come from a large family and I can assure you never have two days ever been the same with all our comings and goings and with the vagaries of life that befall us. But we trust in each other and support each other in a manner we hope is also pleasing to our Lord."

"Your husband will tell you more once he returns with Will. You truly need to know who we are and why we are disrupting your busy life. Believe me, I know my mother does not like unexpected company. But I will do whatever chores and tasks you ask of me. I do not want Will nor I to become a burden to you nor a disruption to the custom and order of your home. I must admit that is a pretty piece of cloth you have covering your hair. Is it as a wimple? Or cornette?"

"Actually, it's a just a pretty head covering made from a piece of cloth that Bruce brought from one of his travels when he went to Paris to obtain some herbs and spices. Paul the Apostle wrote in his epistles that women should have their hair covered when in church and that men should not...but as my hair is long and unruly, I like to wear this covering all the time.

Elke gives Racheal a quizzical and so Racheal adds, "St. Paul's reasoning was based on the notion that women in church were in the presence of angels and their flight could get tangled in their long hair. But for me my angels are here beside me every day in the form of my children, husband, and family. And so, my head covering keeps my unruly hair from flying about whenever I must chase after them as a practical solution. Do you know covering a women's hair has become quite the fashion for society ladies in Paris and around France not only for its need to be worn to church but as an everyday item?

"Thanks for explaining that. I do not know how many days we will be here, but I do want to help with anything that will ease the burden of keeping a large household from turning into chaos."

"Elke, there are so many children and relatives nearby that we all help each other as the good Lord intended. It has pretty easy to put another potato in a pot or a carrot in the venison stew as on most days I never know who will be here for supper or who is staying overnight. I have learned these many years of being married to Bruce that he is very generous with his time and his earnings from the apothecary. But, enough of me, what I really want to hear is all about you and Will. Why did Bruce bring you here?"

Elke responds by first putting her arm under Racheal's and then turning to look her in the eyes says, "I can see, and with no hesitation say that you genuinely love Bruce and your life here. I feel the same way about being with Will. Let us talk more about us when we are inside."

The two women walk arm and arm up to the door of the Seifert's home. As they walk in Elke notices its warmth and its timbered ceiling great room. She also notices white-washed walls

and a large fireplace as its source of heat. A cooking pot on its tripod of blackened iron legs sits over wood embers smoldering in the fireplace. Adding to the ambience is the smell of cooked meat and vegetables. Additionally, a plate attached to one of the legs keeps the smell of warm, fresh, bread wafting throughout the area. Such sights and smells cause Elke to remember her home back in Antwerp. Her reminiscence causes her to hesitate about her decision to marry and go to England, then she thinks about all the events and feeling she has gone through since meeting Will and her heart tells her that her feelings for him are truly those of love.

-Chapter 30-

Friday night, 26February 1537 to Thursday 4 March 1537

The home of Bruce and Racheal Seifert

The bond between Elke and Racheal grows strong. Elke helps with childcare, and housework, enjoying the new friendship. It is as if she has become a member of the family and because of that sometimes feels guilty when thinking of her own family in Antwerp. She also tries to relate to the home she and Will may create.

As the days pass Racheal hears from Elke how she and Will first met in front of the statue of Silvo Bilboa, how she immediately was attracted to him, how she was impressed with his intellect in telling her family of the knowledge gained from Paracelsus, how her decision to leave Antwerp was triggered by love for Will, and why she had to leave because of a bullying suitor. She also reveals to Racheal some of the incidents on their journey from Antwerp south and why they passed Calais, Dunkerque and Dieppe and decided to come to Caen.

Elke reiterated how once they neared Caen, "We were in awe of its size. walls, gates, town square and cathedrals," then added "It was Wills idea to find a friendly and helpful apothecary. Finding Bruce was a true blessing."

Elke avoids revealing to Racheal that their wagon has one thousand Bibles hidden in it nor any of the still-disturbing incident with Gagnon.

By week's end Elke and Will were introduced to about two dozen family members, some were children but most adult nieces, nephews, uncles and aunts, and grand-parents, all of whom lived nearby causing them to agree, "How nice it is for Bruce to be part of this large family. This closeness makes his life safe and make his day joyful and lively.

One evening Will says to Elke "It is pretty obvious why the Siefert's are members of the French Reformed Church and why this Protestant sect, the Huguenots, has been embraced by them...they truly have accepted that it is God's desire that we all love one another and be kind to our neighbors."

Elke nods her agreement and say's "I think it's more than that. They are quite intelligent, so it is no wonder they hold a desire for religious freedom. But I fear that even though they are highly regarded folk in the community that regard may wane if the Catholic Church pushes back. For now, thankfully, they have the God's word written in their own language to guide them."

As more of Racheal's relations learn of the young couple they come to meet them at the Siefert's home and enjoy getting to know them through chatting, idle banter, sharing good food and drinking a little honey mead or cider. Similarly, Will and Elke find they too like all these friendly and gracious folks who have come to meet them. This is especially true among the women folk who relish arranging Elke and Will's marriage feast. However, once the menfolk learn the two are betrothed to each other, through hand-fasting, they immediately use that as an excuse for copious quantities of more music, ale, mead, cider and of course more feasting.

About a week after their arrival Bruce introduces Will and Elke to Bernard Gylpen. Bernard is like Bruce, an Englishman, but he speaks fluent French. He is also a Protestant minister. After meeting with Elke and Will, Bernard after an evening meal he draws them aside and says, "I may live in England, but I love being in France. I am a brother -in law to Bruce. Because Racheal she has asked me, I have agreed to conduct your marriage ceremony and bind you together as husband and wife. However, it is the custom here in France, as well as in England that marriage banns be published.

In France banns are done at a local courthouse and must be done ten days before the marriage. In England banns are announced in church for three consecutive Sundays before the marriage. But as I can see no opposition to your marriage arising in this town, I can have that requirement waived. But also know this, we cannot gain access to the church until Saturday next. From what Bruce has told me you are in a hurry to get to England. Thus, would you rather wait for a week and be married, or would you rather take your chances and leave on the first ship that can get you across the channel?"

Will looks at Elke hoping for a response, but she just looks at him and shrugs. Then after a short pause she is the first to speak, "What is it about these marriage banns that is so special?

Bernard replies, "The banns of marriage are simply a public declaration or announcement of intent to marry. As Will should know they are popular in English churches where their purpose is to allow anyone to raise church or civil impediments to a marriage. For example, it helps prevent someone from marrying more than one wife or marrying a child unable to think for herself... such as one who is noticeably young, pressured into it, or is addled. Such folk cannot consent to the union. Banns also prevent the marrying of someone who has taken a vow of celibacy. Banns help stop the marrying between folks who are of close kinship like a daughter, sister or niece to a brother, father, uncle, or cousin. Such impediments to holy matrimony would make the marriage invalid once known and so, as it is in England, France and everywhere, banns, or proclamation of marriage, exist. The only way to avoid the requirement of marriage banns is to have a local bishop issue a special license to marry."

"Goodness gracious," exclaims Elke, "Will, did you know about this? I have never heard of such a thing."

Why is nothing worthwhile t ever easy?"

He then turns to Bernard and asks, "Are marriage banns the same in every country or in every faith?"

"No, they are not. I the Netherlands, couples who marry must register with town officials beforehand. This is a process called an "ondertrouw." Couples in France have a civil requirement that banns of marriage be displayed in a town hall at least ten days before a marriage.

Elke thinks for another moment then, looking at Will, speaks "I believe it would be better if we travel as man and wife. There have been some issues already by travelling as brother and sister. What say you Will?"

"If we are to be married I too believe we should take the opportunity before us to be married so when we do arrive home, I can introduce you as my wife"

Elke nods.

Then Will continues, "The London Society of Apothecaries has waited long enough for their wagon so a few more days should not matter. We still can get the wagon to them long before their need to travel in late spring and early summer. So, let us take up this opportunity we have here in Caen and tackle the problem of these banns."

Elke takes his hand and squeezes it, "I know the good Lord has made all things possible, so let's just keep moving forward in faith that the folks we have met her in Caen are part of His holy work."

"Well then," says Bernard. I take that as an affirmative and so now I will move forwards with making the arrangements to have you married by the time a week has passed. I can either get a dispensation from a bishop or I can speed up the process of going through the officials in the Caen town hall. Do you have any preference?"

"I do not. What would work best and easiest for you," replies Will.

"Let me think on that a bit., By the way, what are the full Christian names that will be placed on the marriage certificate and into the official register?"

"Mine is Elke Louisa deBergdorf"

"I never knew you had a middle name. I guess I was just too smitten to ask, "says Will rather sheepishly.

"And what about your full name young man?" Bernard asks.

Will gulps and appears startled, he looks at Elke, and then at Bernard with a look as if he had just stolen a King's crown jewels and was caught with them in his pocket. "I have a confession to make," he says to Bernard

"What is this all about? What's amiss?" asks Bernard with quizzical looks as if he has just been betrayed by a friend.

"It's nothing really bad, but my name is not Will Hutchins, rather it truly is William Tyndale. I have been on a mission related to the work of my uncle who was recently martyred in Belgium. However, I truly am an Apothecary and I truly am a member of the London Society of Apothecaries, And I genuinely love this lass and I genuinely want to marry her. Have you ever heard of my uncle or his work?"

"Unfortunately, I do know of the martyrdom of William Tyndale and the great work he accomplished. His death was inexcusable and the work he did should live on for another five-hundred years or more   Are you thinking that if I publish the banns in the Caen town Hall, some ne'er-do-well, would recognize the connection between you and your uncle if he saw your true Christian name?"

"Yes, I certainly do. You already have Bibles in the French language, and you have seen the Protestant movement grow strong here in Caen, but all it takes is one person to stir up trouble. Perhaps our marriage is not such a good idea. If we wait until we get home to England, it would be safer for us to be married in my hometown, and if not there, at least in London. I trust that you can keep my real name a secret until we are long gone from here. Would you give your word on that that?"

"Yes, I will keep your secret, but does Bruce know who you really are?"

"Unfortunately, Bruce knows only half our story. I value his friendship and since we both are Apothecaries, I want our friendship to remain solid. At first, I did not think it would hurt him to know my real name. But he has enough to think about without being burdened with keeping a secret."

"I understand your reasonings and I am sure Bruce will not mind knowing who you really are."

Will looks at Elke and can see the look of disappointment on her face and says to Bernard, "If you can secure a marriage license from a bishop willing to keep my name from being bandied about, then I think it is worth the risk. I know Elke and Racheal have talked about a marriage feast to celebrate our union and be an excuse for your French family to make merry and to drink more of Bruce's mead and wine. I would hate to be the cause of slowing any preparations already in place"

Will takes a deep breath, pauses, then continues talking to Bernard "You have my permission to get us the license we need to be married but only on the promise my real name is kept quiet until it's too late to draw the attention to mw. Are you content with that limitation?"

"Certainly, I will let you know what I find out tomorrow or the next day. Caen is a sizable town, but I cannot imagine anyone here would want to act badly knowing a Tyndale was heret. But then again, we Protestants are truly in the minority. Before I leave let me also ask a small favor, I think it best you reveal everything about yourselves to Bruce and do it as soon as possible."

-Chapter 31-

Friday, 5 March 1537

The home of Bruce and Racheal Seifert

The next day Will and Elke, along with the whole Seifert household, sit down to enjoy a hearty breakfast of cooked eggs, smoked ham, and fresh warm bread. Will looks at Bruce after the children have gone outside to play and once Elke has left the room and is helping Racheal clean up after the morning meal.

Once Will knows they are alone he says to Bruce in a hushed tone "Bruce, you and Racheal have been wonderful to us and your hospitality has been the best I have ever enjoyed. The friendship between our two ladies has really blossomed and I trust the one between the two of us has as well. I would like to tell you a little more about who, what and why I am here and what Elke and I have before us. Is that alright?"

"*Mon Dieu mon ami,* Oh! Pardon me! My God my friend. What is the matter? Surely by now you know you can tell me anything."

"Well, it is a situation most delicate. William really is my first name. Hutchins is a name several of my family members have used when faced with persecution or some other reason they want to remain silent. I am named after my uncle who was recently burned alive for his viewpoints deemed heretical by the Roman church and the King of England. Thus, because of my being here representing the London Society of Apothecaries, they and I all agreed I should use the name Hutchins, rather than my real name. Now that Elke and I want to be married I do not want to see public banns issued that place my real last name to public scrutiny. Nor do I want a start a life of matrimony based on a falsehood. And I do not want to expose you to any possible persecution because of who I am. I trust you can understand this and forgive me? "

"Is that all there is? That is not a bad thing. You would be amazed the number of people I have seen and treated in my apothecary who never reveal their true names. In many of these cases the reasons are flimsy. So out with it my friend, what is your true last name?

Will looks Bruce straight in the face, leans forward, and says in a hushed tone, "My real name is William Tyndale. Have you ever heard of my uncle? I hope that it won't make a difference to our friendship."

"Well I'll be ...... I always suspected there was more to you than you let on ...but it was not my position to pry ...of course I know who your uncle was. I was saddened to learn of his martyrdom. I never did understand why it happened. It seems heresy is only supported by unthinking, superstitious folk, those who have something to gain, or those who cry heresy when they see their power waning."

"I have to agree with you," Will says.

Bruce continues "I could never understand why the Bible could not have been made available in languages other than Latin. After all there were Greek and Hebrew versions long before Latin. Here in France we have a version of the Bible in our native language. It was translated by Jacques Lefevre and published in Antwerp in 1528. He did this using those new movable type printing presses. I believe Lefevre was a professor at the University of Paris, much like your uncle who started out at Oxford University.

Will is almost speechless at hearing Bruce's display of such knowledge and matter-of-fact acceptance of common language Bibles. When Bruce pauses to reflect on this situation and Will wonders what to say next, Bruce breaks the silence between them saying, "About two years ago, in 1535, another fellow, Pierre Robert Olivetan from

Picardy, France, and who was said to be a cousin of John Calvin, published a Bible. It was a revision of the Lefevre Bible. Olivetan's revisions used the best Hebrew and Greek references and he did his work in Switzerland. I would not be surprised if John Calvin were not working on one as well as I have heard he is closeted in Geneva on a mission of some sort. But I digress from what you have just told me. Yes, I can certainly understand why you have been traveling under an assumed name because your real name may be abhorrent to many in the Catholic faith and it might cause some well-meaning, but favor-seeking horse's ass to stir up trouble for you."

"Thank you for being so understanding. I never did want to deceive you, especially as we are brethren in the same fraternity of Apothecaries. There was a time I thought becoming an Apothecary was the most important thing in my life but meeting you and Racheal has shown me otherwise. Watching you and Racheal these many days I have been in your home, has made me realize that the most important thing in life is love and being loved, and it is all the better when tied to being part of a large and wonderful family."

Bruce then takes Will's hand, shakes it, smiles and says, "Well my brother Apothecary, if you have learned that lesson, then you have learned well. I wish you and Elke every happiness from here to whenever your time on this earth is over."

As the two men smile, Will chimes in, "Not to digress, but do you have any news of a ship that could get Elke and I across to England?"

"As a matter of fact, I do. I was hoping you might stay another week as I know of a perfect ship and its crew leaving for Brighton. But I also know of a smaller but adequate ship that is leaving for Brighton this coming Monday morning. If you and Elke are determined to leave in a few days I can arrange that. I also know Racheal and Elke have been talking and planning a wedding, but the danger of publishing banns, whether civil or church related, is quite real if you use the Tyndale name. You cannot use the Hutchins name as it would make the marriage invalid."

Will interjects "Before we say any more about this, let us invite our two women into our conversation and see what they have to say."

"Yes," says Bruce with a wry smile, "Your willingness to ask the ladies for input tells me you have every chance of being successful as a husband. Seeing a wife as a partner, and not an obedient and silent servant, will make your life incredibly happy."

Bruce then calls out to Racheal and Elke asking them to join the two men near the glowing embers in the fireplace. Once all four are seated Will and Bruce explain their reasoning for leaving Caen as soon as possible and why they should cancel the ladies hopes for a wedding ceremony and feast.

They then ask the women for their input to all this. Elke speaks first, "Will and I are hand-fasted, so I know his pledge to me is real. A few days more to arrange a wedding when we have such a long life ahead of us would not make a difference to me as I know where we are headed in our relationship. Will and I are also pledged to get the Apothecary's wagon to London. The longer we delay on that matter the more worried they will be that something bad has befallen us."

Will says," I would like to add to that how much we both have loved being here. We are dreading having to leave but that does not mean our friendship has to stop. Elke and I can always come back for a visit and you both can always come to visit us wherever we end up living."

Now Racheal, looking rather pensive, sits forward in her chair and with a somber face says, "I have genuinely enjoyed having the two of you in our home and Elke's help and her friendship have been a true God-sent blessing. However, I know now that a risk exists every day that you are here, and it will continue until that wagon is delivered. Whatever happens next, I cannot foretell. Perhaps instead of a wedding feast we can have a farewell feast to wish you Godspeed and safe passage back to London."

At that, the two women hug and embrace, and Will and Bruce shake hands and nod giving their tacit approval to the women's support and their agreement to move forward with their leaving Caen as soon as possible.

As they sit down again in front of the fireplace, Racheal says, "I have some English breakfast tea in a cupboard. Since the kettle is still hot why don't I make us all a nice cup of tea?"

Elke responds to Racheal's invitation. "my dear lady, a cup of tea would be most kind and generous. Let me help you make it. I believe the men have a little more to talk about."

Will looks at Bruce, once the ladies have left, and says, "I have another small imposition for you to consider. Is there any way I can have you put a letter on a ship sailing to Antwerp? Our original plans were for Elke to return to Antwerp and by now her mother and brother will be wondering what has happened to delay her. Her family had hoped we would have been able to put the wagon on a ship leaving either Calais, Dunkerque, or Dieppe. Their expectation is she would return home before now. Our decision to marry and our time in Caen has upset those original expectations. But please know I did receive permission from both her brother and mother to court this wonderful lady."

"If you have your letter ready, I can take it with me into town today. I know of several ships that regularly sail to Antwerp. Getting a letter to Antwerp will be quite easy."

"Thank you again, I really mean it, but not just for the letter but for all you and your wife have done for us."

"Glad to do it, after all it's the Christian thing to do… helping someone in need."

-Chapter 32-

The docks of Caen on the Orne River, where it opens onto the English Channel

It is early in the morning as Bruce, Racheal, Will and Elke watch a huge lifting crane latch onto the Apothecary wagon. It takes a team of six dock men to accomplish it. They watch in awe as the crane gently and slowly lifts the wagon onto the main deck of the ship. The sailors gently place it between two of the ship's three masts and throw a large tarpaulin over it. Then they secure it by expertly lashing it down with ropes. The men all nod their approval that the wagon will not move once they are out of the River Orne and onto the rough waters of the English Channel.

They next watch as one of the same crew walks Betsy up a long gangplank onto the same deck and place her into a special pen for her and a few other livestock. It seems the ship will ferry several cattle across the channel. The pen is in the middle of the ship as that is the part of the ship that moves up and down the least if the ship is buffeted by wind and waves.

Will looks at Bruce and both nod their approval at seeing a crewman leave Betsy with clean water and some hay. Then they watch as the crane is used to load the ship with about two dozen heavy wooden crates Will has no earthly idea of what they contain. Watching the sailors work causes Will to turn a little solemn knowing he will soon be leaving his new friends. He remembers how pleased he was on Saturday when Bruce came to him and said, "I closed my Apothecary for an hour after a sailor on that ship came to me for help with a stomachache that turned into a bad case of diarrhea."

"See that crew member in the blue overcoat?" Bruce asks Will. He is the one that came to see me and for whom I compounded some bismuth earth. While he was waiting he told me he was sailing to Brighton on this Monday morning, which was why he needed to be well.

Bruce looks about the dock to see if anyone is listening then says, "Its fortunate for us he mentioned how large the ship was that he was part of its crew. He also said it was quite often it took on livestock by use of a wide gangplank. The open pens on the deck to hold animals he said were permanent features. This sailor also mentioned he was part of a team assigned to using the ships lifting crane to haul aboard cargo too heavy to carry up a gang-plank."

"Did he mention anything else?" queried Will

"Yes, he told me he had consulted a priest about his diarrhea and was told his condition was divine retribution for some sinful act and to say the Lord's prayer fifteen times, give the priest some coins, and then it would go away."

"What did he do when told that?"

"He told me he was raised a God-fearing man and knew he had done no sinful acts. It did not make sense to him that his "bloody flux" was a "beast of the Lord"."

"How did you respond to that?" asks Will.

"I told the sailor of my experiences with sailors and they often get diarrhea , or the "bloody flux," as they call it, when a ship's provisions run out of wine, beer, ale, or cider and the crew drink water that has become tainted and dirty. So, I suggested to him to be sure the cook gives them drinking water that has been boiled first for at least five minutes. I also told him he should eat some bland food, such as cooked oatmeal until his innards got back to normal."

"You are a pretty smart guy; I am sure your advice was appreciated."

"Thanks, Will, but anyway, the sailor told me how grateful he was and asked me to come to the ship and meet the captain and inspect the cook's quarters for dirty water as several of the crew were suffering the same ailment as him. The captain was so grateful, he said he would grant me any favor within his power. And that is when I found out he was leaving for Brighton and that he would take you Elke, Betsy, and the wagon across for a few small English coins.

Will muses over how fortunate he and Elke were that Bruce has secured a ship that would take them to the port of Brighton. Will knows once they reach Brighton they would unload the same way but in reverse. Then with Betsy hitched to the wagon they would face a three-or-four-day trek to London.... that is barring any unseen events and unplanned delays...but "*si dieu le veut,*" he concluded. "God willing, we will make it."

"I cannot believe you trusted that sailor to help arrange all this with such a brief encounter, God really does work in mysterious ways."

"Not really," Bruce replies, "I have worked with so many folks in my line of work I have found the old French saying truly applies when people complain of an illness. That saying is "*Il ne faut pas prendre les enfants du bon Dieu pour des canards sauvages,* which in your language means "do not take God's children for wild ducks." What that implies is that a person should not judge people too hastily, as they truly may be trustworthy.

"Yes, judging people by how they look can be awkward and dangerous. Folks surely miss getting to know a lot of wonderful people that way. Just imagine if I were to think ill of all people who were short and stocky and hid their face behind a bushy mustache," Will says with a wide grin. Bruce returns a smile with, "Yes, and just you think about what would have happened if I had thrown you out of my apothecary as someone whose use of the French language is just dreadful."

"Ha!! Mon ami, that would be touché,' oui?"

Still waiting for passengers to board Will remembers fondly the other special event of the past weekend, a huge surprise feast on Sunday night in their honor. Racheal's friends and relatives all came to wish the couple a "bon voyage." "Godspeed" and a mumbling of other well-intentioned wishes in fractured English. But Will and Elke knew the comments were heartfelt, and genuine, and from people who thought of them as adopted family. All Will could utter that night was that everything was "fantastique."

Interrupting his reverie, the captain waves the few passengers aboard. An almost palpable silence fell the silence among the four of them. Suddenly the silence was broken by the ringing of the ship's bell.

Bruce looks at Elke and Will "That ship's bell signals to crew and passengers that it is time to set sail. You will notice some dock workers have started to untie the mooring lines and a couple of others have started towards the gangplank to remove it."

Again, the two couples look at each other in a wistful way with the two women near tears as Bruce speaks again, "I hate long goodbyes and you must get on board quickly or the ship will leave without you."

"How and why you came into our lives I will never know, "Bruce says with tears in his eyes, "but you both have become a true blessing, As we say in France, *Pourquoi les poules n'ont-elles pas de dent ?* In English it means why do chickens have no teeth? The answer is *les voies de Dieu sont impénétrables,* which you would know in English as something like "because God works in mysterious ways and this we can't explain." So, wondering why good friends come into our lives is a waste of time, we just need to accept that it happens and enjoy the time we are given with them."

"So, you are a philosopher as well as an apothecary." Elke says to Bruce

The two couples embrace, and Bruce looks at Will saying, "My friend we all need a purpose to live for, otherwise we are nothing but skin, blood and bones. Once you deliver your wagon I ask that you and Elke live for each other and keep each other happy. One never knows where one will find love but always be grateful that you have."

Racheal turns to Elke "It is my hope you raise a brood of children who grow to do their parents proud"

"I guess I get the final

word," Will says almost with a choke in his throat and teary eyes. "Rest assured that we will do everything we can to return to Caen to be with you once again."

"Non, mon ami. I get the final word," interjects Bruce, "Your wanting to return is admirable and most welcome, but remember God never tells us what he has in store for us we can only move forward on faith."

With another round of handshakes between the men, hugs, and kisses with Racheal, the two young folks race up the gangplank. They are on the ship just seconds before two dock workers hoist up the gangplank and the ship glides from the dock and turns towards the mouth of the Orne River where it will enter the English Channel. Elke and Will stand at the ships railing looking back and wave to Bruce and Racheal until they can see them no more.

Once they head out into the Channel Elke asks Will, "I have never been on such a large ship, how long will we be on this one?"

"Well, it's one hundred nautical miles across to Brighton. I believe we will be at sea until sometime mid-day tomorrow. At least we are on the last leg of this quest and its end is near. Once we get to Brighton it is about fifty miles or a little less, up to London. That distance is going to add at least two more days to our trip. Lots of folk from London come and go to Brighton in order to take in the sea air and get away from the stink of the city. The road we will take is well traveled and quite safe if we just mind our own business and don't draw attention."

Will puts his arm around Elke and whispers in her ear, "I just can't wait to introduce you to my family and to Humphrey. Once we get rid of this wagon and end my obligation to Humphrey we will travel to Hodthorpe where everyone will love you as much as I do, well maybe not as much."

"Oh Will, you are such a tease."

-Chapter 33-

the docks of Brighton on the Southern coast of England.

Tuesday 10 March 1537

The following morning the huge sailing ship glides alongside a dock in Brighton's Harbor. It has been an uneventful trip across the English Channel. Elke and Will had slept through the night in the wagon agreeing the air on deck was much preferable to the musty smells below deck... even though several cots had been set aside for passengers.

Will convinced Elke they should do this saying, "if anyone is thinking of snooping or disturbing our precious wagon then our being in it might deter their presence. If we keep a candle burning it would also be a deterrent. Besides if being under the stars is good enough for our horse then its good enough for me."

"That's fine by me," Elke responds but she could tell Will just wanted to snuggle with her in the close confines of the wagon. She also knew he was not the type to blatantly spurt out his desires in a place where anyone could overhear them.

The following morning, they to the sound of the crew shouting orders. As they left their wagon they found themselves alongside a dock in Brighton. As the crew fastened down the ship to the dock Will and Elke watched in fascination as a crew member slowly and confidently walked Betsy out of her deck-pen, down the same wide wooden gangplank, and tied her up to a post on the dock.

"It would seem that horse is none-the-worse for wear and endured the motion of the ship. Our crossing from France to England did not seem too rough at all.," Elke says to Will.

"Yes, we were fortunate the seas were not bad. Now just watch as that huge lifting crane swings its long arm over our wagon and picks it up as if it were light as a feather".

"That device is quite remarkable. How long will it take 'till we can hitch up our horse and get on the road to London?"

"It should not take too long now, first a harbor master will come and check all cargo hoisted onto the dock. Then a customs inspector will look for contraband and assess any import duty or tax. We will then have to comply with whatever they say but fortunately I have all the papers and coinage they may require."

Will pauses the whispers to Elke, "Have faith in Humphrey Monmouth. He has planned for everything. As one of England's biggest cloth merchants he should jolly well know how to bring foreign merchandise into this country."

A few minutes later two rather official looking men stride out of the office building at the end of the dock. They both are wearing what appear to be epaulets on their shirt and short-billed caps that match the color of their shirts.

Will looks at Elke saying, "They must be the custom officials. I am getting off this ship to meet them... before they poke around too much examining our wagon. Please stay here and watch me. When I wave to you that all is right, please come in a hurry. I want to leave quickly and before we draw attention."

"Yes, I understand," says Elke, "but be safe and remember they may be the type of officials who love swagger and exert their power if you make them angry."

"Not to worry, I can be polite when I have to... but just keep watching 'til I wave for you to come."

Will walks down the gangplank and over to where the ship's cargo and his wagon are staged. He walks up to the two men," Good Morning Gentlemen, is there some way I can be of help?"

"Yaw," says the older and portlier of the two with a broad country accent, "Whose wagon is this? Do you know for what it is intended? What is inside it?"

"Yes, I do Sir. My name is Will Hutchins. I am a representative of the London Society of Apothecaries. I have been entrusted to travel to Antwerp Belgium as their official representative to retrieve this wagon. They have commissioned it to be a mobile apothecary so they can take it to small towns and rural areas devoid an apothecary. Their wish is to bring into those areas much needed medicines, expertly made, and priced fairly. Do you recall when one hundred years ago the Black Plague nearly wiped out a third of England?

The two customs men say in unison, "We don't be that old!"

"Well that was a time when all poor souls, even those who could afford medicines, could not get any, especially those in rural areas. Thus, the London Society of Apothecary's have seen a need and have deemed it their duty to bring their medical skills to the poor and to any area that may need them."

"Is that so?

Yes, and here, see, …these are the papers to verify my credentials and what this wagon contains by way of imported medications. Plus, I have the coinage to pay any tariffs you may impose. Will that be all right? I assure you I have nothing to hide."

"That depends," says the second official who is a little shorter but only slightly less portly, "Let me examine your papers and let us both have a look inside the wagon."

"That will not be a problem." says Will as a bead of perspiration starts to form on his forehead. He steps to the rear of the wagon.

Dropping down the wagon's tailgate and setting up its compounding table and utensils, Will turns to the officers and says, "Here let me show you how it all works. Please note all these drawers are labelled with the names of the agents, herbs, minerals, and plants within. Look also at this built-in table and storage drawers. They will soon contain English tools for compounding. See also how the wagon can act as a caravan offering a person comfortable sleep… or even two if they don't mind being a little crowded."

As the officials' nod, Will grabs their attention by stating in a matter of fact tone, "Now see how, for security reasons all drawers are made facing inward. You may open as many drawers as you like but you will find all the herbs and medicinal agents within match the list on the manifest I have before you."

The two men continue to snoop and open and close a few drawers. Will holds his breath hoping they do not accidently open one of the false panels and set some Bibles tumbling out. After a few minutes one of the men says, "This wagon seems very well-made what kind of wood has been used to construct it?

"Why do you ask? says Will

The craftmanship is excellent and I believe it is made from imported wood. If this is imported wood, there is a heavy tax on wood brought in from other countries."

"Yes, I am sure there is, but I hate to disappoint you. The wagon is made of is good English oak and some English walnut. This wood and the plans were sent to Europe about a year ago, then seasoned there by wonderful

Belgian craftsmen before they constructed it using English drawn plans. In reality I am expatriating all the wood you see before you."

Will breathes a little easier as one of the official replies, "Well, that's good to know as taxes on imported wood are quite heavy. I believe what you have told us, this wagon is for a work of charity. Let me see the papers you have listing all the materials you have brought."

After the two officials confer for a few minutes they turn to face Will who asks them "What are the tariffs going to be on all the medicines on the list?"

"As your papers seem in order we don't think we need to impound your wagon and tear it all apart looking for contraband. Apothecaries are known to be honorable and we have much more pressing matters to attend to. Thus, we believe eight English pounds, five shillings and six pence should cover your tariffs."

"That's more than fair. The Worshipful London Society of Apothecaries expected it to be near that amount and have given me adequate funds to pay it. Here it is in full."

Will watches the men put his coins in their satchel, then turns to them asking, "Now, with that official business done may I trouble you for a receipt, just to keep the accounting straight upon my return to London.

"That can be arranged. You can pick it up at the Customs House at the end of this pier when you leave the

Harbor. Since it is getting late in the day you might want to stay another night before heading up to London. There is an area for caravans on the beaches to your left as you go past these piers. Lots of people come and stay there in wagons or caravans. They see it as a means to enjoy a holiday away from their work and the smells of London."

"Thanks for the suggestion. I will do that. I believe I do need a day in sunshine and some additional rest. A good meal of your local seafood would be refreshing as my channel crossing has made me a bit queasy."

With that, the two officials walk back to their office building at the end of the pier giving Will the opportunity to wave at Elke and beckon her to hurry. They retrieve Betsy, connect her traces, and harness, and start down the long wooden Harbor onto the cobbled streets of Brighton.

Will tells Elke what transpired with the two customs officials. "Will, why are you not stopping to pick up that official receipt for the tariffs? Are you really thinking about camping here for another night before heading to London?"

"No, my dear we are not stopping nor staying here. The demeanor of those two officials was such I did not completely trust them. They did not do a thorough search of the wagon. They did not ask about Betsy the horse. As she is imported livestock there would also be a tax placed on her. Additionally, their asking me to stay the night seemed like an opportunity for either them, or some local brigands to waylay us. I think it best if we put as much distance between us and this harbor as fast as we can."

"I can understand your reasoning. I wondered as I watched the proceeding from the ships rail if the two were asking for a bribe to let you through. Did you think of that?"

"I was prepared for anything they might ask, but my heart was in my mouth the whole time wondering if they were truly honest folk. If they were truly honest they would have made more than a casual look about the wagon. Besides, we do not know what scallywags we may encounter on the road, so the sooner we get this trip done and over with, the better I will feel. They were also well overdue for their yearly bath. You would think living near the ocean they would bathe in it once in a while. They really stank to high heaven and I could not shake the feeling they may have been trouble."

"Heaven's above, Will, you are scaring me with such talk."

Will drives the horse to the edge of town and then with Betsy at a brisk walk, points her north towards London.

-Chapter 34-

Thursday, 11 March 1537

the estate of Henry Monmouth, London England

   Two days after leaving Brighton, Will and Elke arrive at the outskirts of London. They had not camped the first night and took turns driving Betsy through the night. They had both decided pushing on would bring them closer to finishing their quest as they were on a road well-lit by a moon and one that seemed pretty safe. At the end of the second day they stopped earlier than usual, at wayside pull-in. It had several families vacationing and who were staying overnight. It relieved and comforted Will and Elke to see most campers were families with children. Once they were settled Will noticed a small child with a cut on his hand from a nearby thorn bush. After he tended to the child the parents came over and expressed their gratitude and asked the pair to share in their dinner of boiled beef, potatoes, turnips, onions, and carrots.

The next morning the wagons at the campsite had left early. Will and Elke heard nothing and slept soundly through all the departures. Waking up mid-morning Elke and Will shared a hastily prepared dish of porridge before setting out again in a northerly direction towards London. About five hours later, as they rounded a corner going over the brow of a hill on their two-lane dirt road Elke was overcome with awe as she sees the biggest city she has ever encountered spread out before her.

Will notices her unblinking wide-eyed stare "In just a few more minutes you will be able to smell the stench raised when one hundred and twenty thousand people live close together. These same folks have no compunction about living in a dirty town wherein disease, miasmas, urine, feces, fleas, flies, rats, and other vermin are more populous than its people.

"Goodness me and Saints alive!" exclaims Elke, "Is it really that bad?"

"Well to me it is. I will drive Betsy in a route to avoid some of the areas where filth is rampant. Oh, remember too that London has no laws governing prostitution nor use of alcohol. I will have to be on guard to make sure some drunken sod or unsavory character doesn't approach the prettiest girl in the city."

"Oh, my heavens above, I had no idea this great city of worldly commerce was so filthy, as for its other vices, remember that all cities have unsavory men and behaviors, even the town where my brother and I were raised," Elke says.

"Well, it's a lot cleaner and healthier if one can live outside London. But only people with any wealth can afford to do so. But even Humphrey Monmouth with all his wealth finds bathing a luxury and hot water costly."

After a short while Will says to Elke "This wagon is sure to attract some curious passersby. The ones to really watch out for are the church officials. They are more powerful than the King and his city government officials. The Church believes clerics are subject only to church law and can only be tried by church officials. Thus, another reason Protestantism is on the rise is because the church has a voracious appetite for funds and for avoiding secular law and convention."

About two hours later Will pulls the wagon up to the front of Drapers Hall. He jumps down enters the Hall and inquiries about the presence of Humphrey Monmouth from a butler. Will is told, "Humphrey has been staying at home the past few days, likely due to a recurrence of an old illness."

After hearing that Humphrey is not at the Draper's Guild Hall, Will returns to Elke and asks, "What do you think we should do? The Society of Apothecaries Hall is nearby but the Monmouth Estate is about another hour away?"

"My best thought would be to go to the Monmouth Estate. Your uncle's Bibles are our first priority. Perhaps Humphrey will have storage there. The Society of

Apothecaries can always wait another day for their wagon, after all they have waited long enough as it is. Besides, we have to think of security for both. Having come across some unsavory looking characters as we crossed London I have some worries about who may be lurking about and watching where we park this wagon.." Elke says.

"I agree, Let us head to Monmouth's estate. It is near the edge of the city …about an hour away. It also a place where the air is definitely fresher."

About an hour later they pass through the gates of the Monmouth estate. As they get near the front of the driveway the wagon and horse make a crunching noise on the gravel and the driving pad under the mansion's porte-cochere. As they halt Betsy near the ornate front door, it flies open and Humphrey Monmouth and Will's parents rush out to greet them.

"Great Saints above," exclaims the startled Will, "I never expected to see you here. Mother and Father what brought you here? Has something bad happened back home?''

Before they can answer, Will's two sisters also rush out. They climb up onto the wagon and hug and kiss his cheek. Then the younger says "We are so happy you are here. Are you coming home to Hodthorpe?"

Before Will can answer them they notice Elke and in unison say, "Who is this bonny lass?"

Will raises his hand, as if asking for silence, then he looks down at his parents, his two beaming sisters, and Humphrey. He rises from his seat and says, "I want you all to meet Elke DeBergdorf. We met while I was in Europe. We have fallen in love. I have asked for her hand in marriage and have the blessing of her family. We are hand-fasted, and now we need your blessing and that of the church."

"Well, I'll be a ...", says Will's father

"Hoorah for you both,", say the sisters in unison.

"Looks like you got more than just Bibles, a wagon, and medicines on this trip," says Humphrey stoically but with a twinkle as he looks at Elke.

"Welcome to the family, Elke. I can hardly wait till you give us grandchildren. I know the both of you will be incredibly happy. I am so proud of Will and what he has done. I trust him to have chosen wisely and to genuinely love you. You are a beautiful girl" Will's mother blubbers as she brushes back some tears.

"How on God's green earth did you come to be here?" Will asks facing his parents.

Humphrey answers instead, "I sent a letter with coach fare to Hodthorpe. The letter asked your parents to come and celebrate your return. Once I received a letter from Antwerp saying you were heading south to either Calais or as far as Caen, I knew about what it would take, in time and effort, for you to get here. That letter also convinced me I had chosen the right person to recover your uncle's Bibles. Incidentally a second note came with your letter. It was from Elke's brother. In it Ahren said Elke was accompanying you as far as Calais or even Caen. He also said that you both were in love and betrothed…through hand-fasting. We did not expect her to come all the way to London."

Humphrey reaches up and takes Elke by the hand saying, "Now, you have alighted from that hard seat wagon, let us all go inside to some comfortable seating. There has been some great food prepared for you arrival. Besides, we all want to hear about your adventures. Will, I can see for sure that your family wants to get to know Elke a lot better."

Once the group gathered in Monmouth's sumptuous dining room they spend the next several hours listening to Will and Elke talk about their relationship and how it started from their   first flirtation and banter when Will arrived in Antwerp's Grote Markt, and to how quickly it blossomed into the realization that they were in love.

After they had eaten Will explained to his parents how Humphrey Monmouth prepared him, how the London Guild of Apothecaries trusted him to return with their valuable wagon, and especially what it meant to him to have Cyril Blackham and Mr. Miller present at his induction ceremony as a master Apothecary. Will also showed some emotion when he told his parents about meeting Brother Gregory and the tragic end of the Carthusian Monks.

Will's parents pay rapt attention as Will recounts his fist voyage on a ship, his impressions of Antwerp and the privilege he was given to attend the Paracelsus lectures.

Monmouth and his parents also listen attentively to a shorter version of why the pair had travelled from Antwerp to Calais then past Dunkerque and Dieppe and onto Caen. This gave them a chance to regale how fortunate they were to meet the Siefert Family in Caen and all that had been done by a fellow Apothecary to get them across the English Channel to Brighton. From Brighten Will described their journey as "an easy stroll through the woods up to London."

Will had surmised that his parents would want to know everything that happened since he left Hodthorpe, so before they sat down together Will pulled Elke aside and asked, "I think it best that any details of the encounter with ruffians in the Antwerp alley, the bully on the road to Calais, and the deadly altercation with Gagnon are details best left unsaid. They would only upset my mother to think either of us were in danger. Do you agree?"

"Oh yes, definitely I agree. It's best to let those sleeping dogs lie."

After much good food and questioning Will's mother and his sisters turn to Elke, pull her aside and Will's mother says "Let the menfolk continue to talk while we women retire and get to know each other"

As Elke stands up Will's mother suggests, "Perhaps we should move into the library across the hallway. It is quiet in there. Is that all right with you Elke? I can tell you are a lovely lass and believe you will make my Will a happy man. It's obvious he is devoted to you."

Once they are seated across the hall away from the men, Will's mother looks at Elke and says, "My Christian name is Constance. Only Will and my daughters call me "mother" I would hope in time you may do the same but what I really want is for you to soon be calling me Grandmother."

Across the hall, Humphrey Monmouth says, "While there is still light outside, I have a servant arranged to stable your horse and store the wagon in the barn. It is behind my manor house. The wagon's contents will be safe there until I retrieve your uncle's Bibles.

"Thank you for doing that,'", says Will as his father looks on with a smile.

Humphrey continues," Tomorrow we will drive the wagon to the Apothecary's Guild Hall. They will be as pleased as punch to know its finally home. I can tell it's well-made and has been well-taken care of."

"Again, my thanks," says Will, "I am so grateful I accepted the challenge. I never dreamed it would lead to my returning with a wife.'

"Again, you are most welcome. I am happy I played a part in your finding more than what was intended. Elke is obviously smart and intelligent girl and also very pretty. Now! Back to business. I have heard a rumor, which is... the Apothecary Guild's officers want to reward your herculean effort to bring them their prized wagon."

"Good Heaven's above!," exclaims Will, "I have no need of a reward. My mother said this was an honorable task. I admit I had some trepidation about accepting it. Now I know it was part of God's design to bring me out of my comfortable shell and show that with faith in him and the mettle of hard work and perseverance that Tyndale folk are known for that I would be successful."

"That's nicely put Will, but now that your mission is over is there something I can do for you?" asks Monmouth

"There' s nothing that I need but a good night's sleep and preferably on a soft bed. However, Elke and I want to get married. We need to have Church Banns published so we can. How do we do that? Can we do it sooner rather than later?"

"That's not a problem for me," Will's father interjects, "Just tell me when and where and I will take care of it."

"Father, if you and mother are going back to Hodthorpe soon, Elke and I could follow shortly after all our affairs are done in London. I would like to get married in St. Peters Parish Church where I was baptized. Elke has agreed to this. And I hasten to add she is a person of faith and a Protestant. When are you going back to Hodthorpe?"

"We already have tickets for a coach to take us back home. The coach leaves two mornings hence. We will go happy knowing you are safe."

"It would be great if we could have our wedding on a Sunday about a month from now. Elke and I will come to Hodthorpe as soon as all business matters are finished here in London. I want to introduce her to all my friends, and especially Cyril Blackham."

"Son, have you decided on where you two will live? What do you think you will do to support a home and wife once you are married?"

"Father, Elke and I did speak about these things while on the roads and ship but, with all the excitement in our journey, we thought it best to wait for quieter times before making any firm commitments, other than our desire to marry. We do have options and London has some possibilities, but we are not sure we want a life here. But London does offers quick and easy transport for Elke to visit her family. However, as of today I have no work prospects in London."

Well, son, I truly am proud of what you have accomplished. I know your mother and sisters are as well. Thus, whatever you and Elke decide to do with your lives, we will support those decisions."

"Thanks Father, your support means more than you will never know."

Monmouth picks up the conversation again "Gentlemen, this has been an exciting day indeed. A son has returned, a new member of a family has been introduced, and two wonderful treasures have been brought to England. I suggest we all retire for the evening with a prayer that life ahead for our young couple be travelled on a road smoother than the one that brought them here."

-Chapter 35-

Early Friday Morning, March 12, 1537

The Monmouth Manor House, London

Will awakens early the next morning. He is not totally refreshed but slept alone out of propriety and social custom. Elke occupied a room with single beds, one each for Will's two sisters and one for her. Once Will dressed he left the manor to attend to Betsy. He knew from a servant she would be stabled in the large barn.

Once he reaches the barn's front door Will is startled to hear voices, especially since it is so early. Will shouts gruffly through the door, asking "Who is in there?"

He is hoping it may startle any ruffians or robbers who saw Betsy and the wagon on the streets and followed them hoping to steal some of its cargo.

"It's only us," a boy's voice cries out, "Robert and Michael, the stable boys, Master Monmouth asked us to rise early and hitch one of his best draft horses to this wagon. We did not want to disturb anyone. If you are Monmouth's guest you will see your horse is alone in the stall to your left."

Looking a bit sheepish at almost scaring himself and the two boys, Will enters to find them working at the task set before them. "Pardon my brusque interruption, I am Will Tyndall a guest of Humphrey Monmouth, I had not expected folks would be out and about doing chores before breakfast".

"No harm there, said Robert, "Master Monmouth often asks for things to be done at strange hours."

"Yes, I can understand that. I will leave you alone and tend to Betsy."

A few minutes later Monmouth enters the stables and with him is a man Will has never met. Monmouth sees Will and offers a cherry voice, "Good Morning Will. My but you are up early. I would like you to meet my trusted friend and colleague Gerry Barnes. Once the boys are through hitching one of my horses to the Apothecary Guild's wagon, Mr. Barnes will drive it to London. The Guild will take possession of it there. I know they are excited as it's been a long time since they first conceived of it."

"Uh! Nice to meet you", states Will offering his hand

After a hearty handshake, Gerry states, "Mr. Monmouth told me about you. I am happy we have met. You have done the Guild a huge service."

"Well, I was happy to do it."

Monmouth says, "You will notice my boys have left your horse in its stable. Its tired and I have several horses here. The one being hitched now belongs to the Guild. This horse might as well get used to pulling that beautiful traveling apothecary."

Will watches the man attach his harness and traces and is interrupted again by Monmouth who says, "Later this morning, you, I, my wife, Elke, and your parents will ride into London in my carriage. We will witness the official acceptance ceremony of the wagon and then afterward there is to be a reception in your honor for bringing it here. You may be asked to say a few words and my advice is… the fewer words the better…if you catch my drift."

"Assuredly."

"Since that's settled let us walk back to the dining room and start the day with a hearty breakfast. I am sure others are up and wanting to see what lies ahead on this fine day in England."

As they walk back to the house, Will drops back and motions to Monmouth to attend to his whisper, "I can't help but wonder, when and how are my uncle's Bibles going to be removed from that wagon?"

"Don't fret my boy. They were removed last night while everyone slept. I had a three-person crew do it. They had plans of the wagon's construction and knew how to open its secret compartments. All they needed was my word the barn was devoid of human eyes so they could remove the Bibles and take them to a secure place. Those Bibles will start to journey throughout England by when we finish breakfast."

"Humphrey, you never cease to amaze me." Will smiles.

When the Monmouth and Tyndale families are seated breakfast is served and it is eaten in silence. Afterwords, Monmouth rises and states "Today we all are invited to the Guild House of the Worshipful Society of Apothecaries to witness their acceptance of the traveling apothecary. The Guild members have a few details of what Will and Elke have done to get it here. I can only guess that Will is going to be asked to state a few words about his journey to help them. Newspaper folk will be there so Will may be quoted in one of their daily or weekly broadsheets."

Elke, who is absolutely delighted at the invitation blurts out, "Oh yes, Will, how nice of them to give you an honor. Let us all go."

Before Will can answer her Monmouth says. "Will it really is a special occasion. Since I am a cloth merchant, I have some finery here for both Elke and you to wear. These clothes you may freely take with you to Hodthorpe. I trust you will find them suitable wear for your wedding."

-Chapter 36-

Friday evening, March 12, 1537
the Guild Hall of the Worshipful Society of Apothecaries.

Elke, Will, Monmouth and his wife and children, plus Will's parents and his sisters, are shown to seats on a platform outside the front entrance of the Guild Hall. There are about ten other dignitaries on the platform. Will assumes they are officers of the Guild. About fifty people mill around on the street in front of the platform wondering what is about to happen. A blare from a trumpet catches everyone's attention, then the horse Will had seen earlier in Monmouth's barn walks out from around a corner pulling the wagon Will brought from Antwerp.

Will notices the driver is the same Mr. Barnes whom he met earlier. The driver stops the horse in front of them. The horse is festooned with flowers and the wagon is decorated in colorful red, white, and blue ribbon. The Guild's coat of arms is attached to its rear. The Guild's top officer stands and explains to the crowd what the purpose of the wagon is and as he does Will notices two men in the crowd making sketches and writing notes.

Then the Guild official says, "All those here who are members of the Guild are asked to join us inside for refreshment."

Will is a little non plussed by this short ceremony, so on the way into the Guild Hall, he comments to Monmouth, "I thought this event would be bigger, given all that has happened."

"Not to worry." Monmouth responds, "You missed the point here. This was not an event for London folk or Guild members. It was an event to create publicity and get the story of the traveling apothecary to outlying villages. Did you notice a couple of folks scribbling and sketching?"

"Why, Yes I did. Who were they?"

"They were members of the London Daily Times. They made a sketch of all on the viewing stand with the horse and wagon in front. They will write for their newspapers which will be picked up by outlying papers and be spread to many other towns throughout England."

"Well than, I was thinking I would be asked to say something but given all that's happened I realize a simple thanks for the opportunity to be of service to a worthy cause would not be news at all."

"You have the right perspective, my' lad," Monmouth says, "So now, let us go inside the Guild Hall where a sumptuous feast has been prepared. A few hundred Guild members will want to shake your hand and thank you. They will absolutely swoon over Elke. Your mother and father will leave here proud in how they raised you to be the good man you have become"

Following the Guild's sumptuous feast Will is able to shake hands with almost everyone.. Several officers and members of the Guild spoke to him of their understanding of the expense and effort it took to get their travelling apothecary. But Will thought it best to simply say he was proud to do it and turn their attention to the notes he brought back from the Paracelsus lectures and how the knowledge in those notes would benefit many.

While a desert of flaming brandy-soaked fruit pudding was being passed around Will was called to a podium and presented with a life-time membership in the guild followed by a rousing round of Huzzah! Huzzah! Huzzah!

Still Will had not been asked to speak so he sat down with his family and Elke to eat his flaming pudding.

Once the festivities were over a man came to Will and whispered, "Master Tyndale, the Grand Master of the Guild would like to see you in his chambers."

Will excused himself from the table and was escorted into the chambers of the Grand Master. There he was introduced to the Guild's other officers. The Grand Master then asked for silence, tuned to Will and said, "Master Tyndale, it is an honor for me to present you with this purse. Please accept this as a gift of our gratitude as it is little indeed that we can offer as compensation for all you have done on our behalf and at peril to yourself. We will forever be grateful for the effort it took to bring our members their special traveling wagon and all the herbs and other medicinal agents in it. Thank You."

Will looks around the room, and simply says," It was an honor and I thank you. This purse will help my wife-to-be and I start our marriage."

A second officer speaks up, who Will knows is the Secretary of the Guild. "Master Tyndale, while we appreciate your bringing us the wagon we appreciate even more the notes you have shared from the Paracelsus lectures. To us this new knowledge is a gift without measure. Because of your skills we have information that will benefit many. You have a great gift for teaching. The clarity of your notes and of Paracelsus's work is now available to anyone with half an eye to see and a brain to think. As you are an Apothecary yourself you know the scourge that affects most of London today is syphilis. The mercury pills we will be able to make from the chemicals hidden in that wagon will benefit countless people. So, again thank you for all you have done to help so many."

Will is then escorted back to his table and shares what has just transpired with Elke and his parents. Monmouth just sits and listens and smiles without a word.

Later that evening as they all ride back to the Monmouth Estates, Will breaks the silence saying, "I think I know what I will do with this leather pouch and the coins inside it."

"And I pray Dear Boy, what might that be?" asks Monmouth as Elke looks on in silence.

"Well because of you I have been given a chance to figure out why I have been put on this earth. Now I have the means to accomplish this. As Bruce Seifert said to me, God does work in mysterious ways, we just have to accept them. So, I am going to take this purse and give it to Cyril Blackham. It will cover most of the price he has asked in selling me his apothecary. That way I will not be a burden to anybody in the family and Elke and I can start our new lives and be virtually free of any debt. What do you think of that?

"That sounds like a great plan to me," says Humphrey

And I agree...should anybody be asking," echoes Elke.

The rest of their ride home is done in silence.

-Chapter 37-

Saturday March 13, 1537

The Overland Stage Station

The morning following the Guild Hall festivities, Humphrey has his coach hitched and ready to drive Will, Elke, his parents, and sisters to the Overland Stage Line Station. It is the same one Will arrived on his trip to London from Hodthorpe several months before.

As the local station master loads their luggage onto the stagecoach, Humphrey looks at Will and Elke saying to both, "I wish you every good success in life. I can tell you care for each other deeply. I also cannot thank you enough for what you have endured and done to help so many. You will likely never know the blessing you have been."

Humphrey pauses to look around to see if they are out of earshot of anyone close by and says to them in a hushed voice, "Now before we say our final goodbyes, and before this coach loads its other passengers, I have to say this. I have received word from Antwerp from a trusted merchant colleague. It is rumored there that Raemon Gagnon has left town, likely on the news his pal deKlerk, was arrested for taking bribes and stealing. Henry Phillips has also left Antwerp. Phillips went to Rome to plead his case before the Pope but was shunned. He will likely die a pauper as his underhanded dealings ruined his reputation in Europe as well as England. Also, you should know that Sir Thomas More, who was your uncle's bitterest enemy has also been arrested. His trial is likely to be early in July and more than likely it will end with his execution."

Humphrey closes the stagecoach door as two more passengers arrive. He steps backward to let the coach pass where upon the coach driver whistles his four-horse team onto the road taking Elke, Will and Will's family back to Hodthorpe.

-Chapter 38-

Sunday 9 May 1537

The village of Hodthorpe

To say that the Hodthorpe townsfolk had missed one of their favorite sons would be an understatement. Nearly all the town's women and men rejoiced upon Will's return knowing he would settle in their town as its Apothecary. The town women were eager to meet Elke whom they welcomed as if she were a returning sister. Elke especially was taken with Will's childhood friends, Robert, Richard and even Audrey... who could not say enough about Will's skills as a healer and how they had all been best chums since they were children?

When Elke met Cyril Blackham, she knew right away the friendship between Will and Cyril was based on the profound respect each had for the other. Within a few days the Banns were published outside the door of St. Peters Church for all to witness.

Now it was time for them to witness their wedding. Will's mother, aunts, uncles, cousins, and sisters included Elke in as much of the preparations as they could. Every night she declared to Will or her new mother-in- law, "I can't believe how welcome everyone has made me feel. I truly am comfortable with how I have been accepted as the newest member of the family."

When Will responded to her observation he grinned "If you feel that now, after such little time, just wait until you present them with a baby."

As wedding preparations moved forward Will spent more time with Cyril Blackham. He returned to his love of being a working apothecary with gusto. Whenever the day's activities slowed he would ask Cyril questions such as, "What can I be doing to make the transition to proprietor go smoothly?" or "Where do I get better quality herbs and spices? or "What do I do if a customer has no money to pay for a medicine but is desperately ill?" or "How do I best mark-up products so it produces coin to cover expenses and provide a living wage and also pay off my debt to you?"

Cyril is patient with Will and answers all his questions sincerely saying, "Will you have a great sense for understanding how a business works. I know you will apply it as sensibly as you apply your skills as a healer. Just have more faith in yourself."

Cyril suspects Will's nervousness has more to do about stepping into the unknown realms of holy matrimony than about running an apothecary he has been part of for over seven years Elke spends the night before her wedding in the home of Will's Aunt. Will's family still practices the belief that seeing the bride on the day before the actual wedding ceremony was an omen of bad luck.

Will spends the evening before his wedding with his father, uncles, male cousins, friends Richard and Robert, and of course Cyril, imbibing in copious amounts of ale and wine and telling ribald tales, fueled mostly with reading excerpts from Geoffrey Chaucer's Canterbury Tales. Chaucer's work was published almost 40 years prior using middle English. They raised their eyebrows, but only slightly, when Cyril presented his copy before the group but belly-laughed and guffawed when most of its twenty-four ribald stories were read aloud. Will knew the Canterbury Tales were for King Richard's court in 1397 but how Cyril had obtained a rare copy remained a secret in spite of the questioning, bantering, and tongues loosed by ale. By the time, this entertainment was through it was a general consensus Cyril had used his Apothecary skills to heal someone with wealth and position and this was his payment for services rendered.

The morning of the wedding was warm and full of sunshine. Will wore the clothes Humphrey had given him back in London, as did Elke, plus a veil worn by Will's mother when she married. Its blue color complimented Elke's eyes and complexion. Her hair and veil were kept in place by a cordage of braided lavender. Elke carried a bridal bouquet made up of some yellow and purple bulbs that just flowered and were barely poking up out of the ground after a long winter…but mostly her bouquet was created to help ward of any bad smells of some unwashed townsfolk.

Will asked his childhood friend Robert to be his best man, Then, as all looked on and as the bride and groom stood in front of the church's alter the priest intoned the sacred words that united them as man and wife… "until death doth them part."

Halfway through the ceremony Will noticed Elke about to lose her composure and whispers to her, "Are you going to be alright Elke?"

"Oh yes, and assuredly so, my dear husband. it's just that I am so happy."

"From here on, and until we leave this earth, I will do everything I can to add to your happiness… because …you have truly won my heart and I know that I truly love you."

Then taking a cue from Elke's silence the parish priest stated, "Will, you may now kiss your bride".

Elke blushes as Will lifts her veil and presses his lips onto hers amid a rousing cheer from those assembled to watch the ceremony..

Once the all-to short ceremony ended, everyone left the sanctuary for a traditional nuptial feast. Most townsfolk had come to the church to meet the newest couple about to settle into their village. However, it was suspected some of the townsfolk were simply there to eat and drink the honeyed mead about to be served.

As Elke and Will left the church and stepped gingerly into the bright sunlight, they found themselves ducking and weaving in order to reach the hall across the courtyard. It was in this community hall where the wedding feast was to be served. As was the local custom, they were pelted with barley as they rushed to the hall.

The wedding feast was prepared by many Will recognized as patrons of the Blackham Apothecary. The Hall had long tables set up around the room with benches for the guests to sit on. Every few feet on the tables were three-handled drinking mugs… to facilitate the sharing of wine and ale… which also seemed in abundance. Will and Elke were ushered to a smaller table near the front of the room and were given the first course of the feast...a small bowl of "frumentary "or spiced porridge.

The second course was local game, of either roasted wild hog, roasted swan, a leg of venison, or local caught fish. These were served alongside boiled vegetables and dried fruit and berries. For a desert, several women had brought suet cake or a fruit pie, or locally sourced nuts. Of course, the food was either eaten with fingers or splayed on a wooden trencher and picked at with the single bladed knife which most men wore at their waist.

Throughout the meal Will could only marvel at the merriment and feel gratitude for all the well wishes being shown to him and Elke and the obvious respect shown for the entire the Tyndale family.

Fortunately, there was plenty of honeyed mead, wine, and ale for all.

At one-point Will notices his father sitting rather pensively, obviously deep in thought. As Will walks over to his father, his father lifted his head and asks, "What can I help you with, Son?"

"Nothing really," responds Will, "but I saw you alone and thought you were deep in thought when you should be enjoying this special day. We have so many friends and family here and these events do not happen often. But before I forget, I really want to thank you and mother for you have done to make this day possible and especially for welcoming Elke so warmly into our family."

"We all think she is a very lovely and special girl who will make you a wonderful wife. Now that you are settling here we pray you both will be happy and successful and meet your mother's wish to bless us with many grandchildren."

"It's a little too soon to think of grandchildren, father, but who knows I have learned the Lord does work in mysterious ways. Before I forget, and before Elke and I go off on our honeymoon, I do want to thank you for something you have taught me. I am the same man who left Hodthorpe several months ago and the values and work ethic that you taught helped me immensely on the quest I undertook for Humphrey Monmouth. It made me confident, improved my decision making and caused me to discover what I need to be a happy person....to find and to share love with a good woman as I have seen it all my life between you and Mother.

"Thanks for saying that my son, Monmouth told us why you were chosen to undertake the task he set before you. He wanted someone who was genuine, unpretentious, trusted, reliable, and morally sound. He then said he found those qualities in you by talking to townspeople, Cyril Blackham, and your Uncle Arthur. He then said he was looking for someone who was, as Uncle Will translated from Gospel of Mathew and who fit the remarks Jesus used in his Sermon on the Mount, to describe his disciples as being the "salt of the earth." You wear that description well and I am proud of you, my son. Now it is time for you to truly live your dreams.

Historical Notes:

This story in context:

During the 1500's life in England was fraught with danger and incivility caused by:

a) excessive and abusive lifestyles within the Tudor monarchy, b) religious and political intrigue surrounding the Protestant Reformation, c) opposition to the Reformation by the Church of Rome, and d) widespread corruption within the local catholic hierarchy.

While a common sport during medieval times was "heretic hunting" it was also a time that brought widespread change in the arts, philosophy, government, economics, literature, science, and medicine not only in England but throughout Europe.

The Protestant Reformation created new ways for men and women to think; as moral beings, as children of a loving God, and what it takes to enter the Kingdom of Heaven. The Reformation was fueled by people looking for new truths applying reasoning, peaceful means, innate intellect, and friendly civility. What they wanted to avoid were obstructions to those truths caused by self-serving government and religious minions…both of which they saw abuse their authority, toss aside traditions of servitude, and apply false piety in order to accumulate power, wealth, or some other self-serving end.

While this novel is based in an important time period it **still is one of pure fiction.** However, some characters in this story did exist and were part of the life of William Tyndale However it is this author's imagination that introduces them into his fictional story of Will Tyndale i.e.: (Will Hutchins) and others mentioned following the death of William Tyndale.

William Tyndale (1494-1536)

During most of Reformation the Bible was only in the hands of a few wealthy merchants, even fewer clergy, and only available in Latin. It took the financial help of sympathetic merchants in Europe to bring one into England. Then, if a person could not read, nor was unable to translate Latin, the person could hire a private scholar to read it and translate it for them. William Tyndale was such a scholar.

Tyndale was born into a well-to-do Catholic family engaged in the wool trade in Gloucestershire England. He began his education at a prep school in Oxford at the age of 12 and five years later entered Oxford University in 1519. At Oxford he earned a B.S and a M.S. in theology with additional training as a writer and linguist.

While at Oxford, Tyndale supported the Reformation despite being admitted to the priesthood. After graduating in 1521, he tutored for two years, then moved to Wittenberg Germany to pursue a personal quest to create an English language Bible. By 1524 he had translated the five books of the Old Testament, had them printed, and began smuggling them into England. His monumental undertaking was dangerous because England's King, Henry VIII, had declared that to translate anything from the Bible into English was a capital offence and subject to capital punishment... for a crime known as heresy. But despite his personal danger, Tyndale found his work made easier because:

1) recently invented movable-type printing presses made it possible to quickly, cheaply, and easily make thousands of copies of printed works in a short period of time,

2) Tyndale was a skilled, intelligent, and gifted linguist fluent in 7 languages: French, Greek, Hebrew, German, Italian, Latin, and Spanish,

3) Tyndale had a wealthy London merchant, Humphrey Monmouth, fund his endeavors as well as provide him a system for smuggling his printed works into England, and

4) Tyndale joined a well-established Reformation movement that already existed in several European countries and which also created vernacular Bibles in German, Italian, French, Czech, Dutch, and Spanish languages. Thus, Tyndale found Europe a much safer place to work.

The true significance of Tyndale's work was his passion to empower "common folk" into reading and interpreting Bible passages from which they could discuss moral issues on a personal basis. Once Tyndale printed his first New Testament he kept writing additional tomes and reformist tracts as well as updating his Bible translations, Thus, in 1530 he went into hiding in Antwerp where he wrote The Practice of Prelates, a treatise in which he opposed the King's divorce from Catherine of Aragon on the grounds the divorce would not be scriptural. This made him an enemy of both the King and the catholic church. Tyndale chose Antwerp believing it safe from the King of England, but there he was betrayed in 1535, at the age of 40, by someone he believed was a friend.

At the time of Tyndale's betrayal at least 16,000 Bibles were either being sold openly on the streets of London or were already in circulation in private hands Once betrayed, Tyndale was imprisoned in a Belgium state prison where for 14 months he was physically deprived and where he faced a group of paid Inquisitors from a nearby university, However, through all of this they could not break his resolve nor dampen his intellectual prowess. The inquisitors stripped him of his priesthood and had him executed as a heretic by employing secular authorities near the prison. His death happened not because Tyndale was hunted by a King but because of betrayal by a personal acquaintance… all for a pittance of a 40-shilling reward, History records how the life of a kind and simple man was snuffed out for a crime for which very few were ever executed and in spite of appeals by English merchants, by Thomas Cromwell to Archbishop Carandolet, president of the Belgium council of clergy, and to the governor of Vilvoorde Castle in which Tyndale was imprisoned.

Two years after the death of William Tyndale, Henry VIII also died. His death allowed the Protestant Reformation to grow. However, seventeen years later, in 1554, Henry's daughter, Mary Tudor, restored Roman Catholicism to England and had nearly 300 Protestants burned at the stake and nearly 400 more imprisoned who later would die from starvation. Such acts earned her the title of "Bloody Mary".

Today the man who brought forth the first English language Bible remains largely unknown but even more so for his profound effect on the English language. Tyndale introduced many new English words and phrases still in use today and more than any other writer before or since, including Shakespeare. It was Tyndale who created such phrases as; "a moment in time", "the spirit is willing, but the flesh is weak," "my brother's keeper", "let there be light", "the signs of the times", "an eye for an eye, and a tooth for a tooth", "the parting of the ways", "thou shalt love the Lord thy God with all thy soul and with all thy might", "the powers that be", "give up the ghost", and "fight the good fight." Such phrases are still in use today because 500 years ago William Tyndale mastered Hebrew and Greek syntax and cadence.

A few of the single words that Tyndale introduced are atonement, beautiful, fisherman, Jehovah, Passover, peacemakers, scapegoat, taskmaster, and zealous.   This kind and gentle man also created the phrase taken across the seas and used by the slaves in America in their campaign for freedom i.e.; "and afterword, Moses and Aaron went in and told Pharaoh, "Thus saith the Lord God of Israel, *Let my people go"*, (Exodus 5:1).

Tyndale's Bible translations also include explaining Luther's theology of justification by faith, and many of his translations undermine traditional Catholic teachings. For example, Tyndale translated the Greek word "agape" as "love" rather than as "charity" in order to play down its Catholic use of meaning good works".

William Tyndale also coined the phrase used as the title for this story. Thus, when the term *salt of the earth* is used it pays tribute to its Greek origin in the Gospel of Matthew (5:13) to describe "a thoroughly decent person." as Jesus labelled his disciples during his Sermon on the Mount.

Why William Tyndale, and his literary influence of 500 years ago, is not as well-known is a conundrum…. especially since personal reading and application of scripture is the foundation of Protestantism. In 1913 a statue erected in the town square of Vilvoorde Belgium honors William Tyndale. Inscriptions on the statue are in English, French, and Dutch. Also, the town has a small Tyndale Museum and a small Protestant Church i.e.: *Tyndalekirk.*.

King Henry VIII (1491-1547) In 1521 Leo X, the Pope in Rome, conferred upon Henry the title "Fidei Defensor" (Defender of the Faith) for his tract "The Assertion of the Seven Sacraments." Henry gained the Pope's favor by his printed argument against Martin Luther. Then, in 1535 and three popes later, Henry severed England's ties to Rome. He did this by declaring the Church of England (i.e. Anglican Church) a non-Catholic entity. However, it was when Henry VIII, sought a divorce from his first wife, Catherine of Aragon, that he propelled the English Reformation forward as the then Pope (Pope Clement V) rejected Henry's petition to divorce. By setting himself as head of the Church of England, it allowed Henry to confiscate nunneries and monasteries and increase his own wealth by stopping English money from flowing to Rome.

While Henry VIII's deeds led to his excommunication, within two years of Tyndale's martyrdom, in 1536, Henry ordered an English Bible placed in every Church of England parish throughout his kingdom. It is estimated that 95% of Tyndale's Bible translations where was used for this purpose.

Most of Henry VIII's political aims were achieved by either leveling charges of treason or heresy against those who fell out of favor with him…as was done to Tyndale. He would do this by setting one or more of his paid ministers against the man. However, they too could either be banished or executed, such as happened to Sir Thomas More, Richard Crammer, and Thomas Cromwell.

Cuthbert Tunstall (1474-1559)– As Bishop of London, Tunstall rejected Tyndale's original petition for permission to translate and print the New Testament in English. Tunstall publicly burned any Tyndall New Testaments that he could find as well as any other "heretical books". Although he was a learned man, Tunstall became a resolute opponent of seeing any translation of the Bible into English. He was an avid supporter of Henry VIII and served the King as a trusted advisor (Lord Privy Seal) and ambassador.

Thomas More (1478-1535) – More was a lawyer, social philosopher, and statesman. More served as Lord High Chancellor of England (1520-1532). As Lord Chancellor More had a violent dislike of Tyndale, especially his translations of the Scriptures, and thus wrote two scathing books against Tyndale. About a year after Tyndale was executed More was also executed by Henry VIII because he would not recognize Henry as Head of the Church of England. More, like Tyndale, openly disapproved of the King's use of expedient divorce. More is often known for his writing of an imaginary island state, Utopia, which he created as having an ideal form of government. today More is venerated by Catholics.

Bishop John Stokesley (1475-1539) As the Catholic Bishop of London, Stokesley went to France as an ambassador seeking opinions from foreign universities on how to best support King Henry VIII's divorce from Catherine of Aragon. As the Bishop of London and Lord Almoner he had many disputes with the Archbishop of London (Thomas Crammer) but he held a steadfast zeal opposing any English Bible. Stokesley was also staunch in his pursuit of heretics, especially William Tyndale.

Henry Phillips (dates unknown): By 1535, several Englishmen were hunting for William Tyndale, under orders from either King Henry VIII, Sir Thomas More, or Bishop John Stokesley of London. The man who found Tyndale was an Oxford College classmate of Tyndale. A slippery and devious man, Henry Phillips, came to Oxford from a wealthy and notable family but squandered his inheritance and reputation through gambling and other unsavory pursuits. Writing home from Europe in 1535, Phillips hoped to get back into his family's good graces as he was near starvation and destitute. However, being branded a traitor and someone no one could trust he did try to go to Rome to curry favor with the church. It is believed he died there penniless and, in a town where no one would take him in or offer aid.

Theophrastus von Hohenheim (Paracelsus): (1493-1541) born a Swiss citizen he became a lecturer at the university of Basel and earned his reputation as a physician, astrologer, and alchemist. He is considered the "Father of Modern Medicine." for his emphasis on the value of observation, combined with received wisdom, to make a clinical diagnosis. He is also known as the "Father of Toxicology" for his work in using inorganic chemicals and minerals as curatives. Additionally, Paracelsus rebuked the dominate practice of his time wherein diet and bloodletting were used to cleanse and purify bodily juices.

Paracelsus openly defied and rebuked his contemporary physicians and apothecaries, often with outbursts of offensive language. He is also credited with being the first to quantify the dose-response concept. He also observed the mentally ill and called for their humane treatment as he believed them not to be possessed by devils or spirits but rather caught up in a treatable disease. Two of the medicines he introduced were, mercury pills for treating syphilis and a liniment made with camphor, soap, and alcohol. He also was the first to recognize syphilis could be contracted by contact. He gave zinc its modern name and introduced opium to the western world.

His time as an army surgeon led Paracelsus to believe that keeping wounds clean and free of infection would allow nature to heal them and his work became the precursor of antiseptic practice. His belief that the universe was one coherent organism permeated with a life-giving spirit, was found objectionable by the Church of Rome. Finally, he introduced urinalysis as a practical aid for making a diagnosis.

Dirk and Pieter Marten (1446-1534) This Flanders based printer and writer, Dirk, existed just before the time of this story. His printing press was near the University Hall in Antwerp. He set it up in 1497 and successfully ran it until 1512 when he decided to move his shop to the Flemish town of Leuven. He kept his second shop running until 1534 when he retired at age 83. Martens only son, Pieter, took over his father's business but died two months later. There is an epitaph to the elder Marten that Erasmus composed, and which today still hangs in a church in the town of Aalst.

Acknowledgements

The craft of fiction writing truly takes a team to bring it to life. Thus, I would like to thank Dr. Bettie McGarry, Ann Lyon, and Debbie Sears for providing content review and manuscript editing. Another shout out is due Julie H. Turner of www.betterbetareaders.com whose skills polished the final manuscript.

Paul Kim, Barbara Hoffman, and Ken Hubona are due huge thanks for their help and encouragement. Finally, my gratitude is extended to members of the Richmond writer's group, Agile Writers. led the capable Greg Smith. He and they kept me steadfast and focused throughout my journey that ended with this novel.

Made in the USA
San Bernardino, CA
04 May 2020